The Identity Upgrade

Nora Brown
Stella Dunn

Published by
YURIT

1st Edition
Published by Yurit LLC, California, USA
Copyright © Yurit LLC, 2013. All Rights Reserved.

Printed in the USA

ISBN: 978-0-9893829-3-9

Cover credits:
Starfield : gann / shutterstock.com
Savannah: dahl / shutterstock.com
Early man: kindersley / thinkstock.com
Spaceman: wikimedia commons

Also available as:
Multimedia Enhanced eBook for iPad
Original Soundtrack

theidentityupgrade.com

Dedicated to all Self Explorers

Foreword

Gone are the slow changes of the past. It is time for humanity to take an evolutionary leap. The basic life 'software' we have run encourages a linear view, that everything has a beginning and end, that we are nothing more than our bodies and minds. But the evolutionary 'identity upgrade' at the heart of this dynamic novel will awaken us to the exciting broader cycle we are a part of and help us grasp humanity's immortal identity.

To initiate this process, the four Fundamental Forces of Nature materialize on Earth and select a group of five men and women to test the upgrade. They meet one evening at a gathering in California. Drawn by the pull of an uncanny affinity and a tragic event they witness that night, the protagonists will carry their bond through the years, as each undergoes an adventure, crisis, or journey that leaves them transformed...upgraded.

Contents

Cast of Players 6

Prologue...9

Upgrading Mankind...13

Resisting Temptation...23

The Courageous Star...41

In the End lies the Beginning 59

Loving the Enemy...65

A Dream with Impact...79

Software Wizard 97

Master Level Souls 117

Five Paths Cross...127

Stepping off the Roller Coaster...147

A Unique Bond is Formed 155

The Art of Suffering 169

The Declaration...237

Epilogue 281

About the Authors 283

Cast of Players

PLAYER	#	COLOR	ELEMENT
Shiv Singh Sitaram *Indian Fusion Scientist*	1	Yellow	Space
Ali Ben Calif *Egyptian Computer Specialist*	2	Blue	Air
Renato "Reto" Ritter *Swiss Lawyer*	3	Red	Fire
Hakika Hasina *African Medical Professional*	4	Green	Water
Barb Bernstein *Californian Film Director*	5	Orange	Earth
Big G *Gravitational Force* [1]	6	Violet	
Avory *Electromagnetic Force* [2]	7	White	
Marvin *Weak Force* [3]	8	Black	
Victoria *Strong Force* [4]	9	Grey	
'it' *Animating Force* [5]	0	None	

1: Attraction between masses. The main "glue" holding the universe together. Earth's gravitational force gives weight to the mass of a human body.

2: Interaction between electrically charged particles. Bonds atoms to form molecules, and molecules to each other. Gives things strength, shape and hardness.

3: Interaction causing radioactive decay, which generates most of the Earth's internal heat.

REPRESENTS

Knowledge, intellect, teaching, learning, wisdom

Action, work, speed, connectivity, integration

Power, stamina, competition, heroism

Compassion, heart, generosity, caring, the "we"

Creativity, sensuality, individuality, drama, the "I"

Mental and physical tester, examiner

Creation, rising energy in a wave, light

Destruction, descending energy in a wave, darkness

Upholding all matter, stability, twilight

Animator of the universe and all humans

4: Attraction between fundamental particles: it is the subatomic "glue". 100x stronger than the Electromagnetic Force and 100,000x stronger than the Weak Force.

5: All-pervading motionless substance. The source of everything and to which everything returns.

Prologue

Deep below the barren, snow-covered landscape, the Earth is seething. The volcanic cone breathes smoke and gas. In a powerful explosion, it spits chunks of glowing rock into the night sky. Liquid fire streams down its flanks.

High above the spectacle two clouds – one black, one white – hover for a moment, make a swift evasive move, then drift off towards the southwest. They home in on three cube-shaped buildings crowding around a spacious beach house, its wide deck jutting out over steeply sloping ground. Easily passing through the molecular structure of the thick glass windows, the clouds encounter a dense grey mist occupying the front room. Color flashes from within.

"Happy you made it," Grey pulses. "Fantastic show," White fires back, describing how an active volcano distracted them. "We were tempted to pop more of those magma hot spots, and talk Big G into upping the gravitational pull just a smidgen.... Plenty of water to put them all out again!"

Grey quickly modulates its color and envelops the room in a calming blue. "We're not here to wreak havoc, but to upgrade and balance! First things first though: Let's plug in and transform."

The three had come to Earth to set the planetary stage and – unbeknownst to Black and White – to prep humanity for the next act of the play called 'life in human form'. Planet and humans were about to be upgraded with very specific goals. Humanity was being readied to acquire knowledge that only a handful had been able to access in the past. In this third millennium of the earthling's calendar, any interested individual would be capable of logging on to this secret knowledge. The upgrade would broaden intellectual and emotional bandwidth – stimulating new areas of the brain – so humans could finally attain the goal of their layover on this planet.

The tricky part of their current assignment was to precisely dovetail human and planetary evolution. Gone were the slow changes of the past. In the new era, evolution would no longer be determined by the biosphere, change no longer the result of evolution. Instead, evolution would result from enlightened human action.

Grey indicates an iridescent plasma cube rotating slowly in midair, the 'toolbox' Grey has brought along. Floating within its range, Black, White and Grey are struck by a sudden, brilliant particle stream from which each fashions a Chemical Information Database tuned to their particular frequency. This CID not only stores individual talents and traits, its composition also determines how a creature understands and reacts to its surroundings. From slower moving particles the three also form a personal mission cloak: the physical form they will need from time to time on Earth.

In their realm within the building blocks of matter, the three had no form. On Earth they were known as fundamental forces of nature. Were Black and White human, they would be twins – born of one egg, but embodying opposing tendencies. Earthling scientists had tagged Black as the weak interaction. It caused particle decay at the subatomic level. Black ruled over change in the material world and was cause for its constant transformation. White operated quite differently. Known since the late 1800s as the electromagnetic force, White held together atoms and molecules – creating an illusion of permanence in objects humans saw and used in daily life. In reality, though, these items of metal, wood or plastic were mainly empty space. White, being multi-talented, held another important job on planet Earth: he fired up the conveniences of modern life – lights, computers, TVs, phones. Both answered to their leader Grey, the strong force, many orders of magnitude stronger than the twins. This most powerful force in the universe bound everything together at the subatomic level.

While Black and White try to outdo one another with outlandish combinations of hair, eye and skin color, Grey has quickly made her choice: the female version of the ultimate standard design – the total fusion of all physical human varieties – since this best suits her tendency. Eventually she will learn why she keeps attracting many a surprised, shocked or unsure glance when moving among humans. Millions have already seen and greatly admired another face with a very similar expression. It is locked behind bulletproof glass in a securely guarded, climate-controlled enclosure. Each year, some six million people travel to the Louvre's Salle des États to see it. And many feel something inexplicable. A kind of astonishment; as if the world has come to a standstill for an instant. In their words, they have caught a glimpse of eternity. Leonardo da Vinci's famous painting depicts the perfect neutrality of all conflicting tendencies constantly pulling at a human mind. Mona Lisa's face is neither beautiful nor ugly, neither male nor female, not smiling but also, well...smiling.

White and Black balk at this perfect intersection of human design possibilities and keep beaming themselves through forms and sizes, cuts and colors. Black finally settles on skin a few shades darker than average, chocolate eyes and a mop of curls in a glossy black. White opts for lighter skin with honey-colored eyes and hair. In contrast to Grey, they both choose the male mission cloak model, although the end result is pretty similar. Finally they stand all the same height, just under six feet, even-featured and slender-limbed.

Choosing earthling names merits more clowning around. White insists on a female moniker, having developed a particular fondness for Penelope. But Grey isn't having any of it, so White eventually accepts Avory, a combination of sounds that suits his particular tendency. Black finds an acceptable solution in Marvin, and as long as they had dealings with humans, their leader would go by the name of Victoria.

The Forces have touched down a good 150 degrees west of the location where the previous chapter in human learning was set in motion a couple of thousand Earth years before; but still roughly along the 33rd parallel. Not by chance were they to take up residence near the storytelling capital of the world, a place called Hollywood.

1

Upgrading Mankind

"It's a marvel, isn't it? A planet that has nurtured a species with the capacity to consciously fulfill the ultimate destiny of all matter." Victoria stepped out on to the wide deck of their base, whose buildings lay hidden behind shrubs and boulders high above foam-crested surf and fine-grained sand. She enjoyed exercising her unfamiliar voice. Not that they needed speech to communicate, but apparently practice made perfect on this extraordinary little planet.

"What? Eat, drink and procreate?" Marvin sounded a bit throaty as he joined her at the railing.

"I think you've stored the wrong data. Earthlings can actually comprehend the universal animating principle. Their steering center contains a quadrillion synaptic connections, capable of decoding even the subtlest patterns."

"But perceiving the animating force requires extremely accelerated particles! Such bright minds would have lit up like flares, visible even when we were still a fair way up in space. Are you sure Einstein lived here? And Newton and Fermi? They would have illuminated this sea of darkness like searchlights." Marvin waved his hand at the ocean, where a smattering of earthlings floated on slim boards, while others lay prone on the beach.

He gave the humans, flat on their backs or lying face down, a second look. "Are we too late? Have they all dropped their mission cloaks?"

"They're resting, Marv, not dead; catching rays and absorbing salty air. It's beneficial to their bodies."

Victoria smiled at Avory's explanation. Despite comprehensive theoretical instruction ahead of their assignment, the twins had a lot to learn about the complexity of beings in human form.

Watching the earthlings frolicking on the beach, the twins were particularly fascinated by two humans of opposite gender exhibiting a complex progression from visual to intense tactile interaction. Their encounter generated wafts of static in the surrounding air, tinged with a flavor the twins could not decode. Since Victoria wasn't about to explain, they assumed it was some sort of magnetized mission cloak attraction.

On a rustic iron and glass table – stuff Avory had salvaged and tinkered with to get a feel for local materials – Victoria had placed a tray with translucent cups of her own making, which she now filled with pink liquid from an elegant carafe. The twins were reflecting on their discussion with the fourth force of nature, gravity, their partner Big G. They had talked about the humans' fixation on maintaining the status quo.

"This trying to keep things as they are," Marvin ambushed Victoria, "is totally beyond even my comprehension." It was, he pointed out, futile to strive for stability in a universe whose only constant is movement and change, all particles endlessly dancing to Big G's tune. From the smallest subatomic particle to the largest object in space, everything is in constant motion. Every human travels some half a million miles every single night on a planet cruising at about 67,000 miles per hour relative to the sun. With this tiny speck of rocks and water called Earth in tow, the sun itself orbits the center of the Milky Way galaxy at about half a million miles per hour and at a radius of some 156,000 trillion miles. The Milky Way too is moving…

"Care to elaborate on this, Ms Fusion?"

Their team leader acquiesced. Even though earthling science had proven life to be a never-ending ballet of assembling, disassembling and reforming particles, human perception could not yet grasp the reality of this endless dance. With a smile Victoria concluded, "In a nutshell, most humans are simply unaware of their true nature. So Big G's main role is to invite them to wake up to the exciting cycle they are part of."

"Cat got your tongue, changeling?" The voice rolled in like thunder, wreaking havoc in the movement of air around the terrace. Marvin jumped to retrieve a cup caught up in a miniature tornado. "Changeling yourself! Or rather weakling...once I put humans up to your game, Big G! And, please, don't clear out the furniture here!"

Before the two could get into one of their regular friendly spats, Victoria intervened and reminded the twins how important it was that they fully grasp Big G's decisive role on this particular planet. Big G should be regarded as humanity's greatest teacher, constant companion and liberator. "Every human who learns to withstand gravitational pull eventually gains the freedom to probe into the deeper realms of existence," she pointed out.

Marvin wasn't done with Big G just yet, calling him a party-pooper and the proverbial drag. The fourth force wouldn't be goaded and explained instead how drag was just one aspect of his multifaceted personality. In fact, there was plenty of interest in his presence, he said, sounding quite smug. Quite a few of this planet's brightest scientific minds were after him, trying to find his fingerprints – the elusive graviton. Big G emitted a sound like a decrepit steam engine. "I must say, I do enjoy leading them around in circles."

"Oh great imperial mind-twister" – Marvin just couldn't stop himself – "we bow to your mysteries." Again, Big G refused to take the bait. "And I bow to the three of you."

Even though earthling scientists classified him as a force like the others, Big G functioned quite differently. Thus Marvin defined him as the perfect placeholder and particle pusher – their loyal servant – mediator between coarse material and subatomic forces. "And why don't you take form when gracing us with your presence?"

"You know I keep planets in motion around the sun, humans securely grounded, and I prevent the air they breathe from escaping into space. I hold all 'stuff' in place. So what form would you find adequate? Something like this?"

All three watched, fascinated, as a billowing mist condensed into a bizarre figure: large splayed feet, two powerful legs, barrel-shaped armless torso – all topped off where a head would be, by a miniature solar system calmly orbiting in thin air. The whole luminous contrivance glowed a deep shade of violet, Big G's very own color. His voice seemed to come from somewhere behind Saturn: "Like it?"

Even Marvin stared dumbfounded. The overall impression was well beyond weird. He muttered as much when he found his voice again before adding, "You've really outdone yourself this time. Do us all a favor and dematerialize!"

Only the billowing mist remained, out of which Big G rumbled: "Dilettante!"

Avory, straightening his ponytail, looked sidelong at Marvin: "You aren't, by the way, planning on telling humans how they can counteract gravity and giving away Big G's secret, are you?"

Marvin grinned. "You mean beyond inventing airplanes or spacecraft? That's already tricking gravity big time... I'd love to unveil what the game of life is really about. That definitely would thwart Big G's game. He'd probably spit star clusters when more and more humans stood up to him. But I guess we'll be busy enough getting their planet through this transition without it blowing to stardust. Isn't that right, Vic?"

Victoria gave one of her Mona Lisa smiles. "The physical planetary work is actually only part of the job, and the smallest at that."

They were to proceed one step at a time, she elaborated. Planetary adjustments had priority since they directly influence the resident species. As planet and creatures are ultimately one, their evolution always goes hand in hand. The Forces had already discovered how tricky the modification phase would be. They were aware that the planet was in for a rough ride. Marvin wasn't too concerned, though. Compared to where they'd been, this was an extremely tame planet. "A bit of rock 'n roll can't do any harm," he joked, while still trying to make sense of what he'd researched and seen so far. The human concept of existence remained a mystery to him. It seemed a simple enough set-up, but apparently very few were able to understand it. Victoria said this was not a question of failure, but of limits in the current human software. It generally read only the first and second states of matter and thus dealt mainly with the body and – only recently – the mind.

Victoria's next words brought Marvin up short: "The upgrade will change all this, allowing broad access to the third, gaseous state of matter – that which concerns the invisible soul. More and more humans will figure out how these faster moving particles determine outward appearance and how individuals perceive and react to everything around them." Eventually humans would realize that this individual particle mix was put together for each new performance on the earthly stage, depending on what script was to be tackled.

Now she had the twins' undivided attention. "What? What are we supposed to do? Upgrade the human race?"

Victoria calmly topped off her cup and looked at her two companions with luminous eyes and a brilliant smile. She nodded slowly. "Humans are so much more than meets the eye. They are creation's crowning glory – having a singular dimension that sets them apart from all other species. Theirs is a magnificent destiny, and now it is time they learned the true purpose of their life on Earth."

"Wow," Avory said in amazement, looking like a bear that had just discovered the mother lode of honey. "Wow," he breathed again, softly.

And, for once, Marvin stood absolutely still.

Victoria sipped the opaque pink liquid she had created to train her taste buds, while the twins waited impatiently to learn more about this surprising twist their assignment had taken. They were here not only to steer the planet into its next phase, but also to initiate the next act of the play called life on Earth?

"It will be a particularly lively act, I assure you," Victoria said, "since the upgrade will speed up all particles on this planet. All material things will be charged with more energy, moving up towards the third state of matter. Humans will be more likely to focus confidently on what lies ahead, rather than view life and their outer reality through a rear view mirror. Mission cloaks will become lighter, airier, turning into veritable action suits. That will reduce Big G's influence quite a bit."

Marvin had no chance to gloat. Big G immediately pointed out that he would be hugely relieved when humans were no longer so easily manipulated! An increase in personal power would lead to greater physical and mental freedom. "The new program will expedite synaptic connections, giving humans improved analytical ability and a clearer understanding of themselves and the world."

It was important not to judge humans too harshly. Victoria picked up the thread when Big G fell silent. "That's why this planet is so unique: human beings are equipped to find the ultimate clue, reach the top level of the cosmic game and complete the mission." She started to walk away. "We'll talk about that later. I've important things to do right now."

"Hair, nail or makeup artist?" Marvin hooted. "Or have you booked all three today? Kind of into that human body stuff, aren't you, Miz Vic?"

"You know perfectly well we need none." With a flash from her eyes she turned Marvin's hair into a spinach green spiky do, a reprimand intended to make him take his job seriously. After all, they had to get this place ready for another 10 billion arrivals.

"Another how many?" The twins were appalled. How could so many humans crowd this tiny speck of rock and water? They'd most urgently need a major expansion to their abstract thinking capacity, Avory observed, trying hard not to laugh at Marvin's eccentric hair. "They need to urgently lose their fear of planetary change. They don't seem to grasp that the planet is primarily here for them and not vice-versa. After all, it's their performance stage."

Victoria stood by the sliding glass doors, the shimmering white drapes moving lightly in the breeze and shrouding her perfectly proportioned figure like mist drifted in from the Pacific. Her parting remark pulled the twins up short: "We have to discuss the five humans destined to help us with our work!"

"Oh, now we also have human help, do we? Anything else you have forgotten to mention?" Marvin quipped.

"Only that I have already activated their upgrade."

In their excitement, the twins forgot to be angry at being left out. "How did they react? What did they do? Explode, implode, go crazy?"

Forgotten were all plans for making the most of this delicious earth day. Attentively they listened to what their leader was telling them about the exceptional group of five humans selected to serve as messengers of the next act. They were apparently quite accomplished and strong representatives of the five distinct human frequencies. Having developed an admirable amount of personal power, they were capable of withstanding Big G's pull to a certain extent. And no, they had not gone crazy from the upload, since it would not start operating until they met up. The five were spread around the globe but would eventually gather in this area.

Victoria looked at Marvin with a bemused expression, saying she was surprised he hadn't figured out already why the Forces had manifested right here, far in the west between the 30th and the 35th parallels. He should have remembered that these were the latitudes along which knowledge traveled – from the Indian subcontinent to Egypt and onwards to the land of California.

Marvin shrugged. "How could I, Miss V? Ave and I were not invited last time you came down here, for that upgrade a couple of millennia ago." He gave her a chastising look and with a brief "I'm definitely off" vaulted over the railing and landed softly on the rocks below. He scrambled over them like a giant crab, before disappearing on swift feet in the direction of his own bungalow.

Hefting his body from the lounge chair, Avory shook out his hair and gave Victoria a slow wave: "Kid always wants to be the bad boy, can't admit that he's fascinated. You're sure, Victoria, the five humans won't realize something has changed in their brains before the new software kicks in?"

They couldn't be really sure of anything, she answered, since a human was an incredibly complex biochemical masterpiece made up of some 100 trillion cells. For this composite to function properly, all cells, nerves, muscles and organs have to cooperate incessantly, exchanging information in fractions of a second, then acting.... The human brain, their control tower, is the most complex organism in creation. It contains tens of billions of neurons, passing signals to each other via hundreds of trillions of synaptic connections. The brain's wiring alone stretches for about 100,000 miles. It is constantly active: regulating the functions of the mission cloak, processing every tiny morsel the five senses drag in, setting those billions of neurons to work, inducing highly complex activities, and provoking physiological, emotional or physical reactions. This awesome organism allows humans not only to journey outward, ever deeper into space, exploring the workings of the universe, but also inward, observing and studying the workings of this organism itself.

"The brain is infinitely complex, but it is no computer. Up to a point it's unpredictable even for me. I am reasonably sure our five friends won't notice any changes right away. They would probably credit their superior perception to having tapped deeper into themselves. Which, after all, is true, right?" Victoria gave a little sigh.

"No negative consequences then? Would be a pity if we started with a setback...."

"Always my very considerate friend, aren't you Avory? No, I can assure you, there will be no nasty surprises, just joy when the two sides of the brain fuse, when ever-subtler patterns are deciphered and all humans finally comprehend the fullness of the game of life. When humanity discovers its true identity... Joy, Avory, great joy."

2

Resisting Temptation

The peak was still shrouded in darkness, the soft swish of skins under his skis the only sound. Fresh snow had fallen all throughout yesterday, working a magic that never got old. Despite having lived his whole life in the Swiss Alps, the man was as enchanted by a heavy snowfall as the little boy had been: standing at grandma's kitchen window, mesmerized by the large white flakes – handkerchiefs she had called them – descending noiselessly on shrubs and trees, roofs and meadows, blanketing his known world in soft white silence.

When the first rays of the sun touched the peak of Piz Nair, spilling pure gold down its flank, Reto stopped his rhythmic ascent. For a moment he felt like kneeling, paying homage to the goddess of light and life. He always thought of the sun as female, and not only because the sun was a she in his native dialect. For him, warmth, light and the power to enable and sustain life were feminine traits. He stood, transfixed, as she unfurled a brilliant shaft of light around him, tempting him to step on and follow it towards his destiny.

With an impatient shake of the head, Reto remembered that, sun or no sun, he was set on making a record ascent along his favorite route this morning. He allowed himself a short breather and a quick sip of tea from his thermos. Hastening to make up for lost time, he caught himself humming a few bars of the "Ode to Joy". He fondly recalled climbing this same mountain in his grandmother's wake – following the tracks she laid in the virgin snow – her "Freude schöner Götterfunken" floating back to him through air so clear and fresh it seemed to deep-clean body, mind and soul. He could not have been more than six or seven years old. She was fast then, his Nona, fast and strong and constantly telling him what it meant to be a man. "A real man conquers the mountain," she would shout back at him while striding ahead. "A real man does not complain," was her retort when the child demanded a break. She had an entire 'real man' litany: a real man should have no fear, willingly risk his life to save others, and of course the core attribute, "A real man, Reto, knows that when he acts morally, he has god on his side."

They would not rest until the sun's warm rays hit them – Reto usually on the brink of collapse – to drink the same honeyed tea he still prepared for every tour, and a smoked, spicy Salsiz sausage that Nona handed him, along with some of her coarse bread to chew on. His grandmother not only encouraged endurance, to go to the limit of his stamina without complaint, but she also talked about the sun, the star that was key to life on Earth, instilling awe at the amazing order of the solar system. With infinite patience – something she otherwise had in short supply – she had tried to find answers to his endless questions. "Why, Nona, is all this? How did it get to be like this? Who put it there? Why doesn't it all fall down?"

His questions had outlived his grandmother; his answers, however, were much less certain than hers. Reto still wondered whether this amazing universe had come about just by accident. Or whether some kind of force, over billions of years, had created an ordered planetary system, in which the different heavenly bodies moved in endless rhythm. How is it that the movement of the Earth and the composition of its gaseous shell were of such perfect design as to enable and sustain a multitude of life forms? He had read what science said, or rather guessed, about the origins of the universe. But all he read left ample room for speculation.

For Nona, the answer had been simple. Her god in heaven held all of this beauty and perfection in his benign and loving hands. He gazed in wonder upon his creation, whose crowning product had no other duty than to be good and to love; to love him in all of his creatures, large and small, to recognize him in all that swims, crawls, walks or flies. Yet as hard as Reto had tried, Nona's all-knowing, all-loving god had eluded him, just like the definitive answers to his boyhood questions. But he didn't mind. As a renowned lawyer, he was always expected to provide definitive statements for his powerful international clientele. So Reto could accept a small number of open questions, even though he was determined to find the answers one day.

On his descent through the deep powder, carving a new track into the unspoiled mountainside, the man who was normally defined by structures, principles, rules and regulations, gave himself up to the pleasure of being alone and at one with nature – and not knowing what came next. He let his instinct take over, trusting in the memory of his well-trained limbs, focused on the next perfect turn.

Back at the chalet he had lived in all his life, he stood his skis on the porch and carefully wiped them of wet snow. His chalet was one of few original buildings left in the village – a rarity on its own island of undeveloped property. Many locals had considered such an anachronism stupid in this heyday of transformation from sleepy alpine village to Switzerland's glitziest international resort. But in time, and with soaring land prices, scorn had turned to envy.

The front of the chalet had remained virtually unchanged since the mid-1800s, when Reto's great-grandfather built it. The inside offered quite a contrast to all the exterior blackened wood, small windows and ornamental carvings. A spacious hall led directly into an airy room that was kitchen, living and dining room all in one. Floor to ceiling glass panels out the back let in the bright winter sun and opened to a terrace of large granite slabs. From there the ground sloped gently down to what in the few summer months would be a luscious garden bursting with color. Instead of the wide variety of vegetables and berries Nona had planted and harvested year after year, Reto had gardeners put in the flowers and shrubs his grandmother had loved. Fat, round dahlias – in all hues from white and pale yellow to vivid pinks and deep purples – grew alongside sturdy asters and fragrant phlox. He'd even agreed to some bright red geranium planters on the windowsills for old time's sake. There were lilac bushes and snowballs, firethorn and forsythia, all traditional brightly flowering plants. Yet the most precious to him, still, was the small but persistent cluster of edelweiss growing from a small crack in the granite bolder the chalet leaned upon. There was a lesson there, his Nona had always hinted, one that Reto pondered to this day.

All of this abundant floral beauty was but a memory right now. It was hidden under a pure white blanket adorned with myriad tiny diamonds sparkling in all colors of the rainbow.

Coming through the front door, the cell phone in his backpack chirped. He recognized his Zürich office number: "Morning, Mrs. Gyger. You're at work early! The boys ok?"

"They're fine, thank you, Mr. Ritter." As usual, his assistant Beatrice Gyger didn't elaborate on her sons. She was a miracle Reto didn't question but gratefully accepted. She was smart, efficient, absolutely reliable and an epitome of discretion, a veritable treasure in his law office.

"I won't be coming down today. I'm staying for the weekend. If there's anything urgent you know how to reach me."

"That's why I called, Mr. Ritter. That mystery man I mentioned called again, asking for you. That's the third time. He's very insistent, foreign accent – I didn't recognize his voice – and the number was blocked. He said you were recommended to him and he needed to speak with you immediately. So I promised I'd try to reach you and asked him to call me back in half an hour. What should I tell him?"

"You did the right thing not to give him my cell phone number. Why don't you just patch him through when he calls again? He needn't know I'm not at the office. Anything else that can't wait till Monday?"

As he changed into a pair of loose sweats and his favorite FC Barcelona shirt, he wondered about this man who needed him so urgently. His clients came from around the globe. Reto was 100% reliable, tenacious and discreet. He was extremely well connected, and when connections were lacking, he was highly creative. And – a trait that some clients just could not fathom in the beginning – Reto was not greedy. He was well paid, very well paid for his services, but on a scale that hadn't lost all touch with reality.

His office phone rang just as he was on his way downstairs to his state-of-the-art fitness room. Reto had planned on another hard and sweaty workout on top of his early morning outing. Mrs. Gyger sounded a bit breathless: "It's this man again. He refuses to tell me his name, and I still can't see his number. Should I put him through?"

Reto was curious: "Ritter. What can I do for you?"

The man who put down the phone fifteen minutes later was lost in thought, a man with much to ponder. Temptation was raising its snakehead, whispering of quick profits, of a fabulous hourly rate for a couple of perfectly legal phone calls, not asking too many questions, moving some heavy bundles of cash instead.

A few rounds with weights would be just the ticket to clear his head. Reto had stocked the fitness room with equipment any professional outfit would have envied. This after his wife had packed her bags, together with most of the furniture, and taken their two children to the other side of the world, to Queenstown on New Zealand's South Island. Not exactly a short hop from Switzerland, which meant he saw his kids far too rarely. Thank god they still got a kick out of coming for a Christmas ski vacation. His beautiful daughter Emma accompanied him on his tours, she on snowshoes, board strapped to her back. But his son Julian – having just turned 10 and knowing all there was to know about life and the world in general – preferred to take the ski lift up. Walking up a mountain, he kept telling his father with a very earnest expression, was for Neanderthals.

Reto smiled thinking about the pair prodding him every evening for stories of Nona and Grandpa, about how it used to be. What were vivid memories for him seemed to them stories from another era, the Stone Age perhaps. It was strange, but Reto didn't really miss his children, at least not all the time. He loved it when they came to spend time with him, but he also felt relief when he saw them off at Zürich Airport after a few weeks. Kids were hard work – demanding and draining. He was so used to a world revolving around him that it took a lot of effort to transform his universe into a minor planet that orbited around two suns. And by the time he got into the groove of this new status, it would be time for them to leave.

Reto was pumping iron with a vengeance, sweat pouring down his chest, biceps starting to burn. He tried to keep his mind a blank. But once under the shower, the phone call popped up again and temptation struck.

The well-cured birch logs burning brightly in the open hearth gave off a delicate aroma. The contents of the dusty bottle from Reto's vintage collection had been allowed to breathe and now glowed a luscious deep red in high-stemmed crystal glasses. A fragrant cloud drifted through the room from the visitor's pipe. The two men, one well advanced in years and weathered, the other young and glowing from fresh air and exercise, were stretched out comfortably in deep, well-worn, leather armchairs facing the fire. A side table with the wine, some olives and chunks of aged parmigiano stood between them, along with an exquisite inlaid chess board.

"I set a new record this morning on the Piz Nair route," Reto had told his companion earlier, before they had started the game. "Shaved off another 50 seconds...."

All Gian had asked was, "What'd you invest them in?"

It was a typical Gian retort. The mountain guide and ski teacher, in age more like a father, was probably Reto's closest friend. When Reto's parents had moved to Zürich, where his father was taking over an important post at the head office of the bank he had worked for in their home town, the boy adamantly refused to leave his beloved mountains, his friends or school. After much deliberation, he was given over to the care of his grandparents, and the close ties between Reto and Gian had become even closer. He'd known him all his life and all the while the man had steadfastly refused to enter the competitions Reto tried to make out of each and every undertaking – no matter whether they flew paper planes when Reto was a kid, or later paragliders, whether they skipped flat stones over Lake Sils or climbed one of the four-thousanders. Gian simply did not comprehend the value of higher, faster, stronger. Trying to entice the older man to compete – to pit skill, stamina and ability – and seeing all his efforts flow off Gian like foaming water over a rock had driven Reto to distraction.

"I go my own pace. I do things the best I can. That is enough for me. And it should be for you too," the man had said time and time again.

To the highly competitive boy, this made no sense. What fun was it to be good at something if you couldn't measure yourself against others, find out who was better, best? Reto smiled at Gian's question and at the memories it had unearthed. "In what have I invested the saved time? In laughing about myself."

Now Gian was grinning too, his leathery skin cracking into a spider web of wrinkles, as he launched another fragrant cloud from his pipe. "OK, spit it out, boy."

Reto knew better than to feign ignorance. Gian was outfitted with the same radar as his Nona had been. "I had this phone call today. From a man with a very tempting proposition."

"Got your moral compass spinning, eh lad?"

"It's not a question of morals." Reto's voice was rising. "Nobody gets shorthanded or hurt. It's actually a very elegant deal. One that could net me a handsome sum, just by standing in."

"Aha," Gian nodded towards the fire and took a generous swallow of the full-bodied wine.

"Don't aha me, Gian." Reto rose from his chair and began pacing along the glass facade, staring out into the eerie bluish light cast by a half moon over the snow. He was so wrapped up in self-righteousness that he didn't see Gian's gentle smile. "Why do I even bother to discuss this with you," he muttered. "You've never been out of this place. The mountains that have surrounded you all your life tend to narrow your view. The world's turned a few times since the fifties, you know. Things change, accelerate...."

Gian just kept spicing the air with his tobacco.

"OK, OK. You don't need to say anything. I know what you're thinking anyway. You think I'll turn into one of these greedy goons who caused all that toxic fallout, in cahoots with their political gofers." Reto picked up his wine glass and drained it, carefully avoiding Gian's eyes. "I'm fully aware of my dealings with some of these dishonorable gentlemen in the past, but never to anyone's personal disadvantage. You know full well how much I abhor corruption and detest the big shots who are pathologically obsessed with short-term profit, or those oh-so-brilliant traders lining their pockets with fat commissions while feeding their clients fancy named false hopes. Not that I feel particularly sorry for their clients. Bunch of greedy vultures they are too...and don't start on me with your moral code! Morals my ass. Morals are just another instrument of power, manipulated like putty to service this or that self-interest!" Reto hadn't been aware he was shouting, but abruptly came to a stop when one of the logs in the hearth exploded. "What, what?"

Still calmly drawing at his ancient pipe, Gian squinted at his younger friend. "You have said all there is to say. Only it is not I who thinks that way. So who is?"

Reto slumped back down into the easy chair like a punctured balloon. Ceremoniously, he lit one of his stash of obscenely fat Cuban cigars, refilled the glasses from the half empty bottle and grinned at Gian. "It's always so rewarding to discuss things with you. You're eloquence personified, aren't you? Full of stupendous deliberation and sharply honed argument." He laid a big hand on the older man's knee. "There's always someone paying the price, no matter what, isn't there? Thanks, I needed that."

Gian covered Reto's hand with his own, a hand that looked and felt like a piece of the alpine rock the two had conquered together so many times.

"Temptation," he sighed more than spoke. "Always a fine challenge." Then Gian pointed to the simple silver plate hanging over the fireplace. "Whenever it strikes, why don't you just look at that? In his role as mayor, your grandfather played an important part in organizing the Olympic Games here in '48. There was no money and not much help just three years after the war.... But they did it, in less than 18 months. Close to 700 athletes were expected, and more than 20 events had to be organized, all outdoors. On top of everything else they had to gear up for 800 media from around the world. No TV, no satellites, nothing like that. The locals had to provide long distance telephone lines and telegraph services. They even had to increase the capacity of the town's sewer system – for all the bull going down the drains instead of through the radio or into the newspapers." Gian laughed. "They had to build new train stations, enlarge roads.... The Games of Renewal, they called them. Your grandfather called them the Breakback Games." Again Gian pointed at the round silver plate. "This ugly little dish is all he had to show for it."

"And it's enough, isn't it?" Reto concluded Gian's uncommonly long monologue.

The older man just nodded and relit his pipe. "It was enough, because he knew he had done what needed to be done, to the best of his ability."

"He was just like Nona," Reto mused, staring into the red glow of the embers. "Her deep contentedness never stemmed from anything she possessed, but from having applied herself as best as she was able – to even the smallest task."

"Pity she didn't live to see you now," Gian said suddenly. "She'd have been proud."

Reto flushed at this rare praise, all doubts gone. In his mind he watched the tempting two million Swiss Francs go down the drain. And his moral compass pointed again steadily due north.

The melodious peals, a four-part metallic harmony, drew people from their homes like the pied piper's flute. The crowd was unusually large today due to the inauguration service in the freshly renovated protestant church – reason also for Reto's out of the ordinary attendance. Returning greetings left and right, he was well aware of the glances that told him it had been far too long since he was at Sunday service. Much as Reto appreciated the parish priest's open and philosophical mind, the religious rituals struck him as no more than a well rehearsed act, devoid of meaning and drained of power from centuries of overuse.

He felt uneasy sitting in the pew and partaking in a routine that lacked true conviction.

Churches mostly contented themselves with going through the motions, and over the same stories time and again. That's what bothered Reto most, the palpable absence of real power. The fancy clothes, the rituals, the whole attitude was stuck in an age that had little in common with today's world. Of course, the church did great good for the poorest and most destitute, especially in Africa. Reto was well aware that. Scores of kids wouldn't go to school, have enough to eat, or be treated for their illnesses were it not for countless men and women who dedicated their lives to alleviating suffering. That's probably where the church's power lay today, with those individuals who put others before themselves. And yet, Reto was suspicious of too-demonstrative benevolence. He often sensed weakness behind highly visible charity, a neediness that didn't sit right with him.

Nowadays, power was with inventive minds daring to develop their ideas and make pots of money at the same time. These men and women built up successful enterprises, providing goods and services that helped shape the modern world. But rather than clinging to their accumulated wealth, they redistributed much of it to worthy causes. Not in the name of any god or to secure a front row seat in the hereafter, but to solve some of humanity's most pressing problems. Now that was power! People who subscribed to these values were the complete opposite of those who succumbed to greed and built their self-esteem on the pile of rubble they buried others under. Reto almost heard his Nona's voice floating through the pews dotted with mostly grey heads: "Remember always, Reto, wealth means responsibility. A greedy man has no honor. And a man with no honor has nothing."

While the sermon was droning on, Reto drifted off and thought of the upcoming afternoon with Annina. The gap-toothed, freckle-faced kid with the thick blond braids had been part of his crowd at the exclusive boarding school where kids from all over the globe received their education. Mens sana in corpore sano was their motto, which the students had interpreted to mean that you could get away with everything so long as you had a strong physique and a quick mind – and didn't get caught. University had scattered the flock, Annina going abroad in pursuit of her credentials in hotel management. Reto remembered the moment, years ago, when he had walked into the newly renovated Chantarella congress center to be greeted by a perfectly groomed, petite blonde with a warm, slightly gap-toothed smile. "Reteli," she had said teasingly, using the sissy name he had hated as a kid, letting her eyes travel appreciatively over his powerful six-foot frame, clad in an impeccable Italian suit. She noted the expertly cut hair, the direct gaze behind dark-framed glasses, the wide mouth breaking into a slow smile. She had taken his hands. "Look at you, Reto Ritter. What a handsome man you've become."

For his part, Reto observed that time had honed Annina's schooltime traits to perfection – her aptitude for strategic thinking, her enormous organizational talent, her ability to find a solution to just about everything and, when it suited her purpose, to tell the most blatant lies with a look of complete innocence in her glacier lake eyes. After earning her stripes as manager of a luxury lodge in the Namibian bush, Annina had been given the manager's position at Chantarella congress center. The old friends had easily fallen back into familiar closeness and had – over the years – come to depend more on one another than either cared to admit, as protective as they were of their independence, their private space, and their autonomous lifestyles.

When the first notes of the Te Deum began to rise around him, Reto awoke from his reveries and stood with the others. He sang, "Holy god, we praise thy name" not because he really did, but because he liked the melody, adding his strong baritone to the timid voices of the congregation. For lunch with Annina, he'd take along a bottle of champagne to celebrate his standing tall in the face of temptation – the mysterious client had had a hard time accepting his flat no – and then they would hit the slopes.

"Ah, vintage Champagne," Annina smiled across the elegantly laid table. They were sitting in the bay window of her apartment, looking out toward the slopes of Corviglia – already dotted with tiny moving shapes. Winter season was in full swing. With their tightly packed calendars this was a rare opportunity for them to enjoy some free time together. "I'm dreaming of taking a trip, Reto, to the desert somewhere. No snow, no ice, no coldness.... Jordan, maybe Israel. I'd like to see Jerusalem, just because I think it's such a beautiful name."

Reto smiled. That was so like the girl he'd known half his life, the woman he had rediscovered. Something would catch Annina's fancy and she wouldn't give up until she either had it in her possession, seen it or at least understood it.

"Have you been there?"

"Oh yes, I have, and I had quite the revelation. In the Garden of Gethsemane no less."

Annina looked at him with a slight frown. "What, did the resurrected body of Christ jump at you from behind a 2000 year-old olive tree?"

"The revelation had less to do with religion than with property laws." Reto smiled and shrugged. "You know, always the lawyer. Can't seem to help it. But on the Temple Mount for one, you walk among a whole bunch of fenced off sections all claimed by different Christian sects, like the Maronites, the Greek or Syriac Orthodox and half a dozen others. And that's when it hit me: What is it with us humans that we always have to claim ownership of property or ideas? What makes a nation claim a certain piece of land or water and defend it to the death?"

"Yes, I can see being in that part of the world would get you thinking along those lines. I mean when even different Christian factions feel the need to mark off their particular spots, what chance is there of Israelis and Arabs ever coming to an understanding? Besides, some of these zealots who call themselves settlers certainly don't help matters...."

Reto shook his head and looked out onto the peaceful winter landscape where the only skirmishes took place on the slopes or at the bars. "Lets not go there, Annina. I also wish sometimes I could look inside those heads to see how they tick. It's painful to see victims become perpetrators and vice versa. But perhaps it balances the pain?"

"What also really irks me is the limp-dicked reaction of our government to this situation. It's a farce; the whole thing is a farce. Perhaps its only purpose is to emphasize that it's ultimately every man for himself, every nation for itself." Annina poured the champagne, which had been chilling on the windowsill. "There has to be another way, a better way."

"Oh there is, I know there is." Reto toasted his lifelong friend and occasional lover with his glass. "I had this really crazy dream a while ago. About how it could be on this planet, how things could be handled differently. Since then I have sketched out a whole drawer full of contemporary world institutions and legislation that would address the problems facing today's global village – going beyond every man for himself and for me just a bit more. This fear of opening up, of seeking common ground, is blocking all real solutions. This desperate clinging to power, possessions, theories and ideologies is leading us all straight to the edge. But then, you can't decree sanity and reason."

"Now that would be grand! Maybe we should just start handing out prescriptions for exactly this." Annina picked up her own glass, and rising gracefully in one fluid motion – loose silk pants and the gauzy kimono swirling around her – she settled herself on Reto's lap. "Get your daily dose of common sense at your pharmacy! Side effects are to be expected and include a more fulfilling life for more people. You going to show me your drawer sometime?"

Reto was putting his German sports car through its paces, roaring over the Julier Pass. He knew every one of its many curves by heart and this early Monday morning the road belonged to him. The pass was one of a few kept clear of snow all winter and one of Switzerland's most important north-south routes – laid out during Roman times. His glossy black ride enthusiastically ate up the curves, and Reto felt as though he were on the Olympic bob run, since the Julier was flanked on both sides by high banks of snow. The drive to the city was pure pleasure, until he left the autobahn in Zürich Brunau and joined the throng of impatient or resigned commuters being forced back to their cubicles after a short weekend of make-believe freedom.

Mrs. Gyger had already sorted the mail, fired up the espresso machine, and put Reto's young research assistant to good use. The third year law student was working himself through university, and Reto was glad to provide him with a source of income while appreciating the young man's aptitude for putting together background material – the way Reto liked and could use it. Most importantly the assistant did not question Mrs. Gyger's undisputed No 1 position.

"Alex," he nodded at the slim, small man who at 23 still looked barely out of his braces. " Mrs. Gyger, good Morning. Coffee smells great." At this, his assistant rose, and fixed him a foamy cappuccino, his favorite start to the workday. He took the cup into his office and stood by the large window overlooking the busy Utoquai. Traffic was still bumper-to-bumper, the blue and white trams impatiently ringing their bells, their shrill cries shooing pedestrians and bikers out of the way and stopping cars on command. Beyond the thoroughfare lay the lake, its quiet blue-grey surface dotted with opportunistic gulls flying escort to commuter-laden ferries and hoping for leftover breakfast morsels.

Reto liked the city – as long as he didn't have to spend more than four days in a row there. With its population of around 360,000, originating from more than a 100 countries, it worked extremely well. It was large and heterogeneous enough to make it culturally and socially interesting, but not so big that one couldn't conceive of it as a whole. His city residence covered the whole top floor of a sought-after 19th century building in the Seefeld quarter, on a quiet residential side street just a few steps from the lake. If he concentrated, he could even catch a glimpse of his penthouse from his office window. But he was not looking for that right now; he was enjoying the view of the snow-covered Alps rising beyond the southern shore of the lake. This morning he could almost reach out and touch them, brought near as they were by the famous Föhn weather. At the knock on his door, Reto turned from the bright white peaks.

"There's a gentleman to see you, Mr. Ritter. And no, he was not expected," Mrs. Gyger added before Reto could ask. She quickly slid through the door and carefully closed it behind her. "It's an elderly man," she whispered, as if anyone could hear anything beyond the leather-padded wood. "Italian, by his accent, very well turned-out too."

Not the mysterious caller, then. Reto was quietly relieved. The accent had put him in another area.... His assistant intuitively picked up on his train of thought.

"Doesn't have any distasteful odor about him. Actually seems very reserved and, like I said, quite elderly, delicate even. Has a briefcase with him and just said he would like to speak with you, if you had a moment to spare."

"Ok, show him in, Mrs. Gyger, and ask if he'd like coffee. Thanks."

When the door opened again, it admitted a smallish, slightly stooped gentleman, dressed in an impeccable, somewhat old-fashioned dark suit, a starched white shirt and a silver gray tie that matched his wispy hair. He had a fragile air about him, until you looked at his face: the patrician features dominated by a pair of keen, intelligent grey eyes. Through large, steel framed glasses, the look he gave Reto was one of appraisal and appreciation simultaneously. He put his small suitcase down and stretched out his hand. In heavy accented German he said, "My name is Roberto Benedetti. I am professor at the University of Padua, ancient scriptures, languages, things of that sort. I also do a bit of translating...."

"Per favore professore, sedetevi. Dica, cosa posso fare per lei? And how did you come to see me, of all people?"

The old man's eyes lit up at Reto's easy use of Italian. "I'm afraid I won't have time for any of this. You see, I have to catch a train in just about an hour. So let me make this brief. You were recommended to me as a man of integrity and reliability. By people whose judgment I value. I want to entrust this case and its contents to someone who can guarantee its safekeeping." Benedetti looked at Reto, who would have had question marks in his eyes, had he been a cartoon character.

With a faint smile, the Professor added: "No drugs, no illicit money, nothing illegal at all. I guarantee it. Just some old texts that should not fall into the wrong hands." At this,

Benedetti patted the well-worn case like a favorite housecat. "I don't know how much interest you have in ancient scripture, but I'm sure you have heard of the Nag Hammadi library." When Reto straightened in his chair so as not to miss a word, professor Benedetti proceeded to tell him exactly what he expected of him.

3

The Courageous Star

For just a second, Barb forgets to compose her face. You'd have had to be watching the show very attentively to catch it, but you would have glimpsed an abyss of despair, a heart oozing pure pain. When the talk show hostess touches her hand, Barb is reminded of where she is and what the priorities are here. She shakes back her glossy chestnut locks and smiles radiantly into camera 3.

"I am deeply touched, Barb, by your sharing what must be the most tragic, the most heart wrenching moment of any mother's – any parent's life. Thank you so much for being so open with us, with our millions of viewers out there – among whom I'm sure some share your fate." Brilliant smile, lots of gleaming teeth. "We'll be right back after a short break and important messages from our sponsors. Then we'll continue our conversation with Barb Bernstein, award-winning documentary filmmaker, about her latest work on drug-running across the Mexican border, the film that earned her an Academy Award nomination."

As the show cuts to commercial, Barb and Amanda Starr both let out long sighs.

"You did great, Barb, and I mean great. I do have to play to my audience on camera, but I really meant what I said. I am deeply touched and awed by your openness and your strength. And I'm convinced it will mean a lot to those parents who have faced similar tragedies."

"I will never..." said Barb in an unusually subdued tone, "never in my whole life do this again."

Wow, so I have an exclusive! Amanda inwardly pumped her fist. Lucky for her, Barb hadn't come to this conclusion before the show. "I can so relate to you, dearest Barb. It must be incredibly painful to talk about. Must be like goring an open wound." Amanda Starr leaned in as if she would gladly stick her finger right in there and make Barb cry out in front of her worldwide audience. "We'll be changing the subject anyhow. You can talk about your work. That'll be easier."

"I warn you – " Barb's voice had taken an icy tone, her eyes the color of storm clouds charged with lightning – "You come back to the subject of my son, and I walk off your show. Are we clear on that?"

The TV star smiled her serial smile and nodded. "I assure you, this won't happen." But would that be such a bad move? Having an offended guest walk off the set is always a headline. The topic was touchy, however. The death of a child, even if it was drug-related, meant sympathies were with the mother. The press would probably slaughter her if she kept digging and Barb were to break down. And after all, she had what she wanted. The haughty Ms. Bernstein, so full of herself, publicly owning up to being a sorry failure when it came to parenting; incapable of preventing her precious son from going the way of so many rich brats – down the highway to hell. Sex 'n' drugs 'n' rock 'n' roll ... Amanda Starr shuddered. She was so relieved her countless couplings had not produced any offspring. Who wanted that responsibility anyway? You poured all this money, all these emotions, all this time and energy into them. And then the ungrateful buggers not only squandered it all, some of them actually croaked at an age when they should finally begin earning an income. What a loser's game.

"We're back with our guest, Barb Bernstein, who was just nominated for an Academy Award for her bold documentary on drug-running across the Mexican border." Amanda Starr beamed into the camera, having rearranged her features on cue from cranky to happy.

"We just talked, dear Barb, about your motivation to dig deep into the subject of illegal drugs flooding this country, and to expose the many ways they come across the border. For those who have just tuned in: Ms Bernstein lost her 17-year old son last year to drugs. Drugs that ultimately finish up in much younger children's hands, through a network of drug barons, runners, corrupt law enforcement and a vast and ever-changing web of pushers and dealers, including children coerced into this dirty business. Barb, what is the most valuable lesson you learned doing this brave and dangerous work?"

Barb focused on the red light of the camera as it zoomed in on her: "What touched and angered me more than anything is how most deaths that result from illegal drugs are so unnecessary."

Amanda Starr just raised her pencil thin eyebrows and bade Barb to continue. They were getting on slippery ground here, and she would definitely not take any blame.

"Illegal drugs are one of the most lucrative business enterprises in the world, amounting to one percent of the entire global commerce. Staggering amounts of money are involved. Mexican cartels alone rake in close to $50 billion a year, in a business that knows neither crunch nor crisis. And we all know money buys not only goods, but also people. It buys power and influence. And just as the world is learning that enterprises turning over great amounts of money need to be regulated on a worldwide basis – keywords here would be global banking or tax laws – so we need to admit that the same goes for drugs. In this business, globalization has been a fact for decades."

"Are you saying that, let's say, the G-20, shouldn't only talk about armaments or trade or human rights, but also about drugs?"

"Yes of course! Look at the numbers. Drugs are a far greater economic stream than the film industry, for instance. But only a handful profit from it. For all others, it's a losing proposition, especially the taxpayers who pick up the tab for all the sick, unemployed, dead or murdered. Just think about the innumerable law enforcement officers paid to chase down every kid smoking grass. Think about the expenses of all those court cases, the prison sentences...all of this costs the taxpayer far more than a college education would."

Barb looked into the camera defiantly. "Matter of fact, I think all drugs should be legalized, with the state taking over the role of the dealer or of licensing the dealers. After all, it does that with a number of drugs already – with alcohol and tobacco just to name the most popular. This is the only measure that would pull the plug on the immense illegal drug market and prevent all the unspeakable violence, the misery and sordidness of drug addiction." Barb beamed sweetly and innocently into the camera, while Amanda Starr's smile, previously chiseled into her face, was crumbling. Just as Amanda drew breath to avert more disaster, Barb continued with quiet determination. "Making drugs illegal really is one of the best job creation programs, but alas not for the real economy. We should have learned that lesson from the prohibition era. Our country doesn't see any revenues from this dirty business, but it does pick up the enormous tab. The numbers are hard to believe: we make up five percent of the global population, yet we hold 25 percent of the world's prisoners – with every fourth arrest directly related to drugs." Again, Barb beamed into the camera, timing herself so precisely that Amanda Starr could do nothing but let her have her say.

"Humanity has used drugs since the beginning of time. The concept of Nancy Reagan's 'Just Say No' obviously doesn't work for everybody. Drugs are a fact of life, so why not look for the best possible way to regulate them and make them available to those who can't or won't do without? Know what? With the revenue and the savings, federal taxes could be lowered or – better yet – our government could use this money to establish a proper education and health care system for all. Then at least some good would come out of this dreadful business."

Amanda Starr desperately wished for a commercial break. This woman was totally off her rocker. This is not what they had agreed on in their preliminary interview. What was this bitch trying to do to her? Oh god, the show's sponsors would be foaming at the mouth, and she'd probably be presenting the hog prices on Radio Iowa as of next week.

"Well, Barb, these are really quite interesting thoughts you have on this subject, radical even. I wish we had more time to explore them in depth." Her smile was brittle. With the repetition of all of Barb's feats, gleefully sticking her finger into the open wound once more, and the highlights of the next show, Amanda Starr expertly ran the clock down, without letting Barb get in another word. That was it for this broad. She would never be on her show again, even if she got an Oscar. Meanwhile her bosses would be shitting bricks. The sponsors were emphatic: no politics, no sex. It would be Iowa hogs next, definitely.

She did not appreciate being upstaged, especially not by a bimbo like Barb. She herself was not exactly a wallflower, but Barb was one of these women who could make any other feel slightly off, a touch shabby even. This Ms. Bernstein was like a complete work of art. Her thick mane of chestnut curls seemed to have a life of its own. When it moved, it threw off sparks in the studio lighting. And this darkly gleaming fire framed a heart-shaped face dominated by a pair of wide-set and compelling eyes. Like the sky at an approaching thunderstorm, Barb's eyes reflected her mood – from a calm deep blue to a stormy violet. And if you didn't get hung up on those incredible eyes, you would notice that Miz B. was blessed not only with a strong, straight nose but also a mouth full of promises: upper lip just a touch fuller than the lower and forming an alluring cupid's bow over her pearly white teeth – the latter a monument to her dentist's skill, no doubt. This striking head sat on a petite body curving in all the right directions, and clad in a magnificently tailored suit of the palest green silk and mohair mixture, the small feet in a pair of Jimmy Choo's the exact color of her hair. It seemed she wore nothing under the suit jacket, at least nothing visible. She also wore no jewelry, except a heavy man's watch on her right wrist. The overall impression of Barb Bernstein was of a precious item wrapped with immense care and attention to detail: no frills, no bows or ribbons to detract from the valuable content. Next to her, Amanda Starr was uncomfortably aware of all the gold and glitter on her own body. The look she cultivated and usually cherished suddenly felt cheap. This is exactly how Barb made a lot of people feel. It wasn't intentional, but it made her no friends.

A very subdued Barb took her usual seat in Dr. Mader's spacious therapy room. She let the tranquility seep into her, admiring once again the harmony between the few pieces in this room – the pastel colored rugs, the black and white Ansel Adams landscapes on the wall, the low white sideboard supporting a vibrant bouquet of roses.

Dr. Mader waited until Barb was ready to recount her TV appearance. The therapist's sympathetic eyes seemed to embrace her, when Barb concluded, "Underneath it all is so much sadness still. So much pain.... It's like it had just happened." Barb pulled a tissue from the strategically placed dispenser and dabbed her eyes.

"It's good to allow the sadness to rise, you know that. Look at your tears as runoff. The glacier's melting, Barb. Life is coming back."

Barb was sobbing now, bent over from sheer pain, the dam she had desperately held up all during the show was fracturing. The therapist remained attentive but very still, letting Barb's pain flow and finally ebb. The pain from having to identify her son Ethan at the morgue – he had been found naked and dead in a friend's bedroom at a Beverly Hills mansion, OD'd on too-clean heroin. The pain from the gaping hole his death had left in her heart – a hole that refused to close.

"Open your heart to suffering, it is humanity's greatest teacher." This insight had hit her like a bolt of lightning during a session with Dr. Mader. But stubbornly Barb had refused to comply. Suffering was for dummies, for those who didn't know how to get a grip on life and bend it to their personal liking.

Life was a question of the right styling, wasn't it? It was about going out and grabbing it by the horns, laughing in its face, flashing some cleavage, until it just laid down and let you do with it what you wanted. But then her 17-year-old baby had died, and Barb had gone straight to hell.

"The form is gone, his essence remains, remember? You are forever connected."

Even though Barb could not quite grasp what her therapist was talking about, she was calmer now, more pensive. She had gradually learned to let go of her overwhelming fury and hatred of Ethan's circle of fucked-up friends who – she was convinced – had seduced her baby, led him astray, and hooked him on this dirt. They were guilty of his death. At times she had almost choked on the bitter hatred she felt towards their parents, even wished those kids dead too, so there would be some justice at least.

Accepting Ethan's responsibility for the way he lived his life had been a major step towards healing. She had grappled with the idea that each soul taking on a body comes to this planet to experience life in human form, and who are we to pass final judgment on the value of these experiences? The greatest love of her life was free of his material body, free of having to feel pain or fear or disappointment; but also unable to experience love and tenderness and joy. Ethan had followed his own path in this life. It was not up to her to judge. But all she really wanted was to have him back, to touch him, smell him, ruffle his unruly hair – so much like her own. Her baby, flesh from her flesh, blood from her blood, her heart. She'd give anything to have him back.

Barb gave a fat tip to the turbaned and bearded driver, whose cab smelled foreign, rich with exotic spices. She had been grateful for his silence while he drove her back to her retreat in the Hollywood Hills. She felt at home here, rooted, her family having settled in the area generations ago. Her great-grandfather, a Jewish physicist, had sailed from Germany for the Promised Land at the turn of the 20th century. He had settled with his family of five in what was then named Cahuenga. When the moviemakers came to town, this David Bernstein, until then a sober and somber man, found his true calling. He met D.W. Griffith, and then a fellow countryman from Baden-Württemberg, Carl Laemmle, who talked him into investing in his company: Independent Moving Pictures. The rest, as they say, is history. Unskilled in handling money, grandpa Bernstein had lost his fortune just as quickly as he had made it, giving her father Ethan the opportunity to start from scratch and prove his own ability. With this background, Barb could claim to be one of the few true Tinseltownians.

Entering her haven with a small sigh of relief, she climbed down off her murderous heels and proceeded barefoot – and several inches shorter – to her bedroom. She peeled off her suit, grabbed her favorite pair of jogging shorts and an oversized Lakers tee shirt and padded, via the kitchen and a bottle of chilled wine, out onto the spacious deck. She dropped into one of the lounge chairs she had talked her father out of. The contemporary interpretation of the traditional loom chair – so elegantly simple and delicate it seemed to float on its chrome rods – had immediately caught her eye on his terrace. He had been easily convinced how exceptional it would look on Barb's deck.

This was a rare moment of tranquility, and Barb didn't really feel comfortable with it. She got up to find a magazine, lit a Brazilian cigarillo, and took a sip of wine. What she really wanted was some of that great grass her sound engineer on the film used to share with her, or maybe half a Quaalude to take her down easy. But that was no longer an option, not since her baby... Never again would she touch that dirt. Yet she still feared quiet; out of silence crept memories that piled up into dark, heavy clouds laden with grief and sorrow. She went over to the stereo and slipped Dylan into the disc player, her favorite music when she felt this way. She had listened to 'Forever Young' a hundred times, sobbing her heart out at first, then – with time – just letting the tears wash away the pain. When her cell phone chirped, Barb grabbed it like a lifeline.

"Got a couple of things to sign, and need to drop off Luce. I'll be over in twenty!" No question, a flat statement, delivered in an affectionate tone.

Mercedes "Merc" Domingo knew exactly how Barb felt after this horrible TV woman had made her talk about Ethan junior's death. And being the mistress of Barb's calendars, both personal and business, she knew her boss would be facing the fallout alone. Both women knew the signatures were a pretext and that Barb's dog Lucy loved to stay over with Mercedes and her big boys. But Barb was grateful – no way she wanted to fall back into her old pattern of coping with anxiety or pain. Too many white lines, too many uppers and downers and screamers and laughers. Barb had at times felt a close kinship with the infamous Gonzo journalist – too many mornings in alien bedrooms, waking to nameless faces. Nunca mas. She never wanted to be a disappeared person again, as she had become in the aftermath of her son's death. Mercedes had been her lifeline then, and still threw the lifebelt when her internal alarm signaled 'woman overboard'.

Ms. Dog jumped on Barb's lap, gave her face a quick lick, and retreated to her home sofa...British racing green velvet. "Feel like some Thai?" Mercedes called from the kitchen.

"You got Thai sticks? Wait till I tell your children!"

Mercedes was pleased with Barb's feeble joke. With a snappy, "It was actually the kids who scored for me," Mercedes put the cartons on the glass table, laid out some napkins and chop sticks, and poured herself a glass of Pinot Grigio. The smells wafting over made Barb's mouth water. Suddenly she was starving.

"I was just having a really great time by myself. Now you come barging in, completely destroying the mood." Barb's frown turned into a smile as she hugged the big woman. "Thank god for it, too."

When they were well into the spicy green curry, the crisp fish and the deliciously fluffy rice, Barb said, "It was primarily your curiosity that brought you here, wasn't it?"

"What else? I can hardly stand your company at the office, so why would I look for it in the insufficient free time you leave me?" Mercedes topped up their glasses, wiped her mouth and settled her elegant 5 foot 8 inch frame into the other lounge chair.

Earlier that morning, Miz Bernstein had swept into her PA's office, full of enthusiasm and specific instructions. "Clear my calendar for the first two weeks of May, and I mean clear, clean, swiped, zero. Yours too by the way...and call Josh, I need him three times a week as of pronto. Have to get in shape, not much time, sit on him if you need to. You too, little one, yes, you too." She had nuzzled the lumpy creature nestling against her bosom, sat it down on Mercedes' desk and took a big sip of her energy drink. "You don't mind, do you? And while you're at it, reschedule my appointment with Dr. Mader to her earliest possible opening, no matter when. If there's something else on the calendar, change it! Best would be this afternoon after that dreadful TV Show. Should I book the spa this weekend? Next?..." Mumbling to herself she had let the door to her office slam shut before Mercedes could even get out a "good morning."

"What do you say, Ms Hound, manic phase coming on?" Mercedes had looked at the dog perched on her desk – short and square like something out of a car press. Lucy had wagged her stumpy tail once, flicked her fawn colored bat ears and clambered onto Mercedes' lap. "Oh no you don't." The elegantly dressed woman had laughed and offloaded the French Bulldog onto one of the ghastly doggy sofas Barb had made her buy, this one upholstered in burgundy with a border of faux petit-point.

How she was going to clear two weeks of her boss's tightly packed calendar was quite beyond her. But what she really wanted to know was why. Knowing Barb, she wouldn't have to wait long to find out; the woman couldn't keep secrets any longer than lovers. After a full hour of phoning and emailing, wheedling and explaining, Mercedes was set. She readied another can of liquid energy and went into Barb's office.

"Dr. Mader squeezed you in right after your TV thing, Josh promised to drop that C-list actor to accommodate you, and I'm still working on those two weeks. Does it really have to be two full weeks? What on earth could be so important?"

"Ah, you're dying to know, aren't you, Miss Nosy?" Barb had smiled mischievously. "Don't raaaghtly know aah should tell you."

Mercedes hated it when Barb did the Southern Belle thing, not only because she was really bad at it, but because thanks to a former employer who hid her pathological spitefulness behind a graceful and polished surface, Mercedes had had enough Southern Belles to last her a lifetime. "Fine, Miz B, as you wish." She had risen to her full height, glanced down at the glossy chestnut hair and made as to leave, when Barb – just as she had known she would – had cried "No, wait, you won t believe this!"

Like a conjurer, she had materialized an envelope from out of nowhere and dropped it on the table. Then the telephone had rung, and it was time to hop into the tacky limo the TV studio had sent for her.

"This is what you want to get your greedy, greasy little paws on, isn't it?" Barb elegantly fanned herself with that mysterious envelope. "You could read it too. It's in Spanish, ¿oyes?"

"I give you oyes, chica! Really want to get into a little language contest here? One you are sure to lose too? Now spill those beans before they choke you!"

"Aah beans. No, unfortunately not beans, but there'll be plenty of potatoes and once in a while a nice crispy guinea pig. That's probably what we'll be eating lots of during those two weeks."

"And just where is it that you'll be eating these delicacies, amiguita?"

"We, dear one, we!" Barb got a huge kick out of this game with Mercedes. Their routine was as finely tuned as something out of 'I love Lucy'.

"We're going to Peru."

"Peru? In the Andes?"

"Yes, Miz M. You got any climbing gear?" Barb giggled at Mercedes' shocked face. "Naaa. Won't need that, we can go everywhere by mule." Now it was the dark eyebrows, which did the climbing on her companion's smooth brown forehead.

"Whoever said I was going? Can't remember you ever mentioning this before and besides, I'd be dragging my feet on one of those scraggly animals. Plus my children...."

"Your children, as you so quaintly call them, are nearly adults. They don't need you, as you very well know. Certainly not for the short time we'll be away. Besides their abuela loves to take care of them, and they love to be taken care of by her. Grandmothers are cool, less stress with the older generation."

"And what, dear god, are we going to do in that wild country?"

Barb's smile faded. When she spoke, she didn't look at Mercedes but gazed out over the trees and the city to the sun sinking into the pink and purple haze – as if slowly settling into its evening bath.

"I've been thinking a lot about doing something in Ethan's memory, something to sink my teeth into at the same time. The documentary was one thing. But that was just a one shot deal, and it's over anyway. Seen today, forgotten tomorrow. Won't change a thing. I wanted something more, something lasting, worthwhile. Now I think I've found it."

Mercedes' heart immediately went out to her boss, her friend. She wanted to wrap her arms around the delicate frame and hug it to her ample bosom, as she had done countless times in these long months of mourning, let some of her abundant strength flow into the woman. But that was not called for right now. Even though there were tears glistening in Barb's eyes, there was a subtle strength – determination even – underneath the sadness.

"When I was researching my documentary, I followed the drug routes from Columbia to Bolivia and Peru. I got to know this Peruvian family, who has lost one of their children to the drug mafia. The boy was abducted and made to work in the Selva. In addition to oil exploration and logging of this incredible rainforest – land that actually belongs to the indigenas – drug cartels are also very active in this area. The people I met are bright, very clear about what they want, but they have no support. When I asked them what they wanted most, it became clear quickly that they would do anything for a better future for their children. And that's only possible if they are given the chance to learn, to be educated and to connect to the rest of the world. So there...that's what I'm going to do. I'm starting an education project, really small scale first, just a couple of families living in a remote area of the Andes. We'll be using the Internet, so they can take online courses, have access to schools, teachers, libraries, information...." Barb's eyes lit up as she proceeded to tell Mercedes in detail how it had all started and what her plans were.

"Strangely enough, doing something for someone else, complete strangers in this case, makes me feel better, you know? Listening to other people's stories, their difficulties and joys, kind of takes attention away from my own preoccupations. Being in a position to relieve someone else's anguish alleviates my own."

Mercedes nodded. This turned out to be quite a leap for self-absorbed Ms Bernstein, usually a universe unto herself.

"And another thing. These people are so incredibly grateful when someone simply listens to them. You know Merc, I had to go to that remote part of the world to realize it, but gratitude is an unfamiliar quality to me. I certainly have never felt much of it, not for what my father has always done for me, not for you being here, putting up with my antics." After a deep sigh, she continued, "I failed to teach my son gratitude." Then cried, "but how could I, if I didn't know it myself! These Andean children are so happy with the little they have, and we live in the land of plenty, constantly dissatisfied, unappreciative, wanting more or at least something else...."

Angrily wiping away the tears, Barb told Mercedes how she would take the money her father had put in a trust fund for his beloved grandson, who was named after him, and use it as seed money for the foundation that would develop this project.

After an hour or so of enjoying Barb's newfound enthusiasm, listening to her plans, and asking countless questions, Mercedes could even imagine herself on a mule. After all, any Peruvian mountain would be a mere anthill compared to the one they had climbed together over the last year. Barb, who used her looks, charm and considerable draw on the opposite sex to gauge her standing in the inbred Hollywood coterie, was becoming aware of a world not only around her, but inside her as well. She had started to perceive others not only as mirrors of her own splendid self, but as fellow humans with their own feelings and ambitions. They also suffered and learned and lived and died in every way imaginable. And instead of worrying where the popularity meter stopped in her own case, she had this new determination to figure out what this person Barb Bernstein was capable of intellectually, mentally, culturally, socially. And if Miz Barb could develop such awareness, then just about anyone could.

Still, Mercedes wondered how long this new project would hold Barb's interest. Her attention span equaled that of a butterfly – constantly on to the next, the new, drawn on and on by the seductive whiff of a promising bud. And, please Mercedes, don't bother me with routine, mundane, everyday repetitive things – hampers my creativity as if I were in a grinding mill. Mercedes smiled to herself....

"What ya laughin' at, frescales? Making fun of me again?" Barb threw a chopstick at Mercedes who had lost herself in her musings. The lights had come on down below, so many that they drowned out the stars. As if in answer to Mercedes' thoughts, Barb said, "You know, I feel this project is like the start of something new. It will be in Ethan's name, but it will not be born of sadness and mourning, it will not have suffering as its foundation. It's about curiosity. And that to me is a very important distinction. I really want to find out whether I can make this fly."

Mercedes smiled as she got up and pulled Barb into a big hug. "I'm so proud of you, and I know it'll fly sky high with all this good energy behind it. Gotta run now, gotta kiss my babies goodnight."

"Yeah, as if they let you!" Barb giggled at the thought of Mercedes tucking in her three strapping boys – big men really – bigger than Mercedes and as street smart as the best of them.

"Drug victim's Hollywood Mom: Legalize it!" "Government should deal dope, filmmaker demands!" "Dead son not enough: Drugs for all!" Barb was quite unprepared for the fallout from her TV appearance. Even though Mercedes broke it to her gently the next morning, Barb totally lost it. It was like being hit by a natural disaster; all Mercedes could do was duck and cover and watch from a safe place as earthquake, eruption and tsunami played out. Whatever was not too heavy to be lifted, took air. Whatever wouldn't fly, took a kick. The devastation was augmented by a constant stream of ranting and raving and screaming and yelling and profanities that made even Mercedes, inoculated by the colorful language of her sons, blush. Apparently, Barb was convinced this bloody TV star cow was behind it all. The sleazy network would be having a goddamned field day shredding Barb and digging their filthy fingers into her bleeding heart with fat happy grins on their ugly mugs. But they had picked on the wrong person. She'd chop off their private parts. She'd make them eat their drivel, she'd...she'd....

Mercedes stayed calm throughout the storm. She had weathered many. They didn't upset or frighten her. Matter of fact, she was quite pleased with this one, because Barb didn't turn the wrath against herself, something she had done a lot of in this past annus horribilis. Rather, she lashed out at those who tried to slander her by purposefully misunderstanding what she had talked about. It had to be expected, of course. Media outlets like these low-end news networks – and not only those under a tight financial squeeze – lived off sensationalizing every wind some halfway-prominent person broke. Pandering to the lowest common denominator, pitting opinion against opinion. Not to educate and help people reach their own conclusions, but to provoke discord and to slander those who dissented from the official party line – to divide and conquer. How could Barb not have seen the trap? Mercedes smiled affectionately. It was so Barb to get carried away with what she deeply believed in, to advocate whatever truth she had unearthed – within herself or while working on one of her projects. Communication was her lifeblood, but not the way it was understood by so many. She had no time for those who held their own opinions to be Gospel truth and talked only to the people who liked to nod a lot, while ridiculing anyone up for a true debate – a meaningful exchange of views, thoughts and ideas.

This was definitely a double espresso occasion. Mercedes set the machine to brew its magic, arranged a couple of dark chocolate truffles on a tiny porcelain plate, and headed into the disaster zone. Barb was sitting on the deep window seat overlooking the busy street below, manically shredding the newspapers that had sparked her rage.

"Hold on, is that the Times you're destroying? There's something in it that might interest you, in the technology section. Something about a guy putting excellent free mini-lectures on the net, and about CAL."

Barb slowly looked up, the mad grin fading from her face.

"Huh? Cali, what? I certainly wish I were Cali right now, I'd show those hypocritical bastards where the goddess gets her collection of heads from!"

"C A L", Mercedes spelled out each letter. "Computer Assisted Learning, education, Peru – got it?"

"Yeah, I got it the first time, auntie M. Just wiping the rest of the foam off my mouth. Here, take the rag, can't bear to look at any of them. Put the article on my desk, would you?" Barb downed the strong black brew in one gulp, chased it with one of the truffles and stuffed the other one in Mercedes' mouth.

4

In the End lies the Beginning

While delving deeper into the mysteries of human life on this quite agreeable planet, the twins were particularly fascinated by the way the human brain favored linear thinking: everything had a beginning and an end, even the universe. Matter of fact, earthling scientists hunted in earnest for its beginning. Human life too had a so-called beginning, and apparently the fourth force of nature played an important part in this mystifying process. How did Big G tug a soul into a mission cloak for yet another performance on the earthly stage?

When Victoria offered up some answers, the twins were even more baffled: "Imagine your free-floating subtlest particles suddenly being pulled into a dense shell growing in a watery environment. The shock is slightly lessened by the shell floating in warmth and near silence, connected by a cable that supplies all vital sustenance." When Marvin frowned and got up – his imagination was simply not wired that way – Victoria paused. She hadn't planned on bringing this on just yet, but why not. Now was as good a time as any.

She invited the twins to connect with the plasma cube, and in an instant all three had disappeared from their base and were now hovering near the ceiling of a brightly lit room. Below, lying flat on her back, a woman was moaning and panting, finally giving a heave and a sharp animal cry. Between her thighs appeared a frighteningly large head, slick with blood and birth fluids, slightly bent out of shape by being forced through a narrow canal – more like a fissure in a rock than a flexible tube – into cold air and harsh light. A figure dressed in pale green scrubs eased the tiny mission cloak from the woman, then – to the total dismay of the twins – disconnected the life support cable between mother and young, literally cutting it off. Was it a reject? Damaged maybe or perhaps just too ugly to look at? After a few moments of the world seeming to hold its breath, the hatchling apparently decided to trust his new environment and took a deep gulp of air. This jump start induced a remarkable change of atmosphere in the room. A sudden radiance broke through the dense, electrically charged cloud, drawing the Forces nearer.

"Isn't that the couple we saw on the beach just after our arrival? With that complex dance culminating in intense tactile interaction?" Avory indicated the depleted Mom and beaming Dad, who were cooing over the wrinkled, red-faced newborn sleeping peacefully in the protective circle of its mother's arms. Avory was trying so hard to bathe in the radiance enveloping the family that he almost materialized right then and there.

"You mean ogling and fondling?" Marvin flashed.

Totally absorbed in the momentous occasion, the humans paid no attention to the tiny colored light pulses high up in the corner of the maternity room.

"Let me introduce you to a future President of the United States," beamed the father. "I just know that George Jefferson Forrester will play a very important role in our great country!"

Marvin was baffled. "How does he know what role this soul has come to play?"

"He doesn't. He's just voicing his own ambitions." Victoria then reminded them of what they had learned from their extensive research. Of the three shells making up an earthling, only body and brain were visible to the human. They were made of the first two states of matter: solids and liquids, the particles upon which Big G exerted most pull. The much more subtle, faster moving third state of matter was still invisible to humans, incomprehensible even. Those gaseous particles formed the innermost shell, the soul that housed the universal animating force.

A human was put together in distinct sets of pairs and fives, with the former being an expression of the dual forces ruling this planet and the latter mirroring the five elemental energies – earth, water, fire, air and space. In addition to fingers and toes (to keep in physical contact with the material world), humans were also outfitted with five sensors to decode their surroundings – gathering visual, auditory, olfactory, tactile and gustatory information.

Deeper analysis, however, revealed that these physical and sensory feelers led humans in circles. Despite, or perhaps because of, being surrounded by continuous emergence and dissolution, by relentless transformation even of their own body cells, humans longed for something lasting. They sought permanence in this constantly changing environment, but mistakenly searched externally for life's greatest secret. They hunted and failed, time and again, since the secret of secrets, the only thing that forever remained the same, lay hidden inside every human being.

The five elements making up the planet also came into play in every human. Earth and water formed their physical body: their mission cloak or, in Marvin's words, their 'do-duds'. The element fire kept that cloak at a constant temperature, fueled by caloric and physical energy from food. Furthermore, humans were directly dependent on air, needing it to jump start and maintain the mission cloak, as the forces had just witnessed.

The fifth element, space, was the most elusive, since it could not be perceived with the five sensors. Only by bundling all senses into one fusion sense, directed inward, could humans catch a glimpse of the secret knowledge that was stored in the element space. And, as Avory and Marvin had learned from their conversation with Big G, space was his most intimate colleague and partner: the element through which he communicated with all matter, making humans constantly aware of his presence.

The Forces focused again on the tiny bundle swathed in soft white blankets, a cap protecting its still pliable head. At the center of its fragile mission cloak, they looked in awe upon the force that steered all three human shells, the secret of all secrets, the ultimate reality, that immortal spark all humans carry within.

Judging by the emissions in the room, humans deemed it a most joyful occasion when a soul once more donned a mission cloak. But what was there to celebrate? Wasn't it a hassle to get into this most cumbersome costume for the umpteenth time, figure out its mechanics – use of hands, standing up and walking, learning to form words from sounds – and all without the slightest memory and no idea what role one had come to play on Earth this time around? And if that wasn't enough, from the very first breath they were exposed to Big G's drag. His pull – even a light, teasing tug – caused their water to drop south and made them feel heavy, downtrodden and depressed.

Avory recalled Big G saying how difficult it was to find a volunteer willing to play with him – aside from kids, who loved to test him out. But because a mission cloak was more than half water, dancing with gravity was a tremendous challenge for adults. Big G pulled mainly on the first and second states of matter – on solids and liquids – so his influence was most heavily felt on the physical and mental plane. Thus most humans saw him as an oppressor – imposing suffering and sickness and constantly placing obstacles in their path of uninterrupted happiness – even though they had him to thank for their sophisticated mission cloak: bones, muscles, tendons, the upright walk, even the comparatively large brain. But as long as humans didn't recognize Big G's game and pitted their internal firepower against him, theirs would always be a loosing battle.

Without a sound, the three forces vanished from the room and reappeared on the deck of their base. As if pulled by the twins' recollection of their discussions, Big G soon joined them in their secluded spot high above the ocean – not in body, in unmistakable voice only. He figured it was an opportune time to impress Marvin and Avory with another aspect of his abilities. Sounding like a foghorn, he reminded them that he was responsible not only for ensuring that humans stepped on this earthly stage on cue, but also off of it. And since they had already witnessed the first, they would now be privileged to observe the latter as well. As it happened, the newborn's granddad – the leading actor in this particular lesson – was ready to take his last bow.

"How do you know when to give the decisive jolt, Big G? Or do humans drop their costume every time you hiccup or sneeze?"

Unperturbed he explained to Marvin that every mission cloak had its use-by date pre-programmed to the second, like a processor built to last for a specified time and to perform a proscribed number of tasks. "The game plan is that players know this date when they pick up their costumes, but as soon as they step onto the stage – gone and forgotten."

Victoria winked at the plasma cube, re-opening the view. A group of humans crowded around a small square opening in a long wall. An earthen pot had been placed next to the niche. Scanning at lightning speed through his image bank, Marvin first thought "mailbox," but then muttered: "columbarium." When Victoria tapped the cube for rewind they caught a glimpse of a human mission cloak inside a wooden box. Despite his rosy cheeks and carefully combed hair, the impeccably dressed human was no more than an empty wrapper, apparently causing the gloomy, low frequency emissions from the dearly beloved in the room.

After the box was solemnly pushed behind a curtain, Marvin and Avory were fascinated to see doors opening on a raging inferno. Fire consumed the box, causing gases in the mission cloak to expand, urging it into a macabre dance before it exploded into a shower of ashes.

"Why don't they celebrate now?" Marvin sounded a touch unnerved as the Forces watched the urn being stashed inside the niche. "Like they did when the soul of their hatchling was trapped in his costume? Now that granddad's liberated – after a pretty admirable performance on the earthly stage – nobody applauds. Can they not see they've got it backwards?"

No, Victoria explained, not while humans identified so much with the chemical reactions in their brain – with that extremely strong human force called emotions. Only when they learned to penetrate deeper levels of reality would they know and understand the cycle of life on Earth – something the upgrade would shed light on.

The twins were about to butt in, but Big G wasn't finished with the topic yet. Earthlings, he said, identified so completely with their transitory costume that most of them were convinced it was all they were. So they didn't relish letting it go.

Avory drew a parallel with human reactions to his rearrangement of the planet's fauna or flora. There were outcries about loss, damage, depletion and disappearance, about things ending and the earth becoming poorer. But this baffled both of them, and Big G only added to their confusion by reiterating, "humans are convinced that when a mission cloak is broken beyond repair, their whole existence ends, finito, fini…"

As the plasma cube faded the image of the dispersing mourners, Victoria nodded and remarked that the twins didn't know this human concept of beginning and ending because they simply didn't have it loaded.

5

Loving the Enemy

Thank god it hasn't rained in the last few days. Even in the best of circumstances the road from Kizu is a hell of a challenge. But Haki, both hands gripping the wheel, is singing at the top of her voice as she steers the decrepit vehicle down the dirt road. She swerves around deeply washed-out potholes, craters really, big enough to swallow a small truck. Nothing can dampen her high spirits because she is on the road to the port city of Matadi. And her prayers appear to have been answered – the rusted-out heap has been holding up so far. It's wheezing and coughing and sputtering, but not giving up just yet – much to the shared joy of her passengers: some sick, some going to market. The chickens and piglets add their clucking and squealing to the chorus of human voices, while spare auto parts beat a rhythm from the back of the pickup. Haki is on the way to see her fellow sisters of the congregation of Les Filles de la Sagesse – the Daughters of Wisdom – founded in 18th century France. They are her flock, the only family she knows. It is a treat she looks forward to every three months or so. Of course she'll bring back vital supplies, medicines and tools, whatever her little bush medical station needs. But the prospect of being among her peers makes the otherwise arduous and dangerous drive a joyful occasion.

On the outskirts of town she spots a pride of boys with shovels by the roadside and slows down, tooting the horn – a sound like a wounded cow. The boys run to the old pickup, grin at Haki, and guide her around the carefully constructed sand trap. They wouldn't dare make her pay to be shoveled out, unlike other more unsuspecting travelers, who – once stuck – are then generously helped by boys with shovels miraculously appearing from nowhere...for a sweet soda or another small token of appreciation, of course.

Driving into this port city on the banks of the wide Congo River is always a bit of a shock. Every time she arrives, new buildings have risen and more vehicles, bicycles, animals, and people crowd the narrow streets. Smells and noise assault Haki from all sides, as she maneuvers her way through the chaos towards the center of town. The animals going to market have been unloaded, patients deposited at the hospital. Now it's just Haki and her anticipation, honking her horn at the old man who guards the tall iron gate at the entrance to her fellow sisters' compound. It is not only the logistic center for a whole range of services to the suffering and needy, the compound also shelters a dozen girls who have already seen too much of life, a harsh existence on the streets, pushed out there by their families. She's witnessed it countless times, but Haki does not, will not, come to terms with parents, with families who cast out their own, shoving a child out of the nest without protection.

Accusing a girl or a boy of witchcraft was the most common excuse for such barbaric behavior. But getting rid of another mouth to feed was really just one more ugly consequence of desperate poverty. As in much of the world, females here rated less – ranked lower than cattle. This was all the more infuriating because women carried more than twice the load of life and work than men. In a country where the male population mostly talked and drank and fought – since there was no employment to be had – it was up to the women to quietly feed and clothe themselves, along with the offspring these men sired so recklessly.

Haki is greeted with a storm of hoots and cries and kisses – her tall, slender body crushed against countless bosoms. There's warm water to wash off the travel dust, followed by tea and cookies in comfortably sagging chairs under slowly spinning ceiling fans. There's much catching-up to do on the last three or four months: births and deaths, eloping and returning, tears and laughter and – for Haki most importantly – knowing she belongs. This belonging, to a worldwide group of strong and dedicated sisters, carries her through her days and nights out in the bush, through the brighter and darker times.

But Haki cannot really take a rest until she has visited the families out by the railroad tracks. They are especially important to her, and she longs to see how Kandi and Meme and Jasira and Sauda are faring. Had the babies survived? Were they infected with the virus? Had Kandi finally ditched her abusive man? With four fellow sisters piling into the old heap, Haki crawls more than drives over to the abandoned rail yard, home to the families her congregation cares for – as best their limited resources will allow. The painfully young mothers shared a string of busted up, rusted-out freight wagons. There, these children gave birth to children. They cooked and slept in the murderous heat and dug the dry, hard ground to plant a few crops. A nearby spigot would occasionally give up precious water. Otherwise, they just drew it out of shallow puddles alive with all sorts of creeping and crawling and flying things. The railroad families owned virtually nothing. A couple of tattered straw mats to hang up for an illusion of privacy, a plastic bucket the sisters had provided for washing and bathing the children, a pot for heating whatever they could scrape together for a meal, a bit of cloth to wrap around as clothing. They didn't live: they survived.

What was it God had in mind with this scheme? Haki refused to believe that these women – and the tiny shriveled bundles they produced at regular intervals – were being punished for whatever sins they might have committed. Most hadn't even had time to commit any. Barely teenagers, they were trapped in the most vicious cycle of poverty, exploitation, and abuse, ending in sickness and lingering death. She also didn't gain any comfort from knowing they would be sitting on God's right in the hereafter. They had a right to decency in the here and now. But when she draws up to the boxcars, Haki forgets all about God. She is stormed by a gang of toddlers and teenagers with glowing eyes, huge smiles, happy shouts and greedy, sweaty, dirty little hands grabbing at her from all sides, trying to get at the sweets they know she has brought.

On the drive back to the bush, Haki values the silence. She has unloaded her last passenger at one of the footpaths leading to the countless small dwellings scattered throughout the vast empty landscape of the Bas-Congo. The visit has left her happy and glowing, as well as distressed and angry. She can't rid her mind of the images of her visit to the refugee camp on the outskirts of town, where another congregation tries to maintain some kind of environment fit for humans. But while the mothers from the railroad tracks impress her with their inventiveness and the quiet strength with which they face their dismal circumstances, the camp visits just drain her. Hope and confidence simply sink in this sea of human misery, sink without a trace and drown. How was anyone to recognize the creator's hand in this wretchedness, not to mention his boundless love?

Truth be known, these women and children were there because men claiming to act in His name roved the country, maiming and killing and raping and stealing and feeling heroic at brutalizing the weak. How could that make a man feel like a hero? Didn't they have a heart? Did they really embrace an idea, a concept – their version of truth – higher than the fifth commandment? What about the wellbeing of a fellow human, a human who wouldn't even dispute whatever ideology these perpetrators upheld? How could anyone destroy life in the name of God? Haki suspected that Christ's most important message to the world, his personal example of non-violence, had been purposefully ignored – perhaps even distorted from the very beginning. The warrior Romans had adopted Christianity and spread the word, so perhaps the message of non-violence had simply been lost. Or had those in power put a spin on it, to make their bloody métier look good?

What really upset Haki was knowing that it wasn't only the deprived and uneducated men in her own country who were easily led astray by a leader with a loud voice and a few coins in his pocket giving them a sense of purpose, however distorted. The problem seemed to be a global sickness. A glimpse at the newspapers in Matadi had made her brutally aware of that.

She had read an article about the cost of modern warfare. The numbers had been staggering. With the money wasted on one minute of the most recent war involving so-called civilized nations, Haki and her sisters could have built and fully outfitted at least three new hospitals. One minute! Reading this had brought Haki to the brink of despair, even more than seeing people scrambling for a halfway decent life. The senselessness of it all, the sinfulness. Rich countries squandered their money to maintain enormous destructive power. Her own, deeply corrupt government – in cahoots with multinational corporations – pissed away hundreds of millions on heavily arming its own troops, and all the while siphoning off millions more for cars, villas and unimaginable opulence. It was beyond immoral. It was a crime against humanity that developed nations, which had known peace for decades, made billions through arms sales to violent and corrupt regimes in countries whose people were starving. At times the usually gentle, understanding and forgiving Haki has to muster all her willpower not to let hatred poison her heart – or to go at these people with her bare hands.

Time and time again Haki has wished she had someone with whom to share these deliberations. But this is tricky terrain. Her fellow sisters were too busy to delve deeply into philosophical questions, her coworkers at the hospital are simply not interested. Yet pondering these questions has been vital to her, for as long as she can remember. She doesn't feel unfaithful to her church because of such inquiry. After all, the church was and is the mother and father Haki has never had. The church has given her shelter, an education, and a framework within which the lonely girl could grow safely into the woman she is today. But while Haki has never doubted the fundamentals of the Catholic faith, she does question some of the personnel. Even as a lively and curious primary schoolgirl, she had kept asking why, why, why? The answers – platitudes mostly, bible quotes or a smack on the head – neither satisfied nor silenced her. But when she persisted, her faith was questioned – the argument to end all arguments. However great her debt to mother church, Haki would not close her eyes and shut down her inquiring mind, and she would not take the vows. She would be part of the flock, but remain a lay sister.

She was in no danger of going astray. That was something the church functionaries had never understood. Haki had been blessed with a deep conviction that guided her like a beacon through any spiritual or mental storm. She was certain beyond any doubt that Christ's message of love and forgiveness, of compassion and kindness, could heal the world's ills, all ills. Compassion, she would tell anyone who'd listen, held more power than any weapon of mass destruction. She knew every single human heart had a limitless capacity to love and to forgive, a capacity – regrettably – left largely untapped. Hatred chained the heart and curtailed personal freedom, whereas compassion was the bridge connecting the individual to everything else. For Haki, there was nothing more important in human existence. Compassion was the key to true freedom and lasting happiness.

As she rounds the last bend, before the small hospital building comes into sight, the dark clouds slowly lift from her mind and heart. She realizes how much she loves to return to this place – her home for the last few years – where she knows every tree, every chicken, every person, and where the daily routine structures her life and brings order to her thinking.

Almost 50,000 people depend on this medical station, and each month a few handfuls of new souls see the first light of day in the maternity ward. Haki is proud of what her team accomplishes every day with terribly limited resources. A couple of years ago they had added a small agricultural school to the hospital, where kids were taught how to work the land effectively, produce crops and keep livestock healthy. This addition has also helped provide better food for patients whose families cannot stay behind and cook for them.

As the pickup jolts over the narrow path, Haki gives a short prayer of thanks, that the old heap has survived another journey – surely one of its last, the way the motor is spluttering and spewing black greasy clouds of smoke. They would have to find a replacement. They would have to find the money. But they would find a solution. They always did.

Her first duty – after unpacking all the stuff brought back from town, distributing treats to children magically appearing from miles around, and making a quick round through the patients' wards – is to take care of the chickens. Haki has a special fondness for the scrawny hens scratching day after day in the hard earth, now cracking after an unusually long dry spell. She admires the way they never give up hope of a fat moist worm, though they rarely find anything but the occasional beetle. She laughs at the dust storms they create, wiggling around in their sand baths. Haki throws some scraps on the ground, and the hens come running with feathers flying, just as the children had a little while before. The pompous rooster struts over, selects one of the choice bits and calls his first hen to dine on it.... Haki can't suppress a smile. She marvels at the clear hierarchy in the chicken coop. Just like her Church, she often thinks. The same pecking order: males rule and assign females their place.

Haki doesn't mind such structure. It actually gives her a feeling of security. She likes to know who is boss and where she belongs in an organization, but gender-based hierarchy frustrates her. She simply sees no valid reason to exclude women from important functions in the church. Especially in view of the hard, difficult and often dangerous work her fellow sisters do every single day. Were the men perhaps afraid they'd have to take over the hands-on jobs when women moved up the ladder and into office? Was that a reason why they hid behind tradition and kept this gender gap as wide and deep as possible?

Hierarchy had corseted her at an early age. Blessed with a quick mind and an inquisitive nature, she would have loved to become a doctor, but the church sent only boys overseas to study – of course in the hope they would later serve as priests. Still, she had been allowed to train as a nurse, and she was grateful.

The dusty chicken run with the funky feather balls – always hungry for food and new adventures – is one of Haki's favorite spots. She likes to stand there and let her mind drift. Right now it is pulling her in a definitely more pleasurable direction. At feeding time she makes a sport of identifying each of the more than two dozen hens by name. Even though many of them were of the same parentage, if you looked closely, you could make out distinguishing features. A crooked comb here, a slightly different plumage pattern there – even the scrawny feet were distinct.

Inspired by her chickens, Haki has begun paying closer attention, with increasing awe, to the endless variety in nature. What went for her chickens went for all animals, for all humans, for all plants and all rocks. There was no blueprint to God's marvelous creation, with identical leaves or beetles being mass-produced from a mold. There was no repetition, not even one absolutely identical blade of grass, just billions upon billions of distinct entities. The designer of this breathtaking diversity had access to an inexhaustible source of ideas and variety. Yet some said it had all come about just by accident, by natural selection, environmental circumstance, survival of the fittest.... Could that really be true? Haki sighed. Nobody knew for sure. There were indicators, certainly, but there was just as much speculation. And somehow that satisfied her. She liked the space uncertainty opened up in her mind, where wonder and awe could spread without being strapped down by knowing.

Not knowing didn't mean closing your eyes to what was going on, though. She might be content not to understand precisely how all the different species had come about, but she sure knew what led to their extinction. It was vanity, greed and a frightening lack of foresight that destroyed the habitat of ever more life forms. Native forests were razed to make room for cattle or fast growing timber, while traditional crops were replaced by genetically manipulated varieties requiring high maintenance and yielding only one harvest. Terminator technology they called their hare-brained invention, designed to make farmers pay each time they wanted to sow. The oceans and rivers were poisoned by crude oil and toxic wastes, the air by noxious fumes and gases and dust. The planet's temperature was rising like that of a feverish child. Climate change indeed....

Sometimes Haki thought the planet tried desperately to tell the species that had remodeled it so thoroughly, that a change in climate was vital. Haki felt deeply connected to those trying to stem the tide of destruction, save the planet from ruin, natural resources from devastation and different species from annihilation. In her book, environmental destruction was simply a variation of war.

Just a few minutes more, Haki promises herself, standing still amidst her chickens, letting her thoughts come and go, enjoying the peaceful moment before she would open up her office. Then she would slip back into the daily business routine with its never-ending demands on her ability to organize and reorganize at the drop of a hat, to counsel, comfort, command or simply lend an additional pair of hands.

When she hears them, it is already too late. They look like creatures out of a nightmare: glistening skin barely concealed by tattered bits and pieces, shredded green army shirts and ragged camouflage pants held up by rope. Some are barefoot, some clad in high-laced black leather boots. All wear mirrored sunglasses and bandanas, berets or kepis on their shaved heads. And they are armed, heavily armed. When they break through the brush Haki yells "run, run, hide!" And her staff runs, fleeing in all directions like a flock of chickens at the sight of a wild dog. All except Haki. She stands and faces the intruders; a tall, slender figure in a simple white dress, head held high on a long and graceful neck, the empty bowl of scraps like a shield. Her eyes do not betray the terror she feels, the set of her lips speaks of determination.

It isn't foolishness or bravery that makes her stand her ground. It is more an inability to do anything else. After all, this is her hospital, her flock, her responsibility. They want food their leader says: food and drink for 30 soldiers – proud servants in the Lord's Resistance Army. Even though Haki doubts their claim, since this particular rebel group has never come this far south, she knows full well there is no way to refuse. They will take and do exactly as they please. And she has nothing but herself to put in their way.

As she watches how some of the men, boys really, settle on a nod from the leader in the shade of the kitchen building, she feels somebody move next to her. Mbodo, the old man who does chores around the grounds and buildings, steps in front of her, leaning on his garden hoe. "We have nothing to spare," he says in a quiet, even voice. "All we have is for the sick, and those caring for them in the name of the Lord."

Haki holds her breath. The group leader looks up. His heavy jowls spread into a wide grin, and very softly he addresses Mbodo: "We can take care of that, no problem. Takes a couple of minutes and you won't have any hungry mouths – and plenty of food."

But Mbodo will not back down. "How can you call yourselves the Lord's army and behave like that?" he asks earnestly.

The soldier gives a faint nod to the two boys standing next to him. They step forward, grab Mbodo, sling a rope around his ankles and carry him – as if he weighs nothing – over to the tallest tree in the yard. The rope is thrown over a thick branch, and they pull the old man up. When Haki cries out and makes to run and help Mbodo, two more youngsters are waved over to intercept her. They throw her to the ground and hold her there.

"Makele!"

"Yes general?"

"Show us what a man you are!"

The boy cannot be more than 12. When Haki looks at him she sees glazed, empty eyes in a child's emaciated face. Makele swaggers over, already tugging at the string holding up tattered pants that sag around his skinny legs. Haki thinks she can detect a faint odor of fear and shame underneath the acrid stench of sweat and unwashed body. He grabs the front of her dress and rips it open. His hands tremble lightly as he takes a crude knife from his pocket and cuts her white cotton panties. Haki lies still, her eyes closed so as not to aggravate the boy further. She feels strangely detached from her body. Mostly she feels a deep pity for a boy whose childhood has been stolen: abused, misused and soon to be discarded when he had has outlived his usefulness. The boy fumbles and gropes and sweats, while his comrades egg him on, cheering and whistling. He makes as if he is pumping away, but Haki feels nothing but soft, sweaty flesh gliding on her flesh. The boy is, after all, just a boy. He grunts, stiffened in a convincing imitation of orgasm, then rolls off her, hitches up his pants and pretends to kick her in the ribs. When Haki pulls up her knees and raises her hands to shield herself, he spits at her.

"Bitch", he says, just loud enough for the others to hear. "Ugly as sin and dry as a knothole. I should slice you open like a sack of barley."

All the while his eyes beseech her to remain still. The laughing and cheering stops when the general steps up and lifts the boy by the scruff of his neck. "Good show, boy, but we have things to do, places to go. You," he nods at the small group guarding the old man, who still hangs head down from the tree like some strange fruit. "You know what to do." Then he orders the men by threes and fours to go find what is useful. "Don't forget to check the dispensary. But don't touch the patients – we are, after all, the Lord's army aren't we?" He laughs raucously and turns around to watch his boys take sticks and fence posts to the body hanging from the tree, swinging wildly as they bat him around. When at last the group moves off, hooting and hollering – with the general being chauffeured in the fully loaded ambulance – Haki's tears mingle in the dust with blood dripping from a cut on her chin. Her patients are safe, the buildings still stand, and Mbodo is beyond hurting.

By nightfall, those hiding in the rainforest return to help her bury Mbodo's battered and broken body behind the chapel. Haki is sitting on the stoop of the small structure where they worship. Right after the attack she had got on the two-way radio to arrange transport from the main road to Matadi. They urgently needed food, medicine and replacements for what had been looted. They needed new chickens. Haki couldn't bear to look at the empty coop, where only a few stray feathers were left. She couldn't stop thinking about the boy, about all those lost and abused children who were made orphans in unthinkable ways. Some were even forced to kill their own families and accept rifles as their new mothers and fathers. Her heart bled for these children – forced to fight the pointless wars of adults – coerced into becoming allies of those who had violated and abused them most. And in a remote corner of her heart she even found pity for those lost and deluded men traveling straight to hell on their road of violence.

Haki is startled out of her thoughts by a noise coming from behind the chapel. She jumps up and is just about to cry out in alarm, when a small face becomes visible in the moonlit brush, a finger on his lips.

"Makele," she whispers. "What...."

The tears have traced a shiny track through the dirt-smeared cheeks. Haki's heart opens wide at the sight of this child, all alone and desperately lost in this endless darkness.

After the boy has washed thoroughly and slipped into some old clothes that are too big on him, Haki feeds him some watery soup and finds him an empty bed. Makele told her how he had snuck away from the troop in the dense forest and made his way back to the hospital in the desperate hope of being taken in. He did not mention what he had tried to do to Haki. He has not once looked at her since emerging from the forest, but he had handed her his AK-47 so she could defend herself next time.

"That's very thoughtful of you, Makele, but I cannot accept your gift. I would never use a weapon against another human being."

Makele looks at her now, with utter incomprehension. "What if I they come after me? What if I have led them back here?"

"Then we'll just have to see, little one. But they won't come. They would have been here already. What's one boy to them? They will steal another from his home, his family...."

The boy's eyes close. Haki brushes her hand lightly over his shorn head. He looks so innocent, so small, so much like the child he will never be. She will keep him at the compound. He can attend school with the other kids, they will see what talents he has, and teach him how to use them. For a start, he can take over Mbodo's chores.

Gazing down at the sleeping boy now, Haki has a sudden revelation. For months she has fretted over a decision, the due date drawing nearer. The foundation that for years now has generously supported the bush hospital, has invited her to the U.S. They have plans for her: they intend to finance a string of bush hospitals in the Bas-Congo. A supervisor is needed, someone who understands the medical and the managerial side. They will give her the chance to take Business Administration courses and visit modern clinics in their area. It is a unique opportunity, she is well aware of that. Still she has hesitated.

There is the guilt of leaving the others in hardship, of traipsing off into the rich world. There is also her strong sense of responsibility and – if she is really honest – also some fear of the unknown. Ever since being offered the chance, she has been torn between her loyalty to the hospital – to her people here –

and this unique opportunity to realize her dream of doing more good for more people in the future. Now it seems like fate has handed her the answer. It is time to put some distance between herself and this place. As soon as she has their small ship back on course, she will be off. The boy will be cared for. He will get a new lease on life here – through plain honest work in a stable environment.

She lightly brushes the back of her hand over the boy's soft cheek. She will have a word with her assistant first thing tomorrow. She'll prepare her to take over the management of the compound. She'll give Makele into the care of the agricultural section administrator, a quiet and dependable man whose own sons were already grown up. Under his guidance the boy will learn to care for other living beings, hopefully forgetting and healing over time. He will learn to take on responsibility, which will give him a sense of self-worth. He needs stability, appreciation and clear assignments. Thus, with God's help and her treasured little island in the Congolese bush, he will heal.

6

A Dream with Impact

Almost anyone watching Shiv Singh Sitaram hurry across campus towards his lab at the Energy Research Centre would have thought of a giraffe. Not in an unkind way, since the overall appearance was quite appealing, if a touch confusing. The close-cropped, glossy hair was definitely Indian. Yet when you looked into his eyes under thick, long lashes any woman would envy, you'd guess Han Chinese, while his striking features with high, jutting cheekbones took you deep into Tibet. Still, the loping stride of the unusually tall, lanky man, and the way he stretched his long neck forward as if to lead the way, invariably brought a giraffe to mind. If Shiv was aware of that, and it has to be assumed he was (since they had called him giraffe already in primary school) he didn't care. Nothing to do with human vanity caught Shiv's attention.

This morning he didn't even have eyes for the densely set palms spreading shade over the campus sidewalks, nor the elegant red sandstone buildings carrying the inimitable signature of Le Corbusier – who had shaped not only the University but the whole city of Chandigarh. Shiv was, as during most of his waking hours, deep in thought, his mind grinding and polishing away at one of the gems stored in his mind. That's how he saw his brain – the treasure chest he had coveted as a boy, overflowing with promising rocks, some polished to a sparkling brilliance, some still raw and dull, but full of potential. Last night had added a new sort of jewel, disturbing and exciting. Shiv had been jolted awake in the early hours of the morning, drenched in sweat and confusion. The vivid dream still reverberated throughout his system.

As he passed the Centre for Computer Science, Shiv caught sight of a faded portrait of Sathya Sai Baba that some joker had tacked up on the blackboard, advising the reader to "Surf the Innernet – rather than the Internet." A slow smile spread across his face. True indeed. The frizzy haired guru had been well ahead of the crowd. Not that Shiv cared for gurus – not for those in pinstriped suits, preaching the gospel of ruthless economics or nationalistic political beliefs, even less for the merchants of absolute truths, exclusive gods and singular ways to heaven. But he could appreciate Sai Baba's advice: to strive for valid answers from within oneself, instead of chewing the cud of beliefs, theories or philosophies thought up by men long dead.

Shiv had spent most of his life taking a closer look – not merely with his arresting eyes. He knew the mind to be the world's finest instrument, evolution's highest achievement and the most powerful tool in existence. And he was appalled at how few really made use of it. It was this genuine incomprehension that made Shiv appear a bit of an intellectual snob. True, he didn't have much patience for people who used most of their brain capacity to operate a TV remote or figure out the best buy at the supermarket. But he was genuinely baffled why most humans were happy to parrot what others had formulated, instead of seeking their own truths. Why on Earth did people not want to think for themselves?

It was a mystery to Shiv how six billion people could still cling to the same beliefs and concepts as a half billion had done all those centuries ago. 500 million who had barely begun to grasp the basic facts of life, their scientists just beginning to discover the laws of nature. No wonder modern science so often clashed with philosophical concepts created for hunter-gatherers and farmers, along with religious doctrines aimed less at enlightening the human spirit than at consolidating power and wealth. Modern physics sketched out a universe in constant motion with all matter in one endless mathematically fathomable dance of particles, organized over billions of years by only four forces of nature – electromagnetic, weak, strong and gravity – into a myriad of different and ever more complex shapes. But people still clung to inflexible concepts and rigid mental structures thought up and put in place hundreds, even thousands of years ago. Instead of lifting their minds up to the stars, the source of all matter on Earth – planet and people included – they kept their eyes glued to the ground and tried to find safety in being different, different from each other, different from nature, different from all that surrounded them. Searching for safety they found only fear.

And fear, Shiv was convinced, was the soil from which violence sprouted. Some religious and political leaders were particularly adept at exploiting this fear. His country was a prime example of both working hand-in-hand. The Punjabis had been stirred into fear and hatred of their former neighbors, friends even, just because they followed a different prophet. His home country had been torn apart in an indescribably violent frenzy in which hundreds of thousands perished and millions had to flee. In Kashmir, war raged on because the religious convictions of the Hindus and Muslims were being exploited. Not that Christians were any better. One look at the gruesome punishment of the most important and most adamantly non-violent figure in Christianity was enough. Not to mention the atrocities committed in the name of their god by the Inquisition, or the proselytizing that didn't shy away from brutality when words alone wouldn't convince.

Before he hit the lab, Shiv felt he needed a cup of that time-honored remedy for all sorts of ills. He folded himself into a chair under a wide umbrella and gazed at the rainbows playing in the water fountains. The invisible made visible, light split into different colors. But in essence it stayed the same – simply electromagnetic waves of different frequencies. He could not fail to make an analogy to his previous train of thought. We all stem from the same source. We are all stardust – carbon, nitrogen, hydrogen, oxygen.... All life is made of the same building blocks, produced out there in the cosmos. Like light split by a prism into brilliant colors, so do human beings taking their first breath become individuals. Do red, orange, yellow, green, blue and violet also forget they stem from one source and return to it as soon as the prism is taken away?

As he slowly sipped his spicy milk tea, Shiv calmed down. He thought of the evening ahead, when he would join his parents for what would be a most sumptuous meal – with all his favorite dishes. Those family dinners were the rare occasions when Shiv could actually enjoy food. His habitual intake of calories was limited to what the cafeteria had on offer or what he could easily nuke in his room's microwave.

He looked forward to seeing his parents, the man and woman who had taken him home from the Central Khalsa Orphanage, on whose steps he had been left when barely a few hours old. Devi and Gopal had raised him as their own. He had been wrapped in his mother's love and devotion as snugly as in his father's deep affection and reliable guidance. His parents had never felt threatened by their boy's appearance, nor by the brilliant mind that had left his teachers exasperated and in awe even in first grade. And when he sailed through college and university, crowning the years of study with a Ph.D. in particle physics, their love and unshakeable belief in his abilities was the solid foundation upon which Shiv stood. From this platform he set out to become a well-published and internationally recognized scientist, cooperating with like-minded researchers from all over the world. Their common goal was to produce energy through nuclear fusion. Shiv was convinced it was but a matter of time. "In the future," he would tell those who either didn't believe or were exasperated by the task, "we will produce energy not from raw materials or resources, but from knowledge." And what went for energy production was also valid for all other major problems facing humanity, like providing enough food, clean water or stabilizing the climate.

He sincerely hoped that tonight his mother hadn't drawn a fourth dinner guest from her seemingly inexhaustible well of suitable females. They had played this game for a number of years now, with Shiv eluding capture every time. He smiled at the thought, even if a touch pained. Devi just wouldn't quit trying to set him up with a woman, hoping he'd follow up on that first contact. But all she achieved was to make him and the unsuspecting females uncomfortable, so much so that he had started to evade her invitations.

In any case, tonight he'd need their full attention. After due consideration he had decided to share his dream and hear what his parents could contribute from their vast knowledge of the ancient Vedic scriptures. They were deeply anchored in the breathtakingly complex Hindu cosmos, and occasionally he envied those deep roots. As much as Shiv had read and studied, his interest had remained at the level of the intellect. Were he asked to give a name to this deep-seated longing he felt in some rare moments, he would have said it was a yearning to belong – to fuse with and experience what he knew in his mind to be true.

Stirring his spicy tea and gazing at the light dancing on the water, Shiv caught a glimpse of what had been kindled by last night's disconcerting dream. He thought, uneasily as usual, of the astrologer his parents had brought him to almost three decades ago. The wise man had gazed into the compelling black eyes of this eerily quiet, skinny baby. "He carries a message," the old stargazer had said, but refused to elaborate. The message, he added when they had already turned to leave, would reveal itself in time.

Only when a hand dropped on his shoulder did Shiv look up, startled. "You dreamin' of some dark eyed beauty, Shiv, or solving the riddles of the universe?" His lab assistant – a handsome youth with an easy smile and sparkling eyes – grinned at him and hummed a few bars from the latest love-drenched Bollywood blockbuster, imitating the dance steps along with the melody. "You coming? Meeting's about to start!"

Shiv recoiled imperceptibly at being touched. He didn't like physical contact. It was easy to tease him about women, since their absence from his life was so conspicuous. Together they headed for the lab, the only place where Shiv felt completely at ease, where he had built an environment that made sense to him. It was structured according to his needs and provided the few comforts he valued – his beloved fat-bellied teapot and assistants who accepted his quirks and at least tried to follow his erratic leaps of thought. They got his mail, found his misplaced papers, pens or keys, put up with his intellectual snobbery, topped up his supply of Nilgiri tea and ensured that he ate regularly – something he tended to forget when lost in his work of trying to create the sun on Earth.

Once Kavita and Anand Gupta, the elderly couple caring for the Sitaram household, had cleared the last dishes of the sumptuous vegetarian dinner – a delicious kadhi pakora with rice and no coincidental female guest – Devi lightly touched Shiv's cheek: "Something troubling you, isn't there, my sweet boy? Do you want to share it with us?"

Shiv had never been able to hide anything from his mother. Even as a boy, when he had set up elaborate schemes to lead her astray, she needed only one look to find him out. "It's not an easy subject, mother. It's not an area I feel comfortable or even adept describing."

"You had a dream, didn't you?" His mother's large, hooded eyes were full of warmth and golden reflections.

"How do you...?" He shook his head. It was no use to ask. Somehow she always knew. "Yes, a dream, a most amazing dream, a dream like no other. As real as any of my lab experiments."

His parents relaxed into the rather formal dining room chairs, like children settling down for a bedtime story, while Shiv sat up straight – his long neck stretched forward. He started folding and unfolding his heavy linen napkin while he talked. "First, there was sound pulling at my mind, spiraling into an unknown area of my brain; definitely not one I normally use in my intellectual endeavors."

Devi and Gopal exchanged a brief glance and a knowing smile. "When the sound faded, the images came?"

"How do you...?" Shiv just shrugged and grinned. "Yes, that's when the movie started. Three figures appeared, like energy fields, composites of minutest particles. The middle figure was kind of gray, a tremendously strong energy holding the other two – one a lighter shade, the other darker." Shiv groped for words to describe what could not readily be described. He took a sip of fresh tea Anand had silently brought to the table.

"Did the darker figure look familiar?" his father gently interjected.

Shiv nodded, no longer surprised. "I think I saw the god I was named after. But then suddenly Shiva changed into his female form – the mother Cali. She showed herself to me in black skin, adorned with her chain of skulls and skirt of severed arms, accompanied by howls from her pack of female jackals. But she did not come to frighten. Would you believe, she winked at me?"

All three laughed out loud at the thought of the goddess of death and annihilation seductively winking at anyone. "I swear she did, and I found it most erotic, too."

When his father spoke, his voice was unusually earnest: "There was a message, surely?"

"Visit me in my western abode."

Devi bent forward in her chair, her silk sari whispering. "Visit me in my western abode," she softly repeated, her eyes suddenly brilliant with tears. "Oh Shiv, how auspicious. Something most extraordinary has happened to you. The gods...."

"Stop right there, mother!" Shiv interrupted her harshly. "Please," he quickly added trying to take the edge off. "I know, I've brought the subject up; rather, my dream has. But you know I'm not into gods and certainly not into anyone claiming to act in their name." The napkin fell in a crumpled heap on the tablecloth. Shiv had to restrain himself visibly from launching into one of his sermons.

"You should let your mother speak, son." Gopal didn't sound angry, more amused with the age-old ritual between the two. "She may surprise you, if you'd listen."

But Shiv was not going to give in just yet. "Look, that's why I've chosen science. I believe in laws that have steered the universe since the beginning of time. Churches have proven to be wrong about the universe time and time again. Just look at their cosmology! It's still two-dimensional. And despite their claim to be in direct contact with a supreme being, all they have done is carve human perception in stone – a supremely limited perception, I might add. This is one reason why I have focused on particle fusion. I search for unity in all, whereas religion mostly aims to divide – despite all its claims to the contrary."

Not in the least unsettled by her son's agitation, Devi picked up her thread: "The gods...hmmm, those energy fields you saw in your dream...you did make out Shiva in one of them didn't you? The god who destroys?"

Again Shiv couldn't hold back: "See, mother, that is exactly why this god stuff is so ignorant. They were invented to scare people. You know full well, nothing is ever destroyed or created. The total amount of energy in the universe is always exactly the same!"

Devi listened quietly to her son's heated excursion into one of his favorite fields. She waited patiently until he was good and ready to climb down off his high horse, as she knew he eventually would. He grinned at her. "Ok, ok, mother dear, if you want to keep your gods and be scientifically correct, you could call Shiva the disassembler...."

"I like that expression, Shiv, it's most appropriate. Thank you for educating your very limited parents!" she said, smiling affectionately. "Just let me ask another dumb question. Could the other two energies or entities you saw, perhaps represent the rest of the Vedic trinity – Brahma and Vishnu? To use your terminology: Brahma, the god who assembles; Shiva, the god who disassembles; and Vishnu, the god who holds it all in balance. When you look at nature's laws, does that remind you of something?"

It took Shiv a moment to close his mouth. He looked at his mother as if she had mutated into the frightful goddess of his dream.

"Did I grow horns?" she smiled.

"The electromagnetic, weak and strong forces!" Shiv could barely get the words out. Then he slapped his forehead with a loud smack. "How could I have been so blind? How can I call myself a scientist and not make the connection?"

His mother touched his elegant, long fingered hand. "You know, our human tendency to sort everything into good and bad – to put a value tag on everything – can make us blind to reality. So once you chuck the gods in the waste bin, their true nature becomes invisible to you."

Shiv jumped up from the table, suddenly excited. In his research work he had delved deeply into the secrets of the strong force, but connecting it with a Hindu deity opened up a whole new playing field. Then, like a giraffe going to ground, Shiv collapsed his legs under him to kneel by his mother's chair. He took her in his arms and said: "I will never interrupt you again, oh wise woman of the east."

When Devi erupted into laughter, you could see she was most pleased with herself and deeply touched by her son's very rare show of affection. Shiv unfolded his limbs and got up. "We'll have to talk about this western abode business some other time. I need to get back to the lab. I have these new ideas, you see...."

For all his lankiness Shiv was an elegant and excellent golfer. And as he set his ball on the first tee, lining up his feet in the proper position, the burden of that fateful dream seemed to lift. When he had seen his father's message in the morning, inviting him for a round of late-afternoon golf, he had gladly accepted. He really liked the game. The balance, precision, perfectly timed motion – all were challenges Shiv thoroughly enjoyed. As they walked down the fairway amid eucalyptus and jamun trees, between mangos and kikar orchards, Shiv's spirits lifted and his head cleared. He and Gopal fell into an easy banter, complimenting each other's swing, laughing at a ball gone awry. But underneath this lightness something lay in wait. Both men felt it but were equally reluctant to acknowledge it. They wanted to share an enjoyable round of golf – an unburdened outing – being together like friends, rather than as father and son.

When they returned to the red brick clubhouse for their traditional post game drink at the 19th Hole, Gopal asked out of the blue: "Have you ever thought about what is written on the State Emblem of India?"

And Shiv knew the undercurrent had just surfaced. "You mean Satyameva Jayate, 'Truth Alone Triumphs'? No, not really. You know, this whole truth thing seems like a cheap commodity for whoever shouts the loudest."

Gopal smiled. "You definitely have a point there, son. Still, it's a powerful statement, that truth alone triumphs."

Shiv shrugged, pulling his golf shirt out of his trousers to cool off. "I'd have to give it some thought. But I'm not sure I really want to."

When the two had comfortably settled with cold bottles of Kingfisher lager, Gopal said in a most casual tone: "When you give something thought, how do you do it? I mean, how to you 'produce' a thought."

The seemingly innocuous question left Shiv speechless. How did he produce a thought? He poured his beer, licked some foam off the rim of the glass and took a deep drink. Then he looked at his father and came to a decision.

Shiv did not easily confide in anyone. Not even his parents, whom he would have trusted with his life, knew much of what really troubled him. But since he had already shared his dream, they were now involved in this strangest of stories, so he might as well take the plunge.

"Funny you should mention that. I have indeed been preoccupied with precisely this question. The dream has opened a door in my mind, a door I didn't even know was there. What lives in that unknown room? Is it the place where the thoughtmaker is hidden? What do you have to put in, for a thought to come out? What triggers visions, ideas, thoughts? I know all about neurons and synapses firing away, high-speed chemical messengers, impulses traveling along nerve tracts, nerve endings making connections, eliciting physiological reactions. But all this knowledge does not answer the most fundamental question of how the thought process really works. Right?"

"Yes, I guess so. You describe how the hard- and software work, but not where the content comes in that sets the process in motion. We so easily say, 'I had this idea' or 'that thought went through my mind.' But the inner process remains a mystery when you try to grasp it intellectually."

"Come on, bapu, let's not get on that track again." Shiv picked up his beer and clinked it against his father's. "Here's to a sharp mind that can figure out anything, when it is applied properly."

Gopal smiled fondly at his son. "With the intellect alone you will not achieve lasting happiness or peace of mind. Happiness comes from another organ than the brain." He put one hand on his heart, while he saluted Shiv with his beer. "This is the seat of happiness, my son. And I know, I just absolutely know, you will find that out some day."

For a moment Shiv lost himself in his father's smile; it lit up his whole face, his entire being, and seemed to radiate from just the spot where he had placed his hand. It was, Shiv felt, as if his father were radioactive or something.

"Is that one of those truths that will prevail?"

Gopal broke out in loud, hearty laughter that made a few heads turn. "See, I knew you'd get it!"

Devi knew the time had come for Shiv to take the decisive next step. Her brilliant son was on the threshold of a new, a more encompassing understanding of life. All he needed was a little shove. And who better to provide this than a mother?

Barely a week later, Shiv again sat at his parent's table, picking absentmindedly at a colorful array of tasty curries and lentils, rice flavored with a variety of masalas, and stuffed parathas. Not surprisingly, the conversation had been steered towards THE MESSAGE in his dream. But Shiv was being obstinate. He kept maneuvering the discussion towards the attributes of the three gods/forces. Devi lifted her eyes to heaven and said to herself, "We just have to let our Lord Shiva do his bit first...." After all, Shiva, the destroyer of illusion, of false thought, was most capable of ripping apart the veil hiding eternal truth.

"Shiva's abode," Gopal said, "is of course Mount Kailash. Perhaps you should go there?"

The prospect intrigued Shiv. A whole range of political upheavals and nationalistic claims were connected with this majestic peak of rock and ice. Visas could be obtained only with great difficulty. The sacred mountain was a very strong symbol of Tibetan culture, and the Chinese were wary of troublemakers. Mount Kailash was contested territory, just like Shiv – his national identity usually questioned whenever he met new people. Was he one of them or one of the enemy? So he felt a certain kinship with this holiest of mountains.

How utterly antiquated these notions of belonging to one nation or another, especially since space travel had made the planet frightfully small. Wasn't it enough to be a human being, to have an individual identity? And just as Kailash's power lay within itself, so it was with the essence of human beings. All that mattered lay within – in borderless territory. Political or national definitions were nothing but arbitrary restrictions anyhow. Worse, they were the cause of unfathomable tragedy. His country was a prime example of the havoc that could be wrought by drawing random borders. Hadn't national borders become obsolete with the first glimpse of Earth from space? They were a hindrance to his work as well. Science, after all, should overcome all differences. But even scientists were forced to adopt a nationalistic stance, shrouding research results in secrecy, raising a national flag on the findings. Shiv found that particularly irritating. Scientists were supposed to work in the interest of humanity, but even here it was the paymasters – governments, military, multinationals – who made the rules.

"What, what did you just say?"

"Didn't you promise last time to listen to me always?" Devi laughed and lightly brushed her son's smooth skinned hand. She so much loved and longed to touch him, well aware that he didn't want it. So she had taken to sneaking physical contact here and there, especially when her son was deep in thought and no longer aware of his body.

"No, no, no – I promised not to interrupt you any more! Don't try to outsmart me. Just because I didn't make an admittedly vital connection in my dream, my mind's still a well-oiled steel trap!"

"Well said, son, a trap it truly can be, when only used in one direction.... I have meditated on your dream, and what mother Cali told you. I remembered what Swami Vivekananda said in one of his speeches, when he visited Pasadena in California: Great ones, he said, will come from the west. And then I thought about what some of our more enlightened gurus say: The great yogis of our times are not in the Himalayas, they are in the marketplaces of the world." Devi took Shiv's hand in her own and continued: "Times are different. Today, hands that work are holier than hands that pray."

"That's all well and good, mother," Shiv said and gently retracted his hand. "And I'm glad the gurus display some common sense nowadays. But it still doesn't give me a clue as to what I should do? Go east, go west, go anywhere at all? Maybe it's just an allegory. You know how these gods never speak plain language. That's just one of many things that annoys me about them."

"She invited you to her western abode, son. That seems pretty straightforward. Sometimes great souls come together in clusters. Think about the Renaissance. This great period of creativity would never have happened had not a variety of artist souls appeared in the same time span. Or look at the Declaration of Independence in the United States! Impossible, had not a group of great souls united to create that manuscript. Wish we had such enlightened politicians today." Shiv was surprised to hear his mother voice disapproval.

"Do you mean I have to find scientific partners in the west? There is one I would indeed love to meet – this guy they call the new Einstein. He pulled together all these different theories of how the universe was and is formed – from Big Bang to strings – and unified them in his Theory of Everything, the M-theory. He presented his stupendous body of thought and analysis in California. Maybe I should get in touch?"

"Cali, western abode, Cali-fornia..." Devi was lost in thought, muttering to herself.

Gopal had listened silently to mother and son. Now he said: "Shiv, do you remember what we talked about the other day on the golf course? Have you given it more thought?"

Shiv grinned. "Matter of fact, I have. I figured I have to move beyond Descartes. After all, aren't I always criticizing people for adhering to concepts thought up by some long dead white men?" His smile was a bit lopsided. "Truth be told, I'm beginning to detect all kinds of discrepancies within myself. You sure I should go through with this? Maybe I'll turn into a dropout seeking only enlightenment?"

Gopal and Devi both giggled like children: "How absolutely wonderful for you, son. There is nothing more worthwhile!"

"What really intrigues me is no longer 'I think, therefore I am', but how do I think, how do I produce a thought?" He looked at his father. "How about this: We know that we do not make the heart beat or the kidneys work, so how on Earth do we get tricked into believing we make our thoughts?"

Gopal said this was a thought worthy of his son. Devi got up. "Let's have some tea in the library, I want to show you something, Shiv."

This was a real library, not just a presumptuous label tacked on to a TV den; three walls were covered floor-to-ceiling with well read books. There was a large stone fireplace for those months when it gets really cold in Chandigarh, a couple of comfortable leather sofas, strategically placed side tables and intimate lighting. Perfect for spending whole weekends with books and endless cups of spicy tea. Devi picked out a couple of volumes, knowing exactly what she was looking for and where to locate them.

"Maybe this would interest you?" Devi laid a slim folder on a side table exquisitely inlaid with different colored hardwoods.

Shiv could only stare at her in wonder. "How did you...?" He reached into his bike bag and pulled out a second copy of the text Swami Vivekananda had read at the world parliament of religions in Chicago in 1893.

"I thought you two might connect," Devi smiled. "He was, after all, a brilliant and very rational intellectual in the western sense. And he, just like someone I know really well, loved to provoke – especially those professing to know the truth! You know, when someone would talk to him about god, he would ask: 'Well, have you personally met him?' And make them look like fools."

"Man after my own heart," Shiv smiled back. "He also said something I agree with one hundred percent: 'Science is nothing but the finding of unity.' Plus, I read he was an agnostic like me."

"Until he met the eminent Hindu mystic Ramakrishna, yes. He really gave Vivekananda something to chew on. When he put his usual question about god to him, Ramakrishna said, 'Yes, I have seen god, as real as you are standing in front of me.' Vivekananda then let Ramakrishna put him in a state of samadhi, and that's when his path turned decisively towards introspection. His intellect, by the way, did not suffer from this. He was still one of the smartest men of his time. Might interest you that they meditated using intense breathing techniques, to raise the body temperature and thus reach higher states of consciousness."

It took Shiv only a moment to absorb this. His mind, still gliding smoothly along the intellectual highway, made the connection in no time at all. "Heat, ha. Know what happens to solid matter when you heat it? It liquefies; molecules speed up, become looser, more mobile, not so tightly packed. More heat, liquid turns to gas, even more speed and freedom of movement, less rigid form, and then when you really turn the fire on – plasma. Fusion, mother, jeez."

Shiv collapsed on the large sofa as if having run a marathon. This was a lot to absorb in just a few days. First the forces of nature, now the states of matter.... Shiv felt something emerge from deep within – more than intellectual curiosity, more than the excitement that comes from solving a complex equation. He felt as if a connection had been made, as if he himself had been hooked up to what he previously perceived as abstract science. He was no longer on the outside looking in; he was a cluster of molecules that carried his name and form, intrinsically connected to what he had always tried to grasp intellectually. It was not an entirely pleasant experience. The man so proud of his brain was deeply shaken, trying to sort through conflicting emotions. There was more than a touch of insecurity, sensing that his self-awareness, his sense of identity had shifted. But there was also something akin to irrepressible joy that suffused his whole being, seeming to radiate from his heart. With the joy came awe. Shiv knew he had glimpsed a new universe, a cosmos that had no material form. It did not surround you, did not exist outside of you, but was you – and all else.

He suddenly became aware of the silence in the room. His parents sat close to one another on the ottoman, their hands linked. There was so much love and light in their eyes, Shiv had to close his for a moment, before he could look at them again. He was so not used to displays of emotion. He started groping for words.

"No need to say anything, son," Gopal said in his quiet voice. "We are so proud of you. Our love will accompany you on whatever path life leads you. You know that. And also know: Wherever you stand in life, you are in the right place."

7

Software Wizard

"Is there anything else I can get you, sir?" The smile was inviting, the look too. And wasn't that button on her white shirt closed last time she came by? Ali gave the flight attendant an appreciative glance.

"I'm good," he replied, glancing up from his laptop. He knew she'd be back. As much as it flattered his ego, he didn't like the very personal attention some flight attendants bestowed on him. The less-than-subtle hints at being willing to go above and beyond the call of duty; from cell phone numbers discretely served with drinks, to outright offers of dinner "or something" during the layover at destination. He knew they were not really interested in him. They were simply reacting to the trimmings. "Hardware," he thought to himself, uneasy at being fawned over.

Yes, in his first-class seat and expensive suit they treated him like an Arab prince. With a pawnbroker's experienced eye, they appraised his state-of-the-art laptop and cell-phone, the designer briefcase and the Swiss chronometer claiming a long and expensive history. They smelled money, and his looks didn't hurt either. The lack of a wedding band on the appropriate finger was just an added perk. Ali smiled to himself. More the fool who fell for it, and an even bigger fool whose self-esteem relied on attention and accessories. Only 'hardwares' got a kick out of accumulating power, real estate, trophy spouses, or even pet concepts. While 'softwares' stayed light on their feet, regarding possessions as so much dead weight.

Wary though he was of stereotyping, Ali entertained himself occasionally with the classification system he had invented during one of the many long-haul flights that were part of his life. 'Hardwares,' despite their predominance even in his part of the world, were a phased-out model. The future belonged to 'softwares' like him; motivated not by gold and brick and young flesh, but by creative ideas and ingenious solutions. His was a world of infinite future possibilities, not past achievements.

"Can I refresh that juice for you, sir?" The woman's gaze lingered on him while she bent to remove the still half-filled glass. Ali just nodded and started fiddling with his laptop again. He almost felt sorry for the pretty girl. She'd be better off investing her charms in a more worthwhile subject, since he definitely wouldn't bite. Only 'software' types could stir his interest – strong, independent, proud women – equal to his gender in every respect, except they smelled better. Anyway, he'd enjoy this game as long as it lasted. By the time he reached immigration, at the latest, his princely self would be cut down to size. The glances filled instead with suspicion, and the "Sir" sounding like slander. He'd be invited to spend an inordinate amount of time in airport security, undergoing extra checks, answering endless questions as to where from, where to, why and what and how long exactly.... Ali was glad to be headed towards a friendly state this time. Getting through immigration at Abu Dhabi would be a cinch compared to the U.S. or London or Prague.

He was looking forward to his usual suite at the Emirates Palace. Even though it was a bit on the ostentatious side, Ali did enjoy the amenities – the first rate fitness room, the tennis and squash courts, the pools and the en-suite jacuzzi.

But more than wanting to make use of all that luxury, he was itching to get to work. There were good things mapped out for this speck of sand atop an ocean of oil: most notably a new city that would not use one drop of it – CO_2 free, zero waste.

Ali was excited to be in on the ground floor of this project, collaborating on the software design for the underground electric personal rapid transit system. No fossil fuel vehicles cruising the streets. Be great to move his headquarters here from Cairo, once the city came to life. The amount of time he and his staff lost every day, battling bumper-to-bumper traffic was horrendous. Not being able to get ahead at his own speed was pure torture for Ali.

Yes, he was quite thrilled to be involved in shaping a city, where the future was happening now. A city not constructed on the ruins of a distant past, however glorious, but starting from scratch – implementing all the high-tech creative minds had come up with over the last few years. Who would ever have thought the self-indulgent, petrocash-raking Arabs would get off their pampered behinds and show the world how to put clean- and high-tech to practical use.

Ali couldn't suppress a grin. Of course there would be setbacks, lots of trial and error, maybe even failure – in which case they wouldn't have to wait long for people to point the finger and gloat. But instead of wasting time and money on another international conference, producing more hot air to fuel global warming, the sheiks had acted. Besides, producing energy from renewable sources and aiming for maximum efficiency was just so much more challenging than plunking down another fat power plant with the efficiency factor of a dinosaur. And clean energy kept the air clean, something for which a Cairo resident had the highest appreciation.

Sometimes, Ali played with the thought of razing the anthill Cairo and starting over. Modern infrastructure, good governance, equal rules and opportunities for all. Like in a charter city. Now there was a convincing idea! A plausible alternative for the one third of the world's urban population, something like one billion people – probably two billion in 20 years time – who survived rather than lived where megacities split at the seams and spilled out into slums. Shameful for a modern global society.

Instead of providing fertile soil for pandemics, fundamentalism and terrorism, nations should get together to construct new cities on bare ground, cities guided by a charter defining the rules, with experienced managers overseeing the implementation and providing simple, up-to-date infrastructure, security, and economic opportunity. The Middle East with its great desert spaces would be perfect for such an undertaking. Places like that would offer loads of work and prospects and surely attract capital from shrewd investors. While Ali's fingers played over the keyboard, he suddenly grinned. Those cities would jump the cable age and go right to wireless! Not only in communication, but in energy too: solar, hydrogen fuel cells and eventually even nano-based energy production. Forget New Age, they would head right for the Blue Age. Yes, he liked that thought. The electronic age was truly the blue age, information traveling on air, the sky nowhere near the limit.

From Abu Dhabi International, Ali took a cab directly to the Institute of Science and Technology, designated to develop into the heart of the new city's homegrown research and development community. From there, bright minds would hopefully be collaborating worldwide on cutting edge technological solutions to the world's energy and sustainability challenges, spearheading the emerging knowledge society, tackling the challenges of a globalized society with creativity and unconventional ideas, putting clever solutions before short-term profit. With any luck they would help realize the predicted explosive growth in technology and knowledge.

Ali was fidgeting in his seat, itching to move. Imagining the world of the future helped take the edge off having to sit still. And one bright star in that future would be his little sister, no question. She was already among the best of her generation. Maybe she'd get out of Cairo – hidebound as it was by history – and do her graduate studies here, where every building would breathe the future.

Had the cab driver glanced in the rear view mirror just then, he would have seen Ali's face lit by a tender smile. Just thinking about his little sister, the one human being he truly adored, Ali couldn't help but smile. Suddenly he perked up. Why didn't he invite her for the weekend? There was plenty of room in his luxurious suite, so much more than he needed or even wanted. The Emirate paid for it, so he accepted it as an expression of their esteem. What a pleasure it would be to see Lailah's eyes light up, her oohs and aahs as she looked at this and checked out that.... She was such a brilliant and gifted girl. At 17 she was still a child to Ali, but to other young men she was a woman they barely dared look at, intimidated by her beauty and boundless energy. He grabbed his cell and texted Lailah. If she were free, he'd book her a ticket for the one o'clock flight on Friday afternoon, with a return on Monday morning. She could easily skip a few of her Architectural Engineering classes at the American University in Cairo. Her grades were way up there, with no particular effort on her part. It fascinated Ali how his sister's brain combined a quick, almost intuitive understanding of scientific facts with a great talent for music. Lailah had played the violin since childhood and was now at the level of an accomplished concert violinist.

The chime from a text on his cell-phone interrupted his musings: "Boo hoo, no can do, cram for exam, hugs L." Ali felt a stab of disappointment; he had already imagined a fun weekend with company. Ah well, maybe he should try Nasrin, even though she was involved in some dig out by Tell el-Amarna – halfway between Cairo and Luxor – and was difficult to reach. But he tried his luck anyway. The answer came almost immediately, and it was positive. Ali quickly got on the line with Etihad Airways, then texted back: "Ticket ready, me too!"

Ali grinned. Nasrin was more than a substitute for his sister. Next to Lailah she was probably closest to his heart. And like Lailah she didn't bow to the cultural restrictions of large parts of the Muslim world. Cairo University offered co-ed courses, and girls like Lailah took equal education for granted. But it wasn't the norm, far from it. Why couldn't those in power just let go of the past, of the rules of dubious origin anyhow? How could they afford to forego the intellectual potential of half their population? Denying women full access to education and to the job market was a mistake that would cost them dearly. It required the combined uniqueness of both genders for the world to take that decisive step into the future. What would he do without the creative women in his office? They did basically the same jobs as the guys, but with a twist. While men were usually great with systems, women went at assignments in a more playful way. Their brains seemed to possess extra cross-links, allowing them to connect dots which men with their more linear thinking couldn't even see.

Ali had no doubt that Lailah, with her spunk and her high-capacity brain, would be one to pave the way. "How can it be, Ali?" she had glowed with indignation at dinner one day when talking about her idol of the moment – an American astronaut who had been on a shuttle mission to the Hubble Telescope – "that one nation can send its women into outer space, while another forces us to make ourselves invisible underneath a sack of cloth?"

Ali had suggested she look at the issue from the male perspective. "Those who demand the chador be required by law claim that if not covered head to toe, women would be a constant source of distraction and seduction. What does that say about Muslim men? Are we all so weak and one-track minded? Are we no more than animals pouncing at the slightest whiff of a female?"

Lailah had had a good laugh and muttered something about the weaker sex. Then their parents had quickly steered the conversation towards more innocuous topics. While absently picking at his food, his father had mentioned how Muslims had given the world culture and science. "In the Islamic golden age they were the intellectual leaders, the first skilled chemists, architects, medical experts, navigators, timekeepers...but that was more than a thousand years ago. Where has this greatness gone?"

When nobody offered an answer, Ali's mother had surprised them with her opinion that the Islamic world had been hijacked by narrow-minded thinkers who purposefully kept their followers in ignorance.

"You are so right," Lailah had agreed, jumping up to give her mother a peck on the cheek. "Extremism is highly contagious, and it's spreading all over the world like the flu." To which Ali had added his suspicion that it was not their religious convictions that made people so susceptible, but frustration at having no future. Wherever there was no connection to the modern world, no perspective, nothing meaningful to do, then extremists had an easy task luring people with stories of a glorious past that they were determined to restore by whatever means.

"Trying to restore the past is fruitless." Their mother had picked up the thread. "And to attempt to do so by violent means is downright shameful. What tolerant Muslims all around the globe ought to do is to continue putting forth the qualities that have made our culture great: grace, refinement, education! Just look at the Taj Mahal, the Alhambra in Granada...unmatched in their gracefulness."

"Education," their father had muttered. "Education is the key. After all, science is a traditional Islamic discipline. And when we educate our children, they will not be susceptible to the absurd promises of terrorists or backward thinkers." After a moment's reflection he added, "Of course, we also need meaningful jobs for these educated young men and women. And this is only to be achieved if we overcome the embedded hierarchical structures and horrendous corruption suffocating economic progress."

Ali thought with great fondness of his family. As conventional as their lives appeared, they had always been unorthodox thinkers who still managed to surprise him on the rare occasions he joined a family dinner. He felt gratitude. Not so much for himself but for Lailah. Their parents deserved credit for her first-rate education, for allowing her to form her own opinions. Again he shifted impatiently in the back seat of the cab. He wanted to be where he was going, to do something concrete like fitting another piece into the grand mosaic of a future where all who cared to participate had a chance, regardless of gender, race or creed. Ali patted his computer bag. And here was the magic wand that'd make it happen!

This sleek piece of technology was changing the world more fundamentally than perhaps any tool in the past. With a computer and an internet connection, you could give anyone, anywhere, what the world needed most: education and knowledge. Like remote tutoring via the Web – short lessons from elementary to college level – free and accessible to all. Ali loved it. Of course, you had to know how to unearth such gems amidst the explosive growth of data now available. But he figured that inevitably there'd be junk, the side effect of a high-speed evolution. After all, within a few short years the Internet had provided access to umpteen times more information than the knowledge humanity had gathered throughout history.

Within those billions of web pages, it was, for Ali, the planet's largest encyclopedia that took center stage, simply because the staggering amount of data on Wikipedia was not produced by the knowledge-keepers alone, or by experts in ivory towers, or an intellectual elite. The authors were men and women, kids and grannies, black and white and yellow, Muslim and atheist, sectarian and agnostic – people with their individual traits and experiences willing to take an interest and share. The Internet provided a forum, where ideas could take flight, where people acquired and exchanged knowledge, asked questions, vented anger, expressed opinions, debated, participated, socialized; their worldview no longer shaped by a superior cast.

The beauty of direct access deeply pleased Ali. Information and data travelled around the globe on thin air – no passport, no visa. The data just slipped through, nobody could trap it for good. Those who spied and filtered and collected and forbade were only temporarily successful. A fascinating breed of resourceful hackers found holes in the defenses and ripped them wide open. This genie was out of the bottle for good. No way to stuff it back in and make it shut up. And it hadn't even begun to reach its full potential. While nations were busy shoring up their borders, and sectarians bashed in one another's heads arguing about 2,000 year old concepts, ingenious minds were busy creating the nano-future where borders – all kinds of borders – simply ceased to exist.

Ali had read how nanotechnology would make the non-biological portion of human intelligence billions of times more capable, realizing the vision of a knowledge society. Nanoscience was shaping a world where humans transcended their biological roots. Now here was a truly exciting perspective: when humanity moved from the material to the mental, evolution would really go high-speed.

The taxi's radio pulled Ali rudely back from his nanobot future and into a world full of conflict and dissension. The report about dismal living conditions in one sub-Saharan nation was a stark reminder of what stood in the way of the future: lack of education and lack of infrastructure. It was that stupidly simple. How could you participate if you had no access to electricity – couldn't read or write? All it took was a glance at the world at night to see the huge black holes across the globe, particularly in sub-Saharan Africa and South Asia. Despite all international efforts a quarter of humanity were literally living in the dark.

If he were Pharaoh today – Ali still occasionally played his favorite childhood mind-game – the abolition of nations would top his to-do list. They cost far too much – just look at defense budgets – and spawned rulers who had a nasty tendency to attack each other. Besides, too few nations really cared about helping others catch up. Next, Pharaoh Ali would create a United Citizens Department of Infrastructure. Globalize the system. Do away with these thousands of half-assed foreign aid programs. A drip here, a drop there – and usually with an eye on the possible return of profit. Money would be no issue anyway, since axing defense budgets would free up enough capital to rectify just about all that needed fixing on this little rock in space.

In Ali's global democracy, regions would be managed like businesses. He would introduce a United Citizens masters degree in Prosperity Management. It would consist of peace management, advanced diplomatic skills, economic and educational infrastructure development, and anti-corruption strategies. Only individuals of integrity would be installed as area managers, preferably from some other part of the world so as to ensure impartiality and independence from ethnic or religious groups. That would be particularly important in areas like Kashmir or the Middle East. The most brilliant of these managers would be sent to the most war-torn areas to organize peace and prosperity. Nothing was more important than peace around the globe.

Ali had had it up to here with fighting. All his life, he had been a witness to conflict breeding conflict, hate breeding hate. The opposing parties were like lock-jawed animals, incapable of letting go. And when they dropped away exhausted or weakened by age, a new brainwashed generation stood ready to take their place. When his managers took over, this cast would be sent to reeducation camps where they would have regular viewings of movies like 'Gandhi' or 'The Gods Must Be Crazy.'

"We're at the main entrance, sir."

Ali shook his head to clear the images of a slight bushman sedating a group of terrorists. He pulled out some money, enough to make the driver smile and bow, and got out into the pleasant afternoon. Rounding the corner of the computer lab, he was greeted by a booming "Yo, Arab boy, so you finally get here when we've done all the work!"

Ali fell into a tight hug with his best buddy of many projects, his mentor, teacher and friend, Chayim Grunwald. He planted a smacking kiss on the man's shiny dome. "Great, let's get out to the beach then."

Chayim looked at his friend with sparkling eyes. "In a minute, dear boy. First I have this little job for you, just a tiny bug that needs working out. It's a beauty, just your style!"

Ali groaned, then grinned. It was one of Chayim's ways – and he had a whole arsenal – of testing Ali's abilities while at the same time teaching him new tricks of the trade. Chayim was, as far as Ali could judge, the best and most brilliant computer wizard he had ever come across. Not once had he seen Chayim capitulate. He was capable of working day and night, subsisting on Diet Coke and the most disgusting assortment of cookies, cakes and pastries. It said a lot about the Sheik in charge of this giant project that he'd hired the best from around the world regardless of skin color or creed. Ali really liked this aspect of business, his branch of business at least. Know-how, savvy, and skill counted more than which state issued your passport, which prophet you prayed to or even whether you prayed at all.

"I'm surprised they let you out, old man!" said Ali. "Seems your government's foaming at the mouth these days and breaking out in heavy rashes whenever they hear the word 'Arab.' Did they know where you'd be going?"

"Let me assure you, my friend, they know. They know everything. Mossad's everywhere, and should Mossad have to take a leak, my neighbors are only too happy to report on my daily life. But you have a point. It was actually more difficult getting out of my country than getting in here." Chayim scratched the stubble on his chin. With his dark button-like eyes and short, perky nose he reminded Ali of a hedgehog, an amicable, balding hedgehog.

Ali knew it wasn't the time to pursue the subject. The two men had spent countless hours trying to solve the tragedy of the Middle East. At the end of the day they usually came to the same conclusion: be content to have solved it on a personal level. By seeing beyond doctrines, rising above wrongs done to other generations, letting the past be the past, you could then start taking an interest in each other simply as human beings.

You could take an interest in a different culture and belief system, and this could grow into appreciation and – as in their case – into deep friendship.

Chayim put his arm around Ali's shoulder, even though he had to stand almost on tiptoes, and steered him towards what they called their playpen, all the while explaining "the little beauty" waiting there for Ali. The builders had equipped an office with all the necessary hardware; whatever the small group of experts needed, even a wide assortment of sweets. Ali set down his laptop, settled into the swivel chair and got to work.

Once in a while Chayim would turn away from his display with its Matrix-like data streams, and look over at Ali. He admired his friend's powers of concentration. The guy wouldn't be distracted by anything, not even a parade of pink elephants with trumpets playing some Nat Adderley tune. He knew better than to offer him coffee or – god forbid – one of his sweets. The young man wouldn't come back to the world until he had solved the riddle.

Ali was a bit like a computer himself. He gathered whatever information was around him, processed it, and then disseminated it to whoever would listen. And just like a computer, Ali didn't put value judgments on the information. His idea of truth was the distillate you obtained from looking at all sides of an issue and balancing opposing views. There were, though, three things Ali had a very difficult time with and could react quite ungraciously to: boring people, stiff etiquette, and strict timetables. Chayim chuckled remembering the time they were to receive some kind of honor at Humboldt University in Berlin. Ali had talked him into actually leaving the ceremony before their names were called – escaping the speaker's monotonous drone and seeking respite in a shady German Biergarten.

Ali didn't go to the airport to pick up Nasrin, and she didn't expect him to. She had quickly understood that it wouldn't be one of those relationships, and that was fine with her. After all, she prided herself on being a grown woman – one who had already handled her own affairs and made her own decisions, when other girls her age were still hiding behind their mother's skirts. Besides, the hotel provided limo service.

Nasrin was looking forward to these couple of days with Ali. They didn't spend much time in each other's company, but when they did, it was usually enormously pleasant, full of laughter, music, fine food and great sex. Her skin started to tingle just thinking about what Ali's supple body, his sensuous mouth and inventive hands would do to her. The man had no idea how gorgeous he really was. To him, it was just not important; otherwise he'd probably spend a lot more time on his appearance than he usually did.

Instead of picking her up at airports or pulling out chairs in restaurants or sending her flowers, Ali did something much more valuable – he listened to her, truly interested in what she thought and what she did. He would be delighted to hear about her upcoming project, leading a group of archaeology students from an American university in trying to reveal secrets of the sacred city built by Ali's favorite Pharaoh: Echnaton the sun god.

"We're not really expecting to find anything earth-shattering. But you know how much I like to work with students. I really enjoy their enthusiasm, the conviction that they'll find something spectacular. Their ability to make a boring dig into a treasure hunt reminds me of myself when I was their age."

"Ah, my ancient one," Ali looked at the young woman with the mysterious dark eyes, comfortably stretched out next to him on the terrace of their hotel suite. He took her hand and brushed it lightly with his lips. "Soon you'll need to be carried to the digs in a litter.... But what exactly will you be doing there? Using any interesting technology?"

"Yes indeed," Nasrin was smiling at the picture Ali had drawn of her. "We won't do any actual digging, but rather training the students in non-invasive techniques like GPR – sorry, ground penetrating radar – and high-frequency seismic."

"Non-invasive, ha! Now that's a concept I like." Ali was grinning at his delightful companion, their naked feet engaged in a little game of hide and seek. "You know how it's also used in medicine...."

"...even sex is increasingly non-invasive." Nasrin interrupted him. "Virtual sex will be, if the proponents are to be believed, absolutely fantastic. We can finally abolish the old saying: no risk, no fun. A lot of women will probably be relieved."

"Men too," Ali smiled. "Would relieve them of 'using' women for their sexual needs, wouldn't it."

Nasrin conceded the point, and quickly steered the discussion away from a subject that was not without serious stumbling blocks. "The students are supposed to map buried archaeological features in the northern city of el-Amarna and get the hang of their new toys."

"El-Amarna, the city of my favorite pharaoh. You know that, don't you? That revolutionary has always fascinated me. When you think about what the guy did, it blows your mind. And you know what? In this day and age we need the exact same thing."

Nasrin looked out on the water. There wouldn't be any nibbling and cuddling forthcoming any time soon. Ali was obviously in full fast-thinking mode. With a small inward sigh, she obliged: "What do you mean? We should go back to the system of pharaohs? You can't be serious?"

"No, of course not. The time of kings and rulers is over for good. But Echnaton understood something really important. You know, when he cleaned out the pigsty that the priesthood had made of a noble calling, he didn't rebuild on the old foundations, but started afresh, on virgin ground...and with just one god"

"Isn't this where Monotheism really started? Previously the heavens were populated by a multitude of gods and goddesses and then...poof...just one, the awesome disk of the sun."

Ali nodded. "He very effectively pulled the rug from under that horde of unholy men, by streamlining worship to one single god; Aton, the sun. A god that people could see every day in the sky. Gave every individual direct access to the source so to speak."

"And that was not the only bold move! He also elevated women to the same level as men. Didn't he make Nefertiti his co-regent? Surely a lesson for our mullahs, don't you think?"

Ali bent to take her hand again. "Ah, my most esteemed main woman, how right you are...." He gave her an appreciative look and continued in a more serious tone: "It's actually quite simple – most entrepreneurs are afraid of your gender. That's to my great advantage, because I can employ from among the best. Besides, I just happen to like working with women." He lightly kissed her fingertips. "And not only work, either.... But women still make the most marvelous, most valuable partners for men, as long as they have access to the same education and the same opportunities. Only stupid men want stupid women."

"It's quite a relief that more and more Muslim men are starting to think that way. I mean how should we Arabs compete in the global market, when generations of children are brought up by mothers who are kept in the Middle Ages?" Nasrin got up to lean on the railing.

"Absolutely. Virtual reality could do a world of good here! We should introduce some kind of test for preachers, missionaries and mullahs, to find out how much they know about the modern world and new technologies. If they're not up to par, they'll be taken on a virtual reality tour. That would kick them right into the here and now."

"Is that why you keep asking people how much they live in the past?"

Ali laughed. "So you've noticed? Actually I can highly recommend it. It makes them aware of how stuck they really are; in life already lived, in things that cannot be changed, just repeated. Only when you live fully in the present and have your mind geared towards the future does your brain get regularly updated."

"Is that why you so rarely talk about your own history?" Nasrin asked, voicing something that had bothered her since she'd met him.

"I just don't understand why people find personal history so fascinating. What bearing does it have on who I am today? I'm a realtime, here-and-now kind of guy. You should know that by now. Too much past glues you to incidents that have lost real meaning, to emotions that have become irrelevant. Personal history is like schlepping around a dozen heavy suitcases filled with dusty souvenirs. Prevents you from living fully in the present." After this outburst voiced at the open sea, he joined Nasrin at the railing.

"Look at all of our state rulers today, still referring to – and relying on – past glories, instead of opening themselves up to the future. New and unconventional ideas get automatically nixed as unrealistic, while our leaders cling to the tried and true. Listening to them, you'd think the Earth was flat. Look how long ago man landed on the moon for goodness sake. We live in a world that people from three generations ago would barely recognize. That's why I recommend high doses of cultural and historic amnesia for the whole globe." With a laugh he added: "Especially for those living in highly afflicted areas."

"So it's wiping the memory from the hard drives and an Echnaton-like revolution?"

"You're damn right. Forget the past, give people direct access to whatever you want to call the ultimate reality. You know, something like open source shareware, that's what the world needs. Do away with all these password keepers, with all the silly superstition." Ali was pacing furiously, waving his glass to underline his arguments.

Nasrin smiled at him fondly. That was part of his attractiveness, the way he could get fired up about a subject, could spin out an idea, find solutions – and then drop it instantly and turn to something else. He was not given to brooding, but to a quick analysis of the facts and then – boom – a quick, bold way out of seemingly insurmountable problems.

"But you know Echnaton failed in the end. As soon as he was gone, the priests restored the old order."

"I know, I know. The important thing is, he tried. It was also a question of education. The simple people just couldn't grasp that they had direct access to the divine. They were convinced of the need for an intermediary, a conviction cemented in place by the very intermediaries who lived extremely well off their jobs. Might be different today with so many people schooled in direct access to information through the Web."

"Speaking of direct access," Nasrin put in, "how is your education program coming along?"

Ali's program had begun as a computer tutoring aid for Lailah. Now, working with one of the sharp women in his agency, the goal was to develop an educational tool that could be beamed via satellite to specific parts of the world where kids had little or no access to proper schooling.

"I've come up with a good name for it," Ali said. "SAT-ED, you like it?" Nasrin nodded encouragingly.

"It's tremendous fun to develop stuff with Habiba. The woman is awesome. I can throw out an idea, an image of how I would like a program to work or look, and she doesn't stop fiddling and puzzling until she has found an appropriate implementation. We're working on relevant content: basic education plus science – the latter is a great tool for implementing cultural amnesia." Ali smiled. "Eventually these forms of education will tie in perfectly with this other pet idea of mine, the charter cities. As soon as one is set up and people have moved in – bam – education is ready to go."

Nasrin loved Ali's enthusiasm for visionary projects, even if they tended to absorb him more than the physical closeness between the two of them.

"Education is refining human software." Ali grinned. "And with programs like SAT-ED, we can keep the children of the world – as well as all interested adults of course – busy, active and trusting in their future. As a global civilization, we are in urgent need of just that."

"That's totally cool, Ali. I sure hope this project grows legs."

"What irks me is that it would be so easy to implement. You know, it wouldn't cost the world. The G20 or such could finance the programs with 1/1000th of their defense budgets. After all, education is the most effective prevention! Besides we have to do it now. Speed is important in this day and age. We have the know-how, and money could be easily made available. All it takes is a decision." He shrugged.

"When are you ready to introduce your program publicly?"

"Not sure, soon I'll be off to the States! California government wants some ideas on a CO2 free public transportation system. Just imagine, the golden boys wanting to learn from terrorist sheiks."

Nasrin grabbed his arm and drew him close. "Let's make the most of the time we have then," she murmured into the crook of his neck while nibbling at the soft skin. But Ali would have none of this, not yet.

"I need to move, my beautiful one! Your choice – gym or a spin on the bike?"

Nasrin laughed, trying to hide her disappointment, "You're just like a great white shark, aren't you? Always have to move or you drown!"

"You've got that wrong, my precious. I'm not a water creature. If I were another life form, I'd be zooming through the air with a set of solar-powered wings."

8

Master Level Souls

Marvin licked the back of his hand, amazed by the taste of salt crystals left by evaporating water. He dropped his arm back into the cool sea and let the mellow surf rock him on his board like a baby in its cradle. Such were the undeniable perks of their stay on the third rock from the sun – in this solar system located on an outer arm of the spiral galaxy called Milky Way. The rock might have been unimpressive in size, but the set-up was remarkable. And right now, Marvin was content with his form. Floating on lazy waves, just off the beach where their house jutted out over the rocks, he enjoyed the sensation of solar radiation and drying saltwater on his skin – as the outer layer of the human mission cloak was called.

Fascinating piece of kit, this cloak. The overall cut was basically the same for everyone: differing only in size, color and minor detail. No way to tell at a glance whether the costume was worn by a rookie, or a veteran player who'd embodied millions of roles. Males and females were assigned parts as slaves and masters, beggars and queens, prophets and villains, lovers and mothers and fathers and even – Victoria had smiled at him while discussing new and surprising aspects of their assignment – beach bums. Humans slipped into their roles for a short time, then dropped their costume, exited the stage, donned a new outfit, and re-entered to play a different character. The role was determined by the lessons to be learned and experiences to be integrated. All scripts were stored in an individual's CID – their Chemical Information Database.

Sitting out on the terrace, they had besieged Victoria with questions about the five humans destined to play key roles in the opening of the next act. What was so special about them? Why did they get the parts? Did they audition?

Instead of answering, Victoria had slowly moved her fingers through the spectral colors created by sunlight hitting the beveled edge of the glass table. After a moment she said, "A human is like a prism. Each breaks the universal light at a slightly different angle and projects it out into the world. How they express the fundamental animating principle is governed by their CID."

Marvin had really liked that image. Some seven billion individually cut prisms, each breaking the same light in their very own way. To an unbiased eye, this planet would look like an exquisite jewel: every inhabitant an individual, unmistakable facet of the cosmic kaleidoscope.

Victoria had stayed with the color metaphor, explaining that while humans were a composite of all color frequencies, they usually refracted one in particular. "You could say humans are born with tinted glasses", she said and finally conceded some details about the five humans, he and Ave were so interested in. "Thanks to their enhanced CID, our five Master Level Souls are about to figure out the 'spectacle' trick. They will realize that while each person sees life through a particular color filter, ultimately everyone is imbued with the same light."

That's when the fun started. Marvin eagerly proposed sorting the quintet according to the color of their glasses. Avory had seconded the idea but suggested they begin with themselves. Between Avory's own white – indicating creation, light and the rising wave – and Marvin's black – pointing to dissolution, darkness and the descending wave – stood Victoria's grey. She signified the sustaining of all matter, twilight, the crest and trough of a wave where it comes to a standstill. Finally, Big G's violet – the fastest frequency a human eye could see – matched his role as gatekeeper between the coarse material and the sub-visible world. This left the rest of the rainbow spectrum to the five Master Level Souls.

Marvin and Avory had no trouble setting the orange spectacles on the nose of vivacious, creative, dramatic Barb Bernstein. Orange amplifies the outermost layer of reality, the form, shape and individuality of matter. A logical choice, given her obsession with the look of her mission cloak and with what she called her identity. Glued to the plasma cube, the twins had hugely enjoyed Barb's TV performance. The way she sacrificed herself on the altar of her convictions had been simply glorious.

Hakika Hasina's model was most certainly green: an emerald stream flowing around solid forms and smoothing the edges of rigid egos. She was all heart and compassion that one, even capable of understanding and forgiving her attacker – which was typical for a "green". Predisposed to helping, caring, and being there for others – whether human, animal or plant.

The red lenses were easily assigned to Reto: clearly a man with an affinity for power and the heat of competition, needing to fire up his body through extreme workouts. Structured and clear-headed, he knew his rules and laws. Marvin tried to incite Avory to hop over to Europe next time the Swiss was chasing a personal best ski ascent, and overtake the man at downhill speed! That would definitely rock Reto's competitive ego.

Ali's eyeglasses were the blue of the current Californian sky. No question. He would be a trendsetter for the coming age, when air played an unprecedented role in human life. Whoever mastered the airwaves was at the cutting edge, transcending and connecting across all borders. The Arab didn't get hung up on philosophical discussions or fruitless differences of opinion. As the twins had frequently witnessed, Ali was no procrastinator. He was a doer, an action man, always looking for a speedy solution.

Finally there was Shiv, master of Master Level Souls. He wore the most exclusive design, the yellow fusion model capable of perceiving high-energy particles, and giving him a keen view of the underlying reality. He could see solid matter for what it truly was, moving particles. With his inner ear and eye, Shiv had Einstein's perception. He could hear the elemental sound of the universe, fuse all hues and blend them in a new and creative way.

"Ah, I see you're trying to imitate Master Sitaram: classifying, giving structure and order to things," Big G's sonic boom had blasted into their lively conversation. "Not bad ... what you've put together, not bad at all. But colors aren't the only way to catalogue our five friends. Have you considered that they could also represent the five elements, which are – I might add – my particular playground?"

Big G's suggestion set the twins off again. Barb Bernstein, orange glasses, would represent the element earth. Big G had chuckled, sending the dishes clattering: "Bit of a drama queen. I definitely have her on my leash...." The green Miss Haki must be liquid, always flowing obediently south at Big G's calling. Red Reto embodied fire, lifting Haki's energy. Blue Ali belonged to air. All of which just left the yellow, Shiv. "Yes, his element is space, my secret travel partner," Big G growled. "He's already attained a level that's hard for me to control – in his mission cloak and in his thoughts."

And that's when it had become even more interesting. Victoria pointed out that the fusion-sense, which bundles all five senses into one beam, was about to fully activate in the five friends.

"The fusion-sense, humans call it the sixth sense, is built into every brain. It lets the individual 'I' transcend its boundaries and experience the universal animating principle. And it lets you perceive matter, including humans, as a colorful dance, while staying aware of the single light animating it all. Master Level Souls see through the superficial outer attributes of a mission cloak and focus on the ultimate identity embedded in each player. The fusion-sense will be activated when the five meet."

"When, Vicky, when?"

"Soon, Marvin, soon."

Not that the concept of soon meant anything to the timeless twins.

They didn't give up though, persisting until Victoria relinquished additional details about the tricks the five senses played on humans. Without an active fusion-sense, decoding what humans thought of as reality was a major challenge.

"In India it is customary to paint a red dot – the bindi – on the forehead, symbolizing the deep wish for attaining the sixth sense, activating the fusion-sense," Victoria explained. Then, to give Ave and Marvin a taste of this particular tricky bit of humanness, she called them over to the plasma cube and proposed an experiment in which their own permanently operative fusion-sense would be disabled.

Marvin had been dispatched to his favorite beach to test the visual, tactile and gustatory senses. Wandering slowly along the shoreline, fusion-sense fully active, showing him his surroundings as mesmerizing colorful particle dance, he checked out the selection of human mission cloaks dotting the beach. When he spotted a group of the tubbier variety, his attention was caught by their surprisingly slow-moving particles. They didn't match the average mission cloak speed pattern, certainly not for this latitude. Instantly Marvin's database provided the appropriate clue: the particle speed was congruent with species needing insulation against the cold or enough reserves to survive long hibernation.

As he was pondering the contradiction of why a human in a warm climate would want to resemble such well-insulated species, Victoria activated the plasma cube, fracturing Marvin's fusion vision. Suddenly his gaze was drawn towards the ice cream vendor, while his nostrils filled with heavenly smells of fried bacon, greasy hamburgers and bubblegum-sweet soft drinks from other nearby stalls. Marvin was instantly ravenous; overwhelmed by a craving for food. Where to run first? All he knew was that he wanted to get his hands on all of it. Grab one of each delicious item, or better still, fistfuls... and like, right now. As he stormed towards the burger stand, the fusion-sense re-activated, and Marvin was freed from the brutal wrench of the senses.

"I swear those food stands had the gravitational pull of Jupiter!" He still sounded aghast when relating his beach experience. "I never appreciated the full value of our fusion-sense. Without it, you are slave to your five senses. They're dictators and tyrants with enough force to get an inattentive mind into serious trouble!"

Avory had scoffed at Marvin's findings. Besides, he felt he had the better part of the deal. He was to attend a concert: Beethoven's 9th. Great music, world-class orchestra, star conductor, top chorus and soloists. Prior to Victoria deactivating his fusion-sense, Avory had been fully immersed in the harmonious vibrations – he was the music, his mission cloak particles resonating with the sound waves. It was a holistic experience, not just an auditory one. But the moment Victoria "flipped the switch" as Avory put it, "it was like being ripped into five separate pieces. The stupid seat cut painfully into my backside; the dude on my left reeked of garlic; my eyes were held captive by the plunging neckline of the gorgeous woman off to my right...." The music, he sighed, was reduced to just another confusing sensory experience, pulling him into a dizzying spin of perception. It all left a rather bad impression.

This experience had reminded Avory of an occasion when they had looked in on the family of the newborn. The older children had received a largish box of different colored and shaped bits and pieces. The Forces had thought it was a pretty useless gift. What fun was a box of fragments? But the kids had quickly spread them out, studied the picture on the box and skillfully assembled the pieces to recreate the image of a sleek spacecraft.

It was the same with the five human senses fracturing all objects into different pieces. Only with an active fusion-sense could you get a grip on reality. Victoria had nodded, pointing out that this was precisely what the upgrade would provide – the picture on the box.

Marvin shifted on his surfboard and paddled lazily towards the incoming waves, recalling what they had learned from their lessons. They had been eager. It had sounded like fun. In fact it hadn't been particularly amusing, but it greatly increased their respect for what humans had to contend with. It was a major challenge to decode the material world with the limited software human brains were currently running on.

Flicking his fingers at a curious fish nibbling at his hand as it trailed in the water, Marvin inadvertently dissolved the aquatic vertebrate's particles. Oops! He'd have to watch that in future. It was one thing to rearrange Victoria's treasured Venetian chandelier into the shape of an octopus, but living things were a no-no.

Night approached in a spectacular sequence of tangerine, gold and violet bleeding into the darkening ocean. Stepping onto the deck of their base, the twins were a tribute to the handsomeness of human mission cloaks. Marvin's dark good looks were a striking contrast to Avory's golden glow. They'd just finished a couple of sets of bimanual tennis – one of the sports they had invented for exercise and to balance body and brain halves. Playing tennis with a racket in each hand made for a dizzyingly fast and complex game, as did charging at each other while dribbling two basketballs – sinking them simultaneously in side-by-side hoops.

"Got any of that fermented barley juice cooling, Vicky, ma belle?" Marvin asked, already opening the small fridge. "You want one Ave?"

The tall man nodded, but Victoria stopped them with her eyes. They were not to dull their senses, not this evening. She needed them in top shape. "Want me to wrestle Big G?"

Marvin cried. "I can do that with one hand tied behind my back."

"Yeah, I've seen you watch those shows on Earth TV. Maybe Victoria'll whip up a sequined costume for you too?"

Their leader just arched her perfect eyebrows. "It's something far more interesting. You'll get to know the reality of our five new friends tonight."

No, they weren't coming for dinner. They weren't even near the base. But to understand the influence of the five senses on a human's sense of identity, the twins would step into the quintet's disparate environments – not physically, but virtually. Excited, they sidled up to the plasma cube and were whisked away on a whirlwind tour through the sensory perception patterns of the five friends.

They were exposed first to Ali's Arab world. Throngs, crowds, bearded men, women in jeans, in business costumes, covered head to toe. Rhythmic music, muezzins calling, amber pearls clacking. Sand stinging exposed skin, aromatic sheesha clouds, cardamom scented coffee. They dove into Haki's African reality, into unbearable heat, aggression, need, fear. Children laughing, dancing. Impenetrable rainforest, wide lazy river. What a contrast to Reto's pristine and structured Swiss surroundings, the chill air high up in snow covered mountains. The busy streets, busy people. Cowbells and church bells. And off they were to Barb's home, to have their senses filled with a balmy Californian breeze, the ocean smells, buildings high as mountains. Sweet smell of orange blossoms. To complete their tour, the twins were thrown into Shiv's Indian reality with its rich fragrances, saturated colors and multiple languages. Delicate tinkle of gold bangles, spicy milk tea, soft sitar sounds and sandalwood incense. Throngs of people, jumble of languages, congested streets, lofty mountains.

As the scents faded and the heat broke, the twins slowly became aware of the sound of waves lapping the shore, breeze caressing their skin, the salty, tangy smell.... This whirlwind tour into the starkly different sensory environments of the five Master Levels had heightened their sensory awareness.

"Wow! What a ride." Marvin was still caught up in vivid images and impressions. He stretched out his arms as if to embrace the whole planet. "Nooooow I begin to understand! Your CID determines your perception. But your sense of identity is also influenced by your environment and by whatever you absorb through your sensory filters, right?

To a human, 'I' was not only a particular mission cloak – male or female, dark or light skinned, strong or weak, tall or short – but 'I' was also the individual mental interpretation of input from the five senses, filtered by the color of ones "spectacles". Yes, of course, that made sense. It explained much of what had been incomprehensible to the twins. Constrained by their concept of identity, humans tended to exclude as wrong, untrue or simply non-existent anything that didn't belong within the scope of 'I' or 'me' or 'mine.'

With the upgrade, the tendency to absorb and accept the 'not me' would grow, especially since the whole range was already stored in an individual's CID. It just needed to be activated. Victoria smiled. "Humans will want to escape monovision and embrace multivision."

They will grasp that only on the surface was an individual white or black, Christian or Muslim, Indian or American, Communist or Republican. Such perceptions are merely a consequence of their brain wiring, mission cloak design, environment, color of spectacles and mental training. Upgraded humans will see through these differentiations and look for the unifying qualities they need in a global human society. And those who really delve deep into the question of human identity will recognize the single source at the core of all existence.

"This yearning to expand one's identity will grow ever stronger and transform human society", Victoria concluded. "After all it is humanity's destiny to be a united species of brothers and sisters, cast by one director as actors in a common play."

9

Five Paths Cross

"And I tell you, I'm going alone!" Barb Bernstein stamped her foot like an obstinate three year old. Mercedes had to hide her face so Barb couldn't see she was almost choking with laughter. "I'm an individual, a grownup. I don't need some tricked out handbag to cling to or to give me status."

No one was arguing with Miz B., but she carried on muttering and swearing anyway, pulling out clothes from the wardrobe running the length of her considerable bedroom. She was in full drama mode: practically naked, clad in nothing but a whiff of sheer lace and impossibly high heels. Her gleaming chestnut waves tumbled over delicate shoulder bones, the heart-shaped face a tribute to her stylist's artistry – the eyes mysteriously shadowed, cupid's bow glowing a deep red. Barb marched up and down the serried ranks of clothes like a general furiously surveying the sorry state of her troops. The dog watched the parade from her silly velvet sofa.

"What on earth am I going to wear? There's absolutely nothing in here..." she moaned, dismissing with a weary wave the dozens of gowns, blouses, suits and other exquisite pieces making up her impressive collection. "I don't want to look like a Hollywood bimbo. Mercedes! Lucy! What am I going to wear, help me. I'll never make it to that party if you don't help me...."

While Lucy contented herself with a lazy wag of her tail and a sympathetic flick of her bat ears, Mercedes acted as an appreciative audience to her boss' antics. Now she got up from the black-and-white cowhide ottoman, aimed for a point about halfway down the row of clothes and grabbed a hanger. "Try this, honey. It's always been one of my favorites, and you haven't worn it in this part of the world yet."

Barb gave her assistant a hug – careful not to smudge the artwork on her face – then stepped into a shimmering pair of harem pants that rode low on her hips, hung deep in the crotch and were accentuated with large side pockets. On most women, such pants would look like fully loaded diapers, but Barb's were so ingeniously put together that they flowed around her, changing form with every step and setting off her curves without being tight. She then drew on a sleeveless vest made of paper-thin leather and closed it with three of the four buttons. "Where are my car keys? Could you find them for me Miss Merc? You're the best."

"Err, isn't there supposed to be something under or over this vest? You know, it kind of buttons awfully low down...." Mercedes stared at Barb's breasts, ingeniously disguised by the sleek black leather.

"Don't be such a prude! And don't worry; they won't fall out! That's the trick with this vest. See, everyone will expect it to happen and keep staring...." Barb laughed out loud, twirled around in front of the mirror and started towards the front hall in an exaggerated model's hip-swinging stalk. It wasn't only her outfit that would make them stare. Their eyes would pop at the gorgeous Miz B., arriving at the party alone. It was not for a lack of willing escorts. She just felt that in the aftermath of her TV appearance, she had to stand her ground alone. Anyway, she wasn't some insecure babe who only felt worthy as a powerbroker's accessory, or when towing some sculpted bunch of muscle on a leash. She was an Academy Award nominee, a woman at the peak of her game, with the future looking bright.

She'd just received a request from one of the big networks – they'd picked up on her educational foundation idea – to document a number of similar projects in Central and South America. Her foundation was gaining traction; so she would take advantage of the network job to put the final touches on her Peru venture. She just needed a highly skilled and creative person to advise on the computer infrastructure. The negative publicity spewing forth from the relevant or rather, irrelevant, media had only added to Barb's aura as a strong and successful woman who spoke her mind – she didn't keep her mouth shut just to win approval of the masses.

Barb expected to see her father at the bash. He wasn't the party animal he used to be, but he could still work a crowd. Instead of setting up business deals, he now used his vast network to promote aid projects for the foundation he chaired, expertly and shamelessly wringing sizeable donations from those who lent him their ear. Perhaps he'll bring along the African girl who was staying at his house in Indian Wells. Barb was keen to meet her. She would surely have great stories to tell. Besides, she might have some good ideas for the Peru project; after all, the problems were pretty much the same whether you were dirt poor and isolated in Africa or the Andes.

Coming up the long driveway to the spread (calling it a house would have been like calling the "QE2" a boat) Ali was impressed. First off, he could have happily spent the evening just wandering around the parking lot. Sleek and gleaming, a who's who of auto-nobility was discreetly hidden behind a flowering jasmine hedge. Majestic British luxo-barges shared space with stylish Italian aristocracy, while German precision engineering was clearly preferred to anything from the once great U.S. auto industry. Ali coerced his companion into spending just a little more time – please – checking out the handful of powerful motorbikes leaning heavily on their stands.

What the owner called his barn was in fact an architectural showcase of different cubes...straight lines, all light grey concrete and acres of glass. When you stepped inside the lofty spaces, you couldn't tell where indoors ended and outdoors began. The living room floor morphed into a flagstone terrace, and movable glass panels gave the illusion of vegetation growing right into the entrance hall. During the day, these rooms would be flooded with natural light, Ali thought. It would be like living outdoors, but with all the amenities you could possibly wish for. The hosts showed admirable restraint when it came to furnishings. Just the necessary minimum scattered throughout the spacious setting, each piece carefully selected. The reception and living areas were furnished with Italian designs. Here too, clean lines and open space dominated, in keeping with the bold architecture.

The flawlessly groomed Governor's assistant – she reminded Ali of an expensive, pampered purebred – clung tightly to his arm. She fit effortlessly into the surroundings, same clean lines, same stamp of design. And when she had commented on how good he looked in the lightweight suit hanging so well on his lanky frame, Ali had joked that maybe he should change into a sheet, put a dishrag on his head and bring his camel.

He took a glass of champagne from one of the waiters drifting through the colorful throng. Soon his consort was showered with air kisses, while he was greeted with warm smiles, manly handshakes and "nice to meet yous." The high energy of the exquisitely done-up crowd was contagious, and the striking setting the perfect stage.

Murmuring something about a washroom, he escaped his companion's clasp, made his way onto the wide terrace and over toward the pool. The balmy night reminded Ali of home; tall, illuminated date palms in the garden emphasized the connection. He had long been attracted to California. It was the place, outside of his native land, where he felt most comfortable. These latitudes linked California to the North African deserts and their mysterious pyramids – to the lands where his culture had flourished and these same date palms grew.

He glanced again at the trees, separated from the crowd by artful illumination, just one group among tens of thousands of date palms that used to be an important branch of the local desert economy. He remembered that he'd wanted to take the short drive to the town of Mecca before he left. The name intrigued him, another link to the Middle East. But then, California was quite a mecca itself. Bright minds didn't flock here to pray, but to invent, define and shape the future. California was still the mecca of high-tech, with innumerable firms founded and run by creative and innovative people. Their aim was to further communication and understanding between people around the globe, as well as to make information and education available to whomever wanted it. Ali felt very much at home with this future focus, geared towards advance. Besides, his work for the California government had cemented Ali's international reputation – as a man whom you could trust to come up with novel public transport systems meeting the highest criteria of efficiency and ecology. Yes, Ali Ben Calif really liked California. He smiled to himself. How many of those here tonight knew Caliph was the title given to the civil and religious leader of a Muslim state?

Reto felt good about himself tonight. He knew he cut a handsome figure – open-necked, palest pink shirt under a charcoal-grey Italian suit. His work in California was soon to be successfully concluded, and he looked forward to flying home in a few days with a couple of interesting new contacts in the bag. This bash was a great opportunity to expand his already well-spun network, of which his escort tonight was part – albeit more by association. Her husband was a friend, a pretty wild but highly successful wheeler-dealer with his fingers in all sorts of pies, from real estate to luxury yachts. Reto had always liked him a lot; an irrepressible spirit who did things he shouldn't, living life on the edge and all with a boyish charm that made him attractive to the more sober Swiss. But now the IRS had caught up with his friend. It was not a question of fraud, more of a stunning chaos in his financial affairs. Since Peter seemed to lack the gene necessary to keep order, his third wife – or was she the fourth? – had beseeched Reto to please fly over and save her husband from incarceration. After several all-night sessions with Peter and his bankers, they arranged the mess of paper into something resembling orderly books. A deal had been cut with the government people, a heavy fine paid and betterment promised. To commemorate his success, Peter's wife had invited Reto to escort her tonight, not only because Peter currently shunned the spotlight, but also to pay back the favor.

Seated in a lounge chair, Reto marveled at the stylish attire of the very trendy crowd, and at the general health and fitness of the people. Where had the bloodshot eyes, the sunken cheeks of the smokers and drinkers gone? Where were the flab and sag and droop and wither? It wasn't just the men who were fit and trim, the women also displayed toned biceps and strong and shapely calves. Hardly any heavyweights in sight here, but plenty of health-conscious individuals radiating energy.

And suddenly it hit him! There was hardly any visible age difference, even though they had to cover the range between 20 and 60. Everyone looked kind of ageless – just like the stars of the silver screen. Reto sighed. This was close enough to Hollywood after all, where trends that circled the world were set. And what he saw here was an ageless society. Could that really happen? Reto was vain enough to have studied the different anti-ageing techniques and technologies. Recently a clinic, catering to the very wealthy, had set up shop in his hometown. But here, at this party, you could see this future in just about every guest. The bright smiles were the most noticeable. Sure, it was probably their tans, real or cosmetic, that enhanced the whiteness of the teeth, but even the twilight couldn't dull their brightness. Reto looked around, mouth closed. He was aware of his own teeth not making the grade here – his beloved cigars and regular infusions of tar-black espresso certainly hadn't helped... At least he had nothing to fear when it came to bodily shape and fitness, but his self-image as the trendiest lawyer in the Swiss Alps had to absorb a couple of dents this beautiful night. When Peter's wife sidled up and drew him toward the dance floor, he gently released himself. "I'm taking a break, if you don't mind. I'll find a quiet place outside."

As he was striding over the lawns towards the illuminated pool, he inhaled deeply. The air was so very different from home. It's balmy softness so easy to breathe, almost like an antidote to the sharp mountain air of Switzerland. He glanced up at the tall palms dotting the gardens, felt the warmth on his face and thought, "this is how a Swiss mountain guy would imagine paradise."

Hiding in the pool house, safe for another few minutes, Shiv was deep in thought. He still couldn't get used to being here, in Cali-fornia, in Cali-form, in Indian Wells no less! An Indian in Cali-fornia's Indian Wells. He could just hear his mother Devi sigh. "How very, very auspicious, son!" Shiv smiled to himself. He had been amazed at how effortlessly everything had fallen into place, once he had decided to take what was quite a bold step for one reluctant to leave even the university grounds.

The Princeton professor he had contacted – the new Einstein – had enthusiastically answered Shiv's mail, proposing a visit. He had been flattered to learn that this prominent scientist knew of his work in India and, what's more, would be happy to meet him. The professor was soon headed to California to see his brother; Shiv was most welcome to come and spend time with him there. For once, Shiv had not hesitated. More so because he kept hearing a faint whisper in the back of the head: Mother Cali's "Visit me in my western abode."

Well, neither a frightful nor a seductive Cali had accosted him here, but Shiv had at least understood the professor's obvious interest in his visit. He would have been bored to death without a discussion partner to follow the brilliant leaps and bounds of his highly trained mind: probing into the deepest secrets of the material universe, seeking to unify quantum mechanics with gravity, and searching for the ultimate building blocks of matter. Representatives of east and west, they had called their discussions, "The theory of everything and its philosophical consequences."

Shiv had mentioned that the question of "how a thought was made" kept nibbling at his mind, raising still more profound questions. His thoughts, he had observed, seemed to appear in his mind without his contributing anything. If you followed that line to its logical conclusion, you had to ask: where, then, is a man's free will? Is there even such a thing?

The Professor had nodded and smiled, visibly excited by the direction their discussion was taking. He was trying to formulate a unifying theory concerning all particles – all, without exception, including those that made up humans. He had talked about neurological studies proving that before a conscious decision was made, it was already measurable in the brain! As much as a few seconds before you decided to pick up your fork, for instance, the brain had already given the command to do so. So who made the decision? Was man but a puppet of his neurons, of a steering center that not only controlled his organism, but also his presumed willful decisions?

From there, it was a short step to the next topic. If there really was a single energy forming all the universe, then who was man? Was he a mere projection of this one energy, a random collection of particles just like a tree or a mouse or a star? It would surely take a more complex entity to answer the questions they were asking now. It was a bit beyond the average date palm or house cat. Amid laughter about philosophical cats and trees doing equations, they had agreed that the answers to where and how thoughts were produced perhaps also lay in tracking down this elusive singular energy.

It struck them both how modern physics and ancient Indian philosophy seemed to arrive at the same conclusions regarding the central questions of existence. New studies of black holes, for example, indicated that the three-dimensional world was a hologram, a projection of information stored on a thin, two-dimensional surface. Wasn't that pretty much what the concept of "Maya," so central to Indian philosophy, proposed – that the material world is but an illusion, a projection.

And thus the scientists had spent a couple of hours every day, going over topics they were both so vitally interested in, trying to catch a glimpse of the cards the universe still held up its sleeve. And as an antidote to this work, they took time out to play numerous, highly competitive rounds of golf.

Cutting a striking figure in his hip-length tailored Nehru jacket with its small mandarin collar, an outfit that really suited his long slim frame, Shiv observed the goings on over by the main house. His mind was calm, but his body hesitant to join the rest of the world. He hadn't mustered enough courage yet to leave the poolside guesthouse. When he looked up, he saw the professor approach.

"You know, you can't pretend to be a stationary universe all by yourself! Remember we're all just clinging to our particular 'Brane'...." The professor broke into a very unscholarly giggle.

"I'm not thinking about anything else! How could I? You really set my mind in motion. In fact, I'd like to try out some ideas on you...."

"There's a time to think and a time to drink, my man. We promised my brother we'd put in an appearance. After all, we represent the intelligentsia here – so let's jump in and simply have fun, what do you say?" The professor knew Shiv would probably just stay in his quarters all evening if nobody coaxed him out, so he took his arm and gently guided him out the door.

Shiv gave an exaggerated sigh and nodded. "I am willing to sacrifice whatever is needed, as long as we can continue our discussions." He laughed. "There's no such thing as an isolated free quark. Therefore I'm willing to mingle."

"You into sharing?"

Barb jumped at the voice coming out of the dark.

"Over here in the gazebo. Didn't mean to startle you, just caught the promising sound of clinking glass."

She looked around and saw a wrought iron structure half hidden by a large hibiscus. Despite the scare he had given her, she noticed the sexy timbre of the slightly accented voice – eastern maybe. Barb stepped around the shrub and now saw the whole gazebo. It looked like something lifted out of a Jane Austen novel, a place where poor but proud maidens would sit and share their dreams or secretly rendezvous with unbefitting suitors. Very 19th century and an incongruous but surprisingly pleasant contrast to the otherwise stark architecture.

"Don't worry, I'm not Count Dracula waiting for some fresh blood to pass by. But my glass is empty and I could sure use a shot of whatever you're drinking."

Barb slowly climbed the steps. The inside was barely illuminated; a single candle in a large glass bowl. She could just make out the silhouette of a man, leaning back on the semi-circular bench. With a gesture, indicating 'help yourself,' she set the champagne bottle and her half-filled glass on the table. She had planned to sit quietly and alone for a while, but this was much better. Barb felt completely at peace, with herself and with the world. She listened to her unknown friend fill both glasses, take a sip, and give a contented sigh. This is exactly what she had come to the party for, she thought, to sit here and share a bottle of champagne with this stranger.

She still had not said a word.

Into this peaceable silence stepped a wide-shouldered figure who seemed to fill the whole entrance, accompanied by a fragrant cloud of cigar smoke. "Oh excuse me, I didn't mean to intrude. I thought I was the only one here." Another foreign accent, Barb registered. This was turning out to be a United Nations gazebo gathering here. She giggled. Then her invisible friend started laughing too.

"You're not intruding or interrupting, except some shared peace and quiet. If you're looking for some of the same, step on up and be welcome."

The new arrival slowly approached the table in the middle of the gazebo and carefully set down a wine bottle. "Sorry, only brought one glass."

"That's cool, we're already into sharing here. So why don't you decant, mon cher." Barb made a gesture as if commanding her servant. She caught an amused glint in the man's eye.

"À votre service, Madame." He poured and offered the glass to Barb like a minister offering the goblet at Holy Communion.

She shook her head and pointed to her freshly filled glass.

Again, a friendly silence descended on the little oasis. No one felt the need for making conversation or filling the quiet with sound.

When Barb heard a warm, husky voice singing a mournful tune, she imagined it was only in her head. "Great booze," she thought. "Not only brings peace but music too." But then she realized her companions were sitting up and listening too. The singing was coming closer, accompanied by footsteps. They were obviously not the only ones drawn to this peculiar structure. The gazebo turned out to be quite the gathering place.

"Barb! How good to find you here!"

"Hey Dad. Come on in. We're just kind of chilling. Who is that wonderful singer you brought along? This wouldn't be your African ward, would it?"

When Ethan Bernstein stepped into the gazebo, it suddenly seemed crowded. He was a big man, barrel chested, wide shouldered, shaggy head of graying hair and a dusting of silver stubble on his jowls. Since he had given up wheeling and dealing in Hollywood and thrown himself whole-heartedly into development projects mainly in sub-Saharan Africa, his look had changed accordingly. "Let me introduce you to Haki – Hakika Hasina really – who is not my ward, as you so improperly put it, but the budding manager of a string of bush hospitals."

Barb got up on her killer heels and gave the still taller Haki a big hug. "It's so good to finally meet you. Hey, great dress. I hope you like it ... I have a ton of questions and a bunch of ideas I want to discuss with you. We must get together. Tomorrow would be best. You know, I need some information on education issues. I have a really terrific project that's just getting off the ground. And I'm sure you could be a great help if you have time. So what say, should we...."

"Barb dear, slow down, girl." Ethan put his big hand on her shoulder. "Give her time to arrive, breathe, get used to her surroundings. And, besides, I thought you all had come here for some peace and quiet."

At Barb's verbal barrage, Haki had retreated to the other end of the bench – almost falling over the men sitting in the shadows.

"Steady there, lady," the burly one said quietly and helped her sit down.

"Don't you want to introduce me to your friends, Barb?" Ethan, beer bottle in hand, leaned on one of the iron posts holding up the domed roof.

"I'm afraid I can't Dad. I have absolutely no idea who my companions are." She was just reaching for her glass again, when she caught a movement outside the gazebo's entrance. "Whoever you are, come on in, there's one more seat just for you."

A very long, very thin frame appeared in the opening. "Good god, it's a giraffe," Barb thought, but kept it to herself.

The stranger hesitated on the steps, not wanting to be sucked into some sort of Hollywood group groove, but also not wanting to appear impolite. "Good evening," he said, and Barb immediately placed him somewhere in the east, India most likely.

"Please," she said quietly. "Do join us. We were just waiting for Asia to show up."

"Asia? How?"

"Europe, the Middle East, Africa and the Americas seem to be represented already, all we're missing is Asia." Barb laughed quietly. "Welcome to the U.N. gazebo."

"Seems the desire for peace and quiet is universal," the stranger answered and folded himself into the last free space. The candle gave off a small, warm light, but not enough to illuminate the faces of the men and women around the bench. Quiet fell once more within the structure, interrupted by snatches of music, voices and laughter drifting over on the mellow breeze.

"I'm curious." Barb broke the amicable silence.

"You were born that way," Ethan chuckled.

"C'mon Dad, I'm serious."

"That, on the other hand, must be a recently acquired trait...."

"Daaad, we're not in family therapy here! If you don't mind, I'd like to hear who all of you are and how you came to be right here tonight. And no 'coincidence' or 'fate' stuff! Make it as concrete as possible. I find it quite extraordinary that five people from different parts of the world would come to sit on the same bench at this particular time, don't you?" She paused just a moment, then added, "And don't worry, Dad. I can still add, but we're family, so we count as one."

"You are right," Reto Ritter said. "This mix is pretty amazing, even for a country where you normally meet people from all over the world. Seems to me this nation is built on its ability to absorb different cultures, backgrounds, languages. It does so much more easily than in my part of the world." He sighed a little. "But that's not what you wanted, right?"

"Everyone calls our country the great melting pot," Ethan cut in. "That idea has always fascinated me. As a kid I imagined that all of the people seeking a new homeland would be thrown into huge cauldrons in the cellars of immigration, melted down, pressed into a new form, and when they came out at the end of the line, they'd all be freshly-minted Americans...."

"...wearing Levi's 501s," Barb added with a laugh. "Now there's a piece of fashion that has conquered the world."

They all laughed at this image of an assembly line producing standard, jeans-clad Americans out of a variety of ethnic backgrounds.

"It has a lot going for it," Shiv said. "I assume the skin color would also be standardized and language ability too. That alone would make life a lot easier for so many people."

"What about religion, Ethan? When your standard, run-of-the mill Americans come out of the press, do they all pray to the same god?" Haki's voice had a smile in it, but the question was a serious one.

"I wish," Ethan answered with an exaggerated sigh. "Be great if they then all followed the religion of tolerance, where everybody could worship whom or whatever they want, or not worship at all. You know, Hollywood was founded by creative people fleeing intolerance – Barb's and my forebears included. America has been founded on the idea of being a country for everyone seeking life, liberty and the pursuit of happiness," he concluded in a humorous declamatory tone.

"Perhaps it would be best to make science the world's common religion; then we'd have no reason to reject each other." Shiv's lilting English sounded very soft in the open structure.

"I find it truly amazing that hundreds of thousands, or rather millions of immigrants have all brought their specific traits, traditions, and beliefs to this part of the world, and woven them into a country that seems to work pretty well." All heads turned in the direction of Ali Ben Calif. "But now, with all this irrational fear of terrorism, this nation stands to lose a lot of the ground it has already gained."

"You're talking about the Homeland Security situation, intrusion into personal freedom, surveillance of communication, the right to arrest anyone under suspicion of terrorism?" Barb grew very agitated. "It is really atrocious what the warmongers and zealots have wreaked in this country under the guise of protecting the people."

"It is important to have clear rules, transparent legislation, comprehensible laws," Reto interjected.

"You must be a lawyer." Barb looked in his direction. "Correct to the marrow of your bones. Rules and laws first, tick, tock, tick, tock. All else is debatable."

Reto chuckled. "You got me figured out pretty quickly. I do indeed admire the precise mechanism of a fine Swiss watch. And I see beauty in expertly crafted laws, ones that serve the overall common good, with guaranteed equal treatment for each individual. Like you, I abhor self-serving legislation. And I agree that a lot of what has been passed in the aftermath of 9/11 is not in the interest of the American people."

Barb gave a little sigh. "I'm glad we see eye to eye on this, Mr. Advocate. I'd hate to have to leave this cozy little place.... But I really didn't want to bring politics in here. Can we just get back to what I proposed before? Would you be willing to share your story of how you all came to be here? Just bold brush strokes, remember, ten sentences or less."

"That's a dangerous parameter, a sentence is an extremely flexible thing, which could – if someone set his mind to it – probably go on as long as there are decimal places of Pi." The inflection was unmistakable.

"Must be a scientific mind speaking," Barb said in mock exasperation. "Turns out, this isn't only the U.N. here, but a true meeting of the minds, something like a gazebo summit. Maybe I should just go back up to the house and drown myself in champagne and mindless chatter."

"Don't go, Barb. I'd really like to hear where everybody comes from and how he or she got to be here. I think it's wonderful that we all come from different parts of the world – really interesting. So, why don't you go first?" Haki had spoken up and surprised herself with her boldness. She had been looking at Reto and was grateful the darkness hid her furious blushing.

"Ok. I don't think I need ten sentences. My story is quite simple. I am Renato Ritter, Reto for short, a lawyer in Switzerland. I'm from an alpine resort you may have heard of. One of my clients, and a dear friend at that, needed some urgent legal assistance. So I came here to help. His wife asked me to escort her to this party. I figured it would be a good opportunity to do a little networking. Besides, I really enjoy seeing and meeting so many interesting and good-looking people. But since smoking is a cardinal sin in California, I grabbed a bottle of that very good Cabernet and looked for a spot where I could do a little sinning."

While Reto talked, Haki was trying to put her little story in place. She felt uneasy talking to strangers, and she was still a little shocked at having spoken up before. But then something had changed tonight, hadn't it. When Ethan had asked her to be his date, as he had laughingly put it, Haki immediately declined. To tell the truth, she had simply been scared. Ethan, however, had taken her hand and told her she looked just like an incarnation of queen Califia, who once upon a time had ruled this wonderful place called California. According to legend, it was populated by dark, strong, brave-hearted women living like Amazons. They rode wild beasts and had weapons and harnesses of gold, because there was no other metal on the island.

And the eternal excuse of "I don't know what to wear" hadn't cut it, because Ethan had – with expert assistance from his daughter – already taken care of that. Haki had found the large box containing a stunning dress in her room. It was all about the fabric, the cut deceptively simple. When Haki had slipped into the sea-green silk, it looked and felt as if it flowed over her skin. The dress was sleeveless, no neckline to speak of, but plunging down low in the back, making the most of Haki's willowy body and setting off her dark, velvet skin. When she looked in the mirror, she had felt transformed. She hardly recognized herself at first, but then she felt power surge through her, a power she had not known before. "I am this woman," she had thought, "this beautiful woman I see in this mirror." She had seen the same in Ethan's eyes when she descended the stairs to the hall where he was waiting. Thoughtfully, Barb had chosen a pair of elegant flat sandals to go with the dress. Haki wouldn't have known how to walk on high heels.

"You truly are Queen Califia, my dear, dear Haki. Breathtaking. But you don't need a sword or a bow. Your smile and intelligence are your golden weapons. I won't have to fear you falling into any shark pool at the party!" They had laughed, he had offered his arm, and they had been off.

When it was her turn at the gazebo, all she said was, "My name is Haki. I live in a small settlement in the rainforest in the Democratic Republic of Congo, in the region of Bas-Congo. By training I'm a nurse, and now I manage a bush hospital. I came to California on the invitation of a foundation chaired by Mr. Bernstein. I'm taking courses in business administration. Ethan was so kind as to invite me to this party, and I asked him to show me the gardens."

After a moment of silence, the soft voice with its particular cadence broke in. "I am Shiv Singh Sitaram, dabble in particle physics, and call Chandigarh, India my home. I could now lay out for you a grand theory about how we all, like distant stars, have been on a collision course for perhaps eons. But then we could also just look at it as coincidence, chance, destiny.... I came to this party to avoid offending my host by refusing. I'm staying in the pool house of this grand estate, as an invited guest. The party presented a good opportunity to observe the native species in their habitat. After completing my 'field studies,' I came to this spot in search of some solitude. But you could also say I am here because I followed a dream."

Barb gave a small, satisfied sigh. "A scientist following a dream! How very unusual and intriguing. But then, maybe eastern scientists have an extra dimension our Westerners lack?" She would have loved to hear more about the dream. But she had set the rules, so there. Great stories though, what good fortune had brought them all together.

She was really curious to learn more about this cute guy who, she had since realized, was the same man she had noticed immediately upon her arrival, simply because he stood out in a crowd. There was something very self-contained, very detached about him. He was a handsome man with a narrow, striking face, clearly Middle Eastern. Nice suit too. But the guy would look great in anything, whether it came from the thrift shop or a designer rack. He just had that kind of body, and the attitude to go with it: completely unaffected, unselfconscious, not out to make any sort of impression. The classic white shirt set off his dark skin, and even the fashionable three-day stubble didn't disturb the image of one totally cool dude. A tidy blonde had clung to him like a dog to a juicy bone, and Barb had considered luring him away – usually one of her favorite party tricks – but couldn't find the heart for it. She had trailed him for a while, watching how he moved through the crowd, always friendly but aloof, autonomous, not attaching himself to anyone, not sucking up to the celebs, just nodding and smiling and moving on. And now he had come to her just like that, wasn't it – perhaps – a sign? "Your turn, stranger," she said and looked at Ali.

"It's going to be a short story. I am Ali Ben Calif. My home base is Cairo. I have come to California on business. I'm advising the state government on emission-free public transportation systems. The Governor's assistant invited me to the party. Well, and here I am." After a short moment he added: "And you, our charming ring mistress? You're maybe not into sharing after all.... Let's hear your story."

Barb gave a small chuckle. "You obviously haven't read the right rags; otherwise, you wouldn't ask. Or maybe you just can't see me in the dark. I'm Barb Bernstein. I'm from right around here someplace. I make documentaries, and right now

I'm up the creek with the yellow press because I sometimes have trouble keeping my big mouth shut."

Even though Ali – and probably the others as well, perhaps with the exception of Shiv – would have loved to hear more about the particular creek she was up, they kept quiet, and Barb was grateful. Actually she was quite pleased with herself. What an interesting collection. She was sure these were the most extraordinary people among the already remarkable crowd gathered at this party. And Barb was convinced, despite a total lack of evidence, that she had somehow drawn them all to this spot. Even Dad had found her. There he was, still standing on the top step, looking strong and tall, as if he were holding up the wrought iron roof all by himself.

Barb got up to sneak a hug. The affection between them came easy, obviously practiced often. But when she suddenly moved away from him and cried out, "Daddy, what?" the others were instantly alarmed.

What happens next transpires as if in slow motion. The dark brown beer bottle shattering on the iron steps; foamy islands forming amidst shards sparkling like discarded jewels. Ethan trying to gulp air into a chest that has suddenly lost its expansiveness. He takes a step towards the grass, clutches at his chest, rubs his arm. "Hurts," he moans, "hurts like hell...." Sweat drenches his face. "Can't breathe..." Haki automatically starts picking up the broken glass, lest someone gets hurt, a silent prayer on her lips. Ali Ben Calif pulls out his cell phone. Reto thinks, "Coronary, massive coronary," flashing on questions of insurance and legal ramifications. Barb is holding onto her father, shaking him, crying, desperate. Then Haki suddenly flies into action, summoning her medical skills, while Shiv seems to withdraw even deeper into himself, staying intently focused on the dying man. In his mind he sees heart cells gasping in vain for oxygen, functions shutting down. He sees molecular chains breaking, matter already starting to decay.

Like a mortally wounded bear, the big man topples and goes down, dimly aware of five pairs of eyes staring at him, his daughter clutching at him, Haki trying to pound on his massive chest. "Who am I?" he groans. "What am I?" he whispers. "Who am I?" he tries to shout, gripping his daughter's arm, seeking, wanting, demanding an answer. Then he is still.

10

Stepping off the Roller Coaster

The emotions gusting over from the gazebo like high-energy beta particles interfered unpleasantly with Marvin's vibratory speed, as did the emergency vehicle's hypnotically flashing lights, which drew a growing crowd to the dramatic event. Marvin urged his companions to return to mission base.

Avory was reluctant to leave just yet. He wanted to keep studying the five Master Level souls, whose individual behavior so clearly reflected their distinct vibratory patterns. He had been particularly drawn to the vivacious Ms. Bernstein, an unadulterated orange, whose emissions had changed so radically when the big man dropped his costume. Hidden amid the gently swaying branches of a weeping willow, Avory had to keep shrugging off Marvin, who was intent on pulling him away from the scene. Only the promise of a remote viewing via Plasma Cube finally convinced him to leave the electrifying moment.

No one paid attention to the three shifting shapes over by the willow, forms gradually losing their outlines, evaporating like a sun-touched mist.

Back on their deck, surrounded by a soundscape of ocean waves pounding unseen on the dark shore, the twins were keen to delve deeper into the mysteries of human nature. How could the simple and inevitable act of dropping the transient costume provoke such vehement reaction? After all, every human knew the mission cloak was only temporary and that they all had to make their exit eventually, regardless of their inner or outer achievements.

The real crux was the way sensory perception triggered emotions, Big G explained. This induced humans to develop strong ties, projecting on each other's mission cloaks the whole gamut of human emotion: love and need, fear and expectation, envy and admiration. Then, when someone thus 'loaded' stepped off the stage, those left behind reacted with shock and sadness to the disappearing form. When they couldn't touch the costume anymore, couldn't see or smell or hear or taste it, the senses became homeless, and the mind also lost its way. Even the death of strangers affected many humans, not deeply though, since their senses had no direct experience of these people.

"But how about when that American President got shot or the British Princess died in a car crash? There were millions mourning them," Avory objected.

"Ah, my smart friend. You've got a point there," Big G growled. "Perfect example of human senses working at a distance. You may have noticed how many react to famous sports or movie stars, those giving off an abundance of what is called charisma? Which is just an enlarged electromagnetic field, by the way. Well, their so-called fans long to see them, to be close to them, to touch and hear them. So when the adored or admired mission cloak disappears, the admirer's senses get forcibly disconnected and go astray. This leads to what humans call suffering."

Even though death featured so prominently in human literature and religious concepts, the average person was in denial about mortality. When it struck, as it did some 150,000 times a day, humans were unprepared and consequently overwhelmed by an emotional maelstrom. This too would change, Victoria pointed out. The upgrade allowed vision beyond the dissolution of solids and liquids. Dropping the mission cloak would be viewed as a simple fact of life with far less emotional impact.

Avory grew ever more thoughtful, then uttered a fateful remark: "It's like when we talked about identity. I can't really get a handle on this emotion business. Your explanations make sense, but they're just too abstract. There must be a hell of a surge."

Marvin suggested hooking him up to the high-voltage current in the basement to give him a feel for it. But Victoria had a far better idea; an ounce of experience could save her a ton of explanation.

The twins never saw her blink at the Plasma Cube. A burst of iridescence, a flash-cut! The twins just stared at one another, slack-jawed. An unseen force pulled them together. Just before contact Victoria ended the witchery.

"What? What the hell was that?" Marvin yelled. "Ave, man, you looked like a naked Barb Bernstein; all soft, curvy, creamy skin. Jeez! I wanted to bury my face in your knockers for the rest of my earthly existence." Avory, completely stunned, kept wiping at his eyes, as if to erase the image of a broad-chested, muscled body, emitting a strong masculine scent, powerful arms reaching for him, spear jutting out from between the legs, causing an almost painful stab of longing deep in Avory's belly.

No way could he erase what had struck him like lightning, just like the current Marvin had suggested earlier. Avory fumbled for an explanation, trying to put into words what had ripped through him. It was like his whole system was flooded with some kind of battery acid, shorting out the brain but igniting something else, something he had no words for. And Marvin admitted that he had almost jumped Ave's bones. So that's what humans called emotions. What a jolt! First the insane upsurge, then the crash when you couldn't have what you craved.

What a fantastic set-up. What an ingenious trap for unsuspecting souls. From the outside it looked like the five sensory filters triggered this emotional tsunami. In fact, it happened simultaneously. External occurrences flowed in through the five sensors; while the computing of an immense amount of data in specific areas of the brain triggered a neuro-chemical storm and elicited the physiological reactions that humans called emotions.

This close encounter of the weird kind with Ave cured Marvin of his penchant for smirking at humans' total identification with neurological functions. It was like being trapped on a monster rollercoaster – clamped into your wagon by Big G – and no way to ever, ever get off until you slipped out of your costume.

There was method to this madness, though; at least regarding male-female attraction. Certain emotions produced in the brain were like magnets, provoking humans to merge, creating opportunities for Big G to pull souls into new mission cloaks.

"What will happen when upgraded humans see the futility of hunting for their other half on the outside?" Avory asked. Since each individual's steering center is fully wired for both aspects, male and female, would they then stop fusing and quickly be added to the endangered species list?

Victoria allayed his fear. Human extinction was definitely not in the game plan. On the contrary, there were multitudes of souls stacked up there, waiting for their chance! Some would understand that male and female were to be found within, while others would happily go on populating the planet. Since the upgrade would activate additional neuronal connections in the brain – expanding its capacity – all humans would finally realize what a fantastic game life on Earth could be.

"Just like these games humans run on their computers," Marvin jumped in. The better you performed, the higher the level you achieved and the more exciting the game. You eagerly anticipated the next mission, next chance to progress. When human brains could probe ever finer details of a topic or situation, life would really take off! But as in the computer game, the more skilled had more fun; the less experienced would probably have to deal with serious frustration and use up life after life getting to the next level.

Once humans understood emotions and learned to unscramble the triggers, they would quickly become more detached.

"A trained, mature mind," Victoria explained, "is like an experienced surfer, reading every wave then deciding whether to ride it or let it pass. Humans would ride emotional waves with much more elegance. They could even accept the tidal wave of death with inner strength and dignity." She paused for a moment. "Understanding that all other humans are surfers too, trying their best to ride their own waves, empathy will grow."

"Hey, that sounds promising. Is this empathy a new feature?"

"Empathy is the ability to connect emotionally with others, to feel someone else's situation." Victoria continued. Just like the fusion-sense, empathy isn't a new feature; it has been part of all mission cloaks, particularly in females caring for their offspring. Males too have that feature, but regard it more as a weakness and left it therefore largely undeveloped. After the upgrade, jumpstarting this feature, inflicting suffering on others will be considered totally outmoded by society – be it killing, letting others die of hunger, or remaining unaffected by millions living in misery. With an active empathy feature, the mental consequences of shredding another's mission cloak will cause the perpetrator severe mental anguish.

When Marvin ambled over to the deck's refrigerator to retrieve a couple of bottles of barley juice – well deserved in his opinion – Victoria activated the Plasma Cube once more for a glance at the situation by the gazebo. Things had quieted down after the ambulance took off with Ethan Bernstein's costume – shed upon taking his final bow at the end of an admirable performance on this earthly stage. The three men and the woman had formed a protective circle around a sobbing Barb, escorting her to her father's house a few blocks away where Haki would keep her company. A smattering of party guests gathered in quiet groups, their faces mostly somber, thoughtful, contemplating the fragility of life, the inescapability of death. It would come regardless of all the money, time and effort they had invested in staving off physical decay.

Avory was reverberating with an unfamiliar energy while watching the inconsolable Ms. Bernstein being led away. All her water had been pulled way south and she had no means to resist Big G. She suffered.

"Can't you let up, Big G? Give her a break?" he asked.

It was Victoria who answered. While humanity had plenty of time to adjust to the upgrade, she said, the five friends would experience an accelerated program. As they had just witnessed, the lessons had already begun. Quietly she added: "They won't perceive them as very pleasant, but they are necessary...."

"Quite right. Quite right!" Like thunder rumbling over distant mountains, Big G's voice rolled into their discussion. "These lessons in detachment are part of my duties, and as you quite rightly pointed out, they are necessary steps on the path to uncovering the real human identity."

With the current software, suffering made no sense to an individual. It was considered mental or physical torture, triggered by outer circumstances. Humans could not see that suffering was actually mental training. After all, there were quite a few techniques available to detach the mind from where it was trapped – in greed, anger, hate, blame, depression – and to focus the senses inward; calmly and unemotionally assessing the situation. Seen from this perspective, suffering could indeed be a noble teacher. Victoria bowed in acknowledgement in the direction of Big G's voice, when he remarked that the gazebo incident would prompt the quintet to ask the right questions quickly. All the more so since Ethan had given them the cue, before having been liberated from his cumbersome bulk.

"Who am I," he had asked. "What am I?" By now he should have his answer, and might even remember it in his next role. If not, he'd be seeking the answer right from the start and would find it quickly. "But unlike him, many – when their time comes – will not be asking 'who am I?' but rather 'what about my stuff'?'"

"And those get extra laps, right?"

"They will be led to introspection through a bit of suffering until they decide to let go of their 'stuff' and turn to more subtle levels of reality. To access the truth, they must walk the path of introspection. They must merge the five senses – which separately distort the human perception of the outside world just as a prism refracts the one true reality – into a laser beam pointing inward. And that's why pain and suffering are so important on the path to wisdom. They force humans to concentrate on their inner universe, and detach from the material. You could also view suffering as a refinery, where human particles get buffed to a bright sparkle – like processing an uncut diamond. Of course, an inexperienced player perceives this process as quite painful, and I guess it's not a lot of fun, but this is how the game is set up."

Marvin nudged Avory with an elbow to the ribs, while imagining humans being herded through a maze of grinders and abraders. Going in they looked like Neanderthals. Stepping out, all dullness was gone. The shop would probably be out of business, however, once the upgrade fully kicked in. Big G had spoken of it ushering in an epoch of intense learning and profound transformation, where growth was no longer stimulated by pain and suffering but by interest and curiosity.

11

A Unique Bond is Formed

All she wanted was to take off these horribly tight but incredibly elegant shoes. Her feet were screaming in pain, which was actually a good thing. The physical discomfort had helped focus her attention during the heartbreak of a funeral. She had gritted her teeth and concentrated on the immense relief that removing the shoes would bring. Now, though, the release of her feet also opened up the emotional floodgates; tears streamed down her face, leaving multicolored rivulets in their wake. Barb flung herself into her dad's favorite fauteuil, where his smell still lingered. Closing her eyes, she could almost believe the worn-to-softness leather was his skin.

"She looks a bit like a water color.... It's actually quite becoming."

Shiv smiled at Ali's remark. He knew the man didn't mean to be crass. After all, Ali had quietly and efficiently carried Barb through this day, being there when she needed someone, withdrawing when she wanted space, comforting and calming her. The two men stood by the sliding doors leading out to the pool area, beers in hand, looking solemn. Reto had withdrawn to one of the many rooms in the house to make some phone calls. The five newfound friends had congregated once before at Ethan's house in Indian Wells after she invited them to come and sit the Jewish ritual of mourning, Shiva, with her at her father's house for a day. Now they had come back to give Barb support after having committed Ethan's body to the earth in Palm Springs.

Shiv was well aware that Barb's unabashed display of emotion was not Ali's thing. Nor his, but it didn't really bother him. In fact, he was quite fascinated how people got so carried away by whatever wave of feelings washed over them, triggered by factors that were not readily identified.

"You're not the emotional type, I take it," he said, turning to face Ali, who shook himself like a wet dog in response.

"I'd rather have measles than intense emotions." He laughed quietly. "But that's the way it is with us data-based guys. However, I can understand that losing someone you had such a close bond with is not easy."

"You know she lost her son just a year ago, don't you?" Haki had walked over to the two men, after trying unsuccessfully to console the sobbing woman. "This new loss has brought all that raw pain back to the surface. I feel so incredibly sorry for her." Quickly she wiped at the tears forming in her own eyes.

Shiv looked over at the tall cacti standing guard where an artificial waterfall cascaded over rust-colored rock from the nearby San Jacinto Mountains and came to rest in a large pool. He made a sympathetic noise, then said, "Maybe we should take a closer look at the words we use in moments like these, especially the word loss. What exactly is lost? Who is lost to whom? In the cycle of nature nothing can be lost. A form decays and dissolves; the molecules are then available to form something new. So a person, if you will, lives on and on and on, albeit in different physical form."

"But a human being is more than the body," Haki surprised herself with her daring to contradict this serious and obviously highly intelligent man. "It is more the loss of the presence or spirit of a person."

"Yes, of course, I agree with you here. But then again, this spirit – what is it made of and where does it go?" When his question just kept hanging there like some wispy ghost, Shiv changed track: "To lose one's parents is to be truly orphaned, even as a grown up. Especially if you had as close a relationship as Barb and Ethan clearly had. It seems the more people care, the more we love them, the harder it is to lose them."

"It might be better not to have such close bonds at all. You'd probably grow up quicker?" Ali looked at Haki as he spoke, a quizzical expression on his face.

"Oh, I don't know. Where I come from, too many children have to grow up too fast, without any parents at all. I can't see any benefit in that."

They lapsed into silence. The shadow cast by the wide umbrella above their heads tracked imperceptibly east. Reto, who had stepped out of the house, spoke at length: "I don't know about you, but I haven't been able to get Ethan's last question out of my mind. His 'who am I, what am I' keeps haunting me. How can you, at the end of a long and fulfilled life not know who you are, much less what you are? Especially a man like Ethan, who has apparently left his mark, made his own rules, realized his ideas and ideals. I mean this guy seemed not only to have been hugely successful with his advertising agencies. As far as I gathered from various discussions at the funeral he had all the ladies he could wish for, and plenty of political clout to boot. Then he pours most of his considerable fortune, and as much as he can wring from his acquaintances, into development projects in Africa! Could you live a fuller life than that? I mean the man must have known who and what he was, don't you think?"

◆

"Did you hear that? They're beginning to ask the key question." Marvin's voice almost cracked with excitement.

The twins crouched behind the dense oleander hedge separating the Bernstein property from the golf course, observing the goings-on on the terrace. While the four were talking, the fifth was still deeply in pain – in the midst of getting her particles polished, as Marvin put it.

Yes, pain and suffering could indeed put a human firmly on the path. Big G launched into one of his favorite subjects.

Just look at their myths and fairy tales. Hero or heroine endured the darkness of the underworld in order to be freed, to find lasting happiness and step out into the light. On the journey they learned that hell had no reality – it was merely a projection of their own fear. "The hero is freed from believing he is just mind and body, freed from suffering because he realizes there is no suffering. Freedom comes from knowing nothing exists outside the one ultimate reality, and that everything is an emanation of It."

Throughout human history there had always been a few select players who knew and understood the concept of unity – from which everything derived and returned – and that every individual was animated by the same force. Big G's voice had taken on a portentous tone: "Each and every human being is but the universal energy disguised as dense matter. But those who knew were sworn to secrecy. They taught it only to a chosen few in the so-called mysteries."

The closest to revealing this precious fact was probably this fellow Plato. In his famous allegory of the cave, he said that man believes his shadow to be his true self. He was actually pointing out that the actors identified with their costumes, so to speak. The reason they made a secret out of something so crucial, so fundamental to their lives, was simple: the basic software that the vast majority of humans was running on would have crashed immediately. It was not designed to handle this extremely tricky identity puzzle.

Marvin couldn't resist putting in his two bits: "When the upgrade kicks in, human intelligence will be readied to gain direct access to the most subtle levels of creation and to its own source code."

But before this came about, humanity would continue to face an era of major disasters. Whether through volcanic eruptions or earthquakes, floods or fires, economic crashes or civil upheavals, humans would have to come to terms with losing everything at any moment! And their mental concepts –

frozen in time – were about to melt just like the polar ice caps, once thought to be eternal!

"They'll hopefully be shocked into realizing that the only house of any importance is their body – and it even comes without a mortgage."

"...and only you, Big G, can foreclose it," Marvin interrupted.

"Humans are facing a tremendous but enormously rewarding challenge – to realize that there is only one form of energy in the universe. A single source steering this cosmic particle ballet, the force we call It. They will learn that this is a force beyond the material, beyond duality, beyond the laws of nature. And they will finally realize their immortality, their true destiny, through direct access to this highest truth."

Victoria had silently materialized behind the hedge and was floating comfortably a few inches above the dewy grass. "Don't want to get your fushion dirty, Miss fancy-pants?" Marvin pointed at Victoria's elegant silk pants. "So that's what has been keeping you busy. Fusing fashion – fushion... get it? All that, while the world is changing right here before our very eyes!" Marvin shook his head, wagging his finger at Victoria like a displeased parent.

Victoria wasn't fazed. "Once humans recognize it, they will realize that what's bad for one is bad for all. Egotistical action will no longer be seen as good business. The greatest profits will flow from participation and sharing." Then she started humming softly "...imagine there's no countries, it isn't hard to do, nothing to kill or die for, and no religion too, imagine all the people, living life in peace..."

When Big G fell in with her, horribly off key, the twins started rolling on the ground, howling like wolves at the full moon.

The upgrade would also lift human players dramatically out of their past, freeing them from an often fatal attachment to history. Who killed or insulted or exploited whom for whatever reasons in the past, would not determine the present anymore, let alone the future. Knowing one's perceived enemy was animated by the same life force as oneself kind of took away all motivation to kill or maim or cheat – even more so, when you knew souls came to play a tremendous range of roles on this planet, and your opponent at one moment could very well be your mate in the future.

"Be pretty difficult to recruit any of those suicide bombers too," Avory was getting excited. "Imagine the slogan – once in a lifetime opportunity to destroy your former grandmother and perhaps your future kids."

Victoria just nodded and began humming again. "Imagine ... a brotherhood of man, imagine all the people, sharing all the world...." Then she added: "There is only one life force. That's basically what the secret knowledge was ever about – about the unity of all things."

"Isn't it funny that the professor, the one our space cowboy is visiting, has developed the scientific Theory of Everything! Here they are intellectually closing in on the truth, but not daring to believe what they have found."

"Still, humanity is on the road towards the same goal. All players will be molded into a single human race, sharing a single planet ... Earth. And once they have understood what and who they are, then they will be sent on the quest to explore space together."

"Very well put, dearest Victoria, very well indeed." Big G hit his most mellow notes. "Then the simplest but also most complex realization will have moved within their grasp: knowing the ultimate reality is not a separate thing, but steers every single player from within."

"...Yeah, and that'll be the day Mickey Mouse finally wakes up to the truth that he is not the self-determined super-rodent he saw himself as, but just another expression of Walt Disney's creative mind. And just as Disney is Mickey's and Daisy's and Pluto's animator, so is It the universal animator of every single being."

◆

Shiv found himself humming a John Lennon tune, unsure how to react. Should he say something to the others? Would they think him completely nuts? Even though he couldn't see or hear anything clearly, he felt there was something going on behind the hedge, as in a dream where you could almost see, hear and touch some elusive thing.

Was it Cali hiding there, trying to lure him into looking for her? Was the western abode she had invited him to, a golf course? Shiv smiled at the image of the naked, bloody Goddess swinging a club – scaring the checkered pants off the seniors who usually populated the course. Plus, it would mean trusting his dream, going with something that had – well – hand and foot and a bunch of skulls to boot, but nothing real, tangible, material. Then again, just because something was not manifest, did that mean it didn't exist? How about Ethan? Was he in that wooden box they had lowered into the ground? Or was the real Ethan made up of that mysterious essence that made him move, talk, feel and think? And where had that gone? Dissipated into the atmosphere like a puff of smoke?

Shiv remained there, staring into the gathering dusk, humming the refrain to himself: "You may say that I'm a dreamer, but I'm not the only one...."

On this side of the hedge, the suffering was not at all abstract – even if only one of the quintet was deeply stricken. Still affected by the difficult afternoon bidding farewell to Ethan Bernstein, they fell into an animated discussion about the elaborate ceremonies all cultures built around such a commonplace occurrence. Barb lay stretched out on one of the lounge chairs, quiet now, content to let the voices flow around her. She was included by her new friends, without being expected to contribute. While the others still wore their funeral finery, she had changed into a pair of cut-offs and slipped on one of Ethan's shirts that billowed around her delicate frame like a tent.

"Common to all funeral rites is a celebration of the soul, the intangible essence that supposedly moves on when the body decays. But isn't it amazing, that all cultures, all religions talk about body, mind and soul – without having a real concept of it?" Reto looked at the others expectantly.

"I have often thought about this anomaly," Shiv said. "Eastern cultures are convinced the essence of a person moves on. The body is seen as a garment for the soul, a garment that is burnt in the Hindu tradition. As for the human trinity you mentioned, I might have found an answer in – surprise, surprise – particle physics. This subtle stuff called soul could be made up of extremely high-speed particles; ones that are liberated when life withdraws from the denser parts where the particles vibrate at a slower speed."

Shiv shifted in his seat, wondering whether he should go on. Encouraged by the expectant eyes on him, he added, "Shiva is the guardian of transience, of the impermanence of the human body. Some Hindus wear his three stripes of ash on their forehead to remember this transience and lead more conscious lives." Shiv had lapsed into silence again, but his mind traveled on. He thought about his dream, which had not lost any of its immediacy over time. Cali was Shiva's consort. "Perhaps you know of the Goddess Cali," he continued after a moment. "She is usually depicted as a very bloodthirsty, frightening figure, adorned with skulls. But she represents the intangible energy we call soul."

Ali, who had listened attentively, now said, "Perhaps this is why Cali is much misunderstood in the west, because here it is primarily the body that is worshipped?"

When Shiv nodded in agreement, Ali continued, "In the culture of the Pharaohs, worship of the body had probably reached its apex. The complex art of mummification kept a body intact for thousands of years, inside pyramids built to outlast the planet itself...." He gave a small chuckle. "They made absolutely sure they wouldn't disappear from the face of the earth!"

Shiv returned his smile and added, "But you know there is more to those pyramids."

Ali said, "I agree. I have always believed that. Don't laugh, but I see those fascinating structures as some sort of spaceport, where the soul is launched on its journey through the cosmos. That has always been a comforting image to me."

"A much more consoling thought than what death means in parts of Africa. A funeral is a huge financial burden for people who already have next to nothing. They have to come up with copious amounts of food and drink for the mourners – and this goes on for days. The more ostentatious the sorrow, the better." Haki shook her head. "A funeral can easily bankrupt a family."

"At least we don't have to worry about this, here." Barb gave Haki – who had kept close to her throughout the day – a wan smile. "I just want to tell you all how grateful I am that you stayed on and helped me bury my father. I know it would have meant the world to him. You remember how much he loved having people from all walks of life around him. He always talked about integration, collaboration."

Barb didn't mention one vital part of their assistance. There had been no man available to follow Ethan's casket. She had no other family in the States, and her distant Israeli cousins surely wouldn't make the trip, especially since a traditional Jewish funeral service had to be held within 24 hours. She knew Ethan would have approved of an Arab, an Indian and a European doing the honors. Thanks to them, the service at the temple, founded with the help of Frank Sinatra in the late '40s in Palm Springs – had been memorable.

The congregants had all been there for her, even though she was not an especially active member of the synagogue. The female Rabbi, an old friend of the family, had conducted the service, while the Chevra Kaddisha – the sacred burial society of Palm Springs – had prepared Ethan's empty shell for proper interment. Then the five of them had taken turns watching over his remains until it was time to entrust them to Mother Earth.

At the service, the Rabbi had torn black ribbons for family members to pin to their clothes, and Barb had been deeply touched that pieces were also given to her four companions, who had solemnly accepted them. When Shiv, Reto and Ali had stepped forward to carry the casket out to the burial ground, Barb's tears of sorrow were mingled with gratitude and love.

Mercedes had been relieved to see Barb's newfound friends stand by her so solidly. They probably had little idea how sorely Barb needed them, being unaware how closely her life had revolved around her adored father.

Ethan had become the center of Barb's universe when her mother decided to break free. The girl was still in high-school when mommy dearest had upped and settled in Kuala Lumpur of all places, seeing her child exactly twice in all those years. No wonder father and daughter had formed a close bond – for Mercedes' taste a bit too close. Barb his princess, and he her "protector and only love." None of the ladies fighting for Ethan's attention over the years stood a chance of breaking into that exclusive circle. Barb made it abundantly clear she did not tolerate another female in her father's house. This exclusivity played both ways though. As much as Ethan wished for his daughter's happiness, none of her boyfriends made the grade as far as he was concerned. She had a hankering for the handsome and pliable – such as Ethan Junior's father. Yet he, like all others, had faded from view after a few short months. It was Ethan who had felt like a father to his daughter's son – together the three had been a family.

What would Barb do now that she had no one? Mercedes feared the weeks to come, once everyone had left. She knew of no other adult, except herself, whom Barb was really close to. What a stroke of luck, that destiny had brought these four people here from all over the world. Especially the Swiss guy, Reto, and the Arab called Ali; they made a solid and strong impression. Mercedes would do anything to make them comfortable and extend their stay.

She watched them now, forming a protective circle around Barb, who clearly drew strength and comfort from their presence. They were talking about the funeral service, how moving it had been and how many of the Hollywood greats had attended, even at such short notice. And they marveled at the diversity of friends and acquaintances Ethan had touched throughout his life – men and women of all different denominations and backgrounds.

"...And the family was together in peace," Ali quoted, and they all looked at him questioningly.

"Don't you know that Jews and Muslims are family? Abraham's family?" he said, an amused glint in his dark eyes. "It began with Abraham's son Isaac and his half-brother Ishmael. In Genesis it says God would establish his covenant with Isaac, but also bless Ishmael and make for him a great nation. So the conflict between the brothers – which is at the heart of the Jewish and Muslim religions – was established right from the start. Somewhere else in the Bible it says that Ishmael had been "born according to the flesh" and Isaac "according to the promise," replacing the first born as the favored son and heir. When the conflict between the half-brothers became intolerable to Abraham's wife Sarah, Isaac's mother, she demanded Ishmael and his Egyptian concubine mother, Hagar, be expelled from the family. God made good on his promise to Hagar: that her son would beget 12 princes who would found a great nation. So they moved on to the Arabian Peninsula and became the great desert peoples of the Middle East." When Ali paused, his audience nodded thoughtfully.

"In other words, today's conflict stems from the first moments of the biblical history of man," Reto shook his head.

And Haki added, "How incredibly sad that for 2,000 years humans have been unable to overcome jealousy or forgive hurt."

"Yep. That about wraps it, Haki," Ali said with a sad smile. "As a kid on pilgrimage with my parents I walked around the center of Islam, the Kaaba. I just knew that Jews and Muslims were from the same family – even though the Bible and the Koran differ on their renditions of the Ishmael and Isaac story. It was Abraham and Ishmael who rebuilt the Kaaba on the same spot where Adam had erected the first building on Earth. In fact, the Kaaba originally was a sanctuary to all, where no violence was permitted."

Into the quiet Haki said, "Well, we could take this one step further. Since Jesus was a Jewish man, then Christians belong to the same family too."

"...So it's high time we own up to this reality and resolve all these painful and perfectly useless disputes." Reto finished her thought, then added, "The only thing standing in the way of peace in the Middle East is the belief of one party that they have been chosen by the Big One himself, and the others are second class citizens. As long as this is propagated, no political solution will ever last. The philosophical base has to be established first."

Reto took a tall glass of the fresh lemonade Mercedes had prepared. After taking a sip, he said with a little frown, "Knowing we all die – after a pretty short time on this planet – makes it really stupid to waste time hating and killing each other. If you look at it matter-of-factly, killing does not make the slightest sense."

After a short pause, he added, "Not even to a Major in the Swiss army!"

Ali gave him a mock salute. "You know, I see an image sometimes. Judaism, Christianity and Islam are like three giant icebergs, each insisting on being the only true one. But the warmth of the sun exposes their real nature; they melt into one body of water...." He shrugged and smiled at his companions. "One of the reasons I'm all for a global temperature rise."

Shiv had not missed a word of the discussion, all the while staring at the hedge – hoping to catch another glimpse of whatever was going on over there. He shook his head to clear his thoughts. "You've made a very important point here, Ali.

Instead of dwelling on the differences, humanity should really gear their minds towards fusion! You know, when you really crank up the heat – I'm talking temperatures like in our sun – all particles fuse. Fission, on the other hand, creates disaster! The world got a taste of that at the end of World War II, and we've teetered on the brink a few times since then. Fusion is our common future, fusion of nations, philosophies and..." here Shiv smiled and patted his chest. "Of course it would supply endless energy worldwide!"

As if on command, they all looked up and realized darkness had caught up with them. Barb voiced what was on their minds, "It seems impossible we've only known one another three days. I feel I've toured the world with you since our meeting in that weird iron house."

'Where a question was posed by a man so full of life and laughter one moment and so silent and seemingly empty the next,' Shiv thought but didn't say. He knew they didn't yet have the answer to what Ethan so desperately wanted to discover with his last breath – but Shiv suspected they were all determined to find it.

"Please, friends, before you go, I have one more favor to ask." Barb spoke up as they started to rise. "Dad kept a guest book here, and you..." she could hardly speak through the tears choking her voice. "Since you are in a way my father's last guests, please just write down a final thought."

Shiv wrote: "As a scientist I say: the universe knows neither birth nor death, just an endless dance of particles. May we all train our intellect to understand this grand truth, so that we might not get attached to perishable form. As a guest, as a friend I say: I will never forget."

Ali wrote: "Barb, you may have lost a father, but since Abraham was our common forefather, you have found a new family member in me."

Reto wrote: "Ethan has left us with a riddle. Let us then go on the quest to solve it. And – life willing – come back together to compare answers."

Haki wrote: "All my love and compassion are with you always. Know that they have no beginning and no end. They are the fabric of the universe."

Barb read and cried.

12

The Art of Suffering

Ali Ben Calif's Desert

His ingenious solutions for the Abu Dhabi and California public transport systems had quickly raised his international profile and kept Ali Ben Calif in more work than was really good for him. He was the globetrotting prophet of maximally efficient, minimally polluting transportation systems, a busy man – a man in demand and on the go – cooperating with specialists in a number of countries. The most fascinating were the Chinese who were clearly at the cutting-edge of modern public transportation.

Money had flowed in freely, and public recognition of his work was icing on an already sumptuous cake. Ali met challenges head-on, bathing in the glory of success. He expanded his Cairo operation, opened up shop in California, and entered into a joint venture in Shanghai, where his adored Lailah represented his interests. His baby sister had grown into a highly skilled professional, with a Masters in City Planning in her pocket. Her decision to study Mandarin, both out of curiosity and because quite a few of her fellow MIT students had been Chinese, proved fortuitous. Ali had thought he was doing his sister a favor when he took her along to Shanghai to sightsee and sit in on a meeting with his partners. To his great, surprise Lailah had been unperturbed by the complex rituals of negotiation, including the endless procession of delicate teacups that drove him to distraction. Her mastery of their complex language had naturally won over his counterparts. Now four years after settling in this dizzying metropolis, she had taken to the local lifestyle with an ease Ali still couldn't quite comprehend, and which made him feel a touch old.

Lailah had found not only her professional place, but also somewhere to indulge her true passion – playing the violin.

Ali had seen his subsidiaries flourish. A wizard at developing computer programs that were the heart and soul of his ideas, Ali really had it made in an accelerating world, packing his daily program ever denser – master of mobile communications – a true disciple of the higher, faster, farther.

He'd even found time to cooperate with Barb Bernstein on the education project she pursued with a determination bordering on obstinacy. They had crossed paths several times when he set up his LA office. He'd even stayed at Ethan's house in Indian Wells for a few days, letting Barb pick his brains about education software. Yes of course, the sparks from their first chance encounter were quickly rekindled. But both had opted to let them fizzle. Ali was reluctant to get involved, too busy to be drawn into what he knew would cost time and require nerves of steel. And Barb had not given any indication of wanting to do more than joke about it.

But in those rare moments, when nothing and no one demanded his attention, Ali would sometimes feel a deep regret. She was a beautiful woman after all, sexy as hell; but her true allure lay beneath. There was stubborn independence and emotional fragility. She had a quick, bright mind offset by a complete inability to see certain things clearly. She was impulsive, then withdrawn – exuberant one minute, inconsolable the next. She was, Ali thought, just like a kaleidoscope – colorful, fascinating and a constant surprise. But once she sunk her teeth into something she really believed in, like her Peru project, she would focus all her energy on it. He had remained in loose contact with the rest of their randomly thrown together quintet. Shiv popped up regularly on prominent science websites, and Ali had promised to visit Reto for some skiing – but never found the time. Staying in touch with Haki was more difficult, given her sporadic access to a computer. But he knew she was well, had survived the deadly perils of daily life in the Congo, and seemed content and busy with Ethan's legacy – a string of five bush hospitals.

When his internal software upgrade – of which he was totally ignorant – finally loaded the program titled "lessons in detachment," the high-flying Ali Ben Calif crashed. Later he compared the experience to one of those cartoon characters, which – in pursuit or in flight – continued running on thin air, only to plunge the minute they looked down.

He had woken up one day and looked down, realized there was absolutely nothing he wanted to do. For a non-stop action man, it was something akin to death. For a guy who needed to be in motion, to stir things up – and who relished complex assignments – this feeling of just wanting to lie there and not move a limb was as foreign as the Chinese way of doing business had been at first. Incomprehensible.

For the first time in his life, Ali was genuinely bored. Suddenly, complicated problems did not inspire him anymore. The search for the optimal solution could no longer drive him to peak performance. Encounters with people from different countries, novel environments, exotic cultures – all lost their luster. Things started to feel and look and taste universally bland. What had been his highly treasured independence – to pick and choose, go wherever his fancy took him – now felt like a trap.

Like a shooting star, Ali had simply burned out; the bright light he had drawn across the night sky fading. Years later, when he was finally able to talk about this, he'd say it was like waking up to discover he had forgotten the password and lost access to himself ... the screen just stayed dark. He had been swallowed by the void, fallen into a black hole that absorbed everything – joy, sadness, enthusiasm, curiosity, even pain in a way.

Soon Ali couldn't bear being around active, motivated people any more. The anthill of Cairo with its frenetic human and vehicular traffic drained his energy. He stayed home for days, shutting himself away in his gadget-laden house. Utter defeat came on the morning when he didn't even want to power up his computer.

As his life ground to a halt, fears crept in. Could it simply be an early bout of midlife crisis, or something worse? Ali feared his mind was starting to slip. He had tremendous difficulty concentrating for any length of time. He had tried to talk to Nasrin about his fears, but hadn't found the right words to describe what was happening. He drifted around the house like a restless ghost, staring at himself in the mirror, looking for telltale signs of a malignant tumor or mental illness; he considered consulting a specialist, a neurologist perhaps. He was getting older – well past his thirties – and that's when those things started creeping up on a man, didn't they?

The last assignment he'd tackled, writing a none-too complicated program for a new high-speed maglev train in Shanghai, hadn't turned out well. He'd made a number of beginner mistakes. After the initial shock of acknowledging his malfunctioning, he put the errors down to lapses in concentration. Perhaps he should settle down. Have a couple of kids, maybe? He pictured a daughter like Lailah: bright, beautiful and independent. Or should he take an extended leave to gather his wits?

He needed to get away and think, that was a given. Now that he'd slowed down, those close to him finally had the chance to catch up – and were bent on making the most of it. His family's concern about his burnout – as it was officially diagnosed – was as suffocating as it was loving. "You must eat more, son," was his mother's remedy for all ills ... besides more sleep and exercise.

"Why don't you go out and party? Fall in love! All the girls I know have a serious crush on you!" Lailah was deeply concerned about her adored brother's visible decline from shining star to chunk of charcoal. But from a continent away, even she couldn't get more out of Ali than a wan smile. And asking Nasrin was not an option anymore, he reminded himself. He had missed that chance. Just a couple of days ago this gorgeous, vivacious woman he had been close to for so long, had called to say she had moved on. She had finally given up on the increasingly moody, often short-tempered man who had gradually withdrawn from her and their relationship. Letting Ali go was made easier by the good looking, easy-going American she had met at her latest dig.

Ali chose the desert for one simple reason: there was nothing there. Into this emptiness he wanted to bring his exhausted mind and tired body. This craving for the desert had developed the morning when Ali lost interest in everything. He sat on the edge of his bed for hours, head buried in his hands, incapable of stepping into another day. Finally, he decided to go to the edge of the Great Sand Sea. It sounded perfect: a sea of bland, boring, imperceptibly shifting sand dunes.

He flew the 500 or so kilometers out to Oasis Siwa. After all, greater men than he had searched for answers there. Alexander the Great, so the history of this mysterious place goes, had traveled there to consult the Oracle of Amun. Ali booked himself into a small, elegant eco-lodge, hugging the base of a tall pale rock face and built from mud plastered with rock salt, in the manner of the traditional village houses. The rooms had no electricity – which suited Ali just fine – but offered an abundance of silence and a spring-fed pool in the midst of lush gardens. Nearby, a shimmering salt lake added to the eerie tranquility of the place.

Ali lay down on a comfortable deckchair, shaded by gently rustling palm fronds. He let out a sigh from the core of his being. He was deathly tired, weary to the marrow of his bones, as if he had been running in overdrive his whole life – which was pretty close to the truth.

He was dressed in a lightweight cotton galabya he had brought for this occasion. It was a statement: that he wanted to rid himself of all constrictions, even his western clothes. As he looked at the play of light and shadow the palms created on the terrace, he let his mind drift. That's what he had come here for. Unstructured time. No deadlines, appointments, schedules or due dates. He had been taken hostage by his iThis and iThat; running like a demented gerbil on a 24/7 treadmill. Ali closed his eyes ... all he craved now was a lot of nothing.

◆

"How about a nice little sandstorm to give the boy some action?" Marvin was trying to surf on one of the high dunes of the seemingly infinite Great Sand Sea.

"Don't you get it? He's not supposed to have any action. That's what his lesson is all about. The new software has increased his creativity and ability to juggle a bunch of highly complex tasks. But he's used his brilliance mostly to solve technical problems. Now there's a nicely baited trap for you! Success, applause and, of course, the envy of your peers. One can easily get hooked on that stuff."

"You are a good observer, Avory." Victoria had silently materialized next to them, dressed in a perfect desert outfit with plenty of gauzy materials veiling her from head to toe. "Seems the program has reached the introspection bit, where questions arise like 'Who is the man Ali Ben Calif, and what does he really want to do with his life?'"

"So our good lad Ali here has to atone for becoming a success junky?"

"Why suddenly so biblical, Marvin? That's so not like you. It is not atonement you are looking at here, but detachment. And – this logic should particularly please you – before you can become detached, you...

"... Have to be hooked! I get it already." Grumbling and kicking up sand Marvin took himself off to another promising dune and settled down to watch Ali trying his best to do nothing.

Marvin knew it would be a good show. Unlike those who evaded life by moving prematurely into the spiritual lane, when a guy like Ali turned to introspection – a guy who really had lived life to the fullest in the material sense – the change in the energy pattern would be dramatic.

◆

Ali slept. Most days he simply moved from his bed to the palm-shaded deckchair by the spring-fed pool and fell back to sleep. He couldn't stay awake for more than an hour, during which he fueled his body with the barest necessities: a couple of juicy dates – fresh from the 300,000 or so palms providing the oasis with income – and a few spoonfuls of delicious couscous and fresh vegetables from the lodge's kitchen.

After four days of inertia, his body was still content to be prone on the deck chair, but his mind had started to play tricks, jumped on some kind of merry-go-round. It controlled Ali's body like a puppet master, forcing him to change position every five minutes. He'd sit up, then – unable able to suppress the urge – get up and pace around. Then he'd sit again and watch his fingers twitch, his mind spewing endless thoughts – like random noise. He tried to visualize the computer's on/off switch, but nothing happened. "I'll have to cut the power," he thought, "then the hard drive should stop spinning." But he couldn't locate the battery. Soon Ali would give his left hand for just one look at his smartphone, a quick browse through the Internet, or at the very least a few moments access to his laptop.

Time and again he had to chase down thoughts darting through his mind like a flock of starlings. A particularly stubborn one insisted on heading west, to peck at a question uttered by a dying man many years ago. "Who am I, what am I, who, what, who, what am I, I, I...?" ricocheted through Ali's brain chamber, to which he added: "Why do I feel empty when I have everything? Why do I suffer when I should be on top of the world?"

A week later he was still stuck on the same question. What little logic he was still capable of led him to a simple conclusion: since he couldn't define himself by his work anymore, he was in dire need of a new identity. The obvious thing would be to look for it in his native Arab culture, in the religion of his upbringing. Would, perhaps, the five pillars of Islam provide guidance?

The first pillar is shahadah: the belief that there is no god but Allah, and Muhammad is his messenger. Fine, he was ok with the first part. He could live with there being a single energy at the source of the universe. And Muhammad had done the messenger job admirably. He'd obviously been a powerful and charismatic guy; otherwise he wouldn't have continued to inspire so much passion in people a millennium and a half after his death. How strange that so many felt the need to defend Muhammad against the insult of being drawn as a cartoon figure, or written up as a character in a novel. After all, here was a man who had the power to convince almost a quarter of the global population to follow his doctrine for centuries. It was like ants trying to defend an elephant from a mouse attack.

While the thought was quite amusing, what really irked Ali was that at some point in time, a few letters had been interjected between 'his' and 'messenger'. One tiny word that changed everything: the word 'only' implied that Muslims alone were on the right track to heaven. The rest, infidels. As a dyed-in-the-wool democrat, Ali could not accept such a claim to exclusivity. Besides, after seeing what the Hubble Space Telescope had glimpsed at the far reaches of the universe, it was absurd to believe that only one single human being could represent the force that had created this mind-boggling cosmos. Ali did see the humor in this same claim being made by fundamentalists of all denominations. As if this all-encompassing energy could have but one single herald. Pretty limited thinking, as far as he was concerned.

Ali had taken up regular walks to the salt lake shimmering amidst endless sand. He loved to sit at the water's edge and gaze into the deep satin blue. Lost in contemplation of the mirrored sky, he leaned against the 2nd pillar of Islam – salah. It called upon the faithful to pray five times a day, facing toward Mecca. Ali had never much liked to pray in a mosque; too many men, more exclusivity. It was that simple. Men and women were partners, on equal footing. They should not only raise children together, but also work and worship together. Thankfully, his parents had instilled this belief in equality deeply in him and in Lailah. Nor had his educated mother and father insisted on a highly visible demonstration of faith. They had taught him that Allah would hear him and his equally well-educated sister whenever and wherever they prayed, be it riding their bikes or sitting on a bus. And since Ali abhorred attracting attention through conspicuous or ostentatious actions – it just felt like so much overly dramatic playacting – he gladly left the 2nd pillar behind.

The 3rd pillar of Islam – zakah – called on people to share, to give alms to the poor. Now there was a worthy rule. If that were globally applied and done properly, it would change the face of the earth. As long as the gap between rich and poor was growing, there would be no peace. This yawning divide provided fertile soil for all kinds of fundamentalists either to lure the young with promises of income, or to stir envy and hatred toward those who had more than they. His father had regarded zakah as a personal responsibility, and had honored this Muslim duty readily and gladly. Ali too gave away money with great ease – after all, more could be made, should the need arise. He had been far more attached to work itself than to the byproduct it produced. This 3rd pillar, he felt, was one that needed strengthening, and there were signs, the Arab world was doing just that.

The 4th pillar stood for sawm, fasting. Quite a challenge really. Fasting during the month of Ramadan was a difficult test for any international business traveler. On the other hand, sumptuous food, and eating in general, had never been foremost in his mind. And right now, in his own way, he was holding his personal Ramadan.

Finally, Ali reached the 5th pillar of Islam – hadj – the pilgrimage to the holy city. Now there were fond memories! Mecca had been a magic word in the vocabulary of all his Muslim friends, and the six days he spent with his parents on that pilgrimage were probably the most memorable six days of his adolescence. He saw that mysterious black rock and the Kaaba as clearly now as he had then. Abraham and his son Ishmael had worshipped before it. How absolutely strange and wonderful that this holiest of holy Muslim places was directly related to the founding father of the Jews. It was so blatantly obvious Jews and Arabs were brothers, and had always been brothers. Ali also saw that men and women worshipped together at the Kaaba.

It had most certainly not been the Prophet's intent that men and women be segregated, as the modern interpreter's of his mind tried to enforce in even the most unlikely situations. What a contradiction: although men and women were allowed to do the circumambulating tawaf together, they had to stand in gender-separated lines at the nearby Mecca fast-food outlet.

When a gust of wind playfully threw sand in his face, as if to tease him back from Mecca, Ali was startled to find the afternoon nearly gone. Despite having done nothing, he was filled with a deep sense of accomplishment. He had surfed the waves of his mind without having to snap immediately into action. Now that was a brand new experience. What did people call this condition? Contemplation, was it?

◆

Why d'you do that, bro?"

"Well, look at him: too far gone to realize the shade has long since left him behind. If I hadn't woken him up from wherever he was, he'd have had sunstroke in a minute! "

"Too far is not exactly the right dimension, Marvin. Maybe higher would be more appropriate, if we consider the level of concentration." Victoria invited the two young men to come sit with her in the small palm garden by the well. "Check out the vibratory pattern of his particles, see any change?"

"Uuuh yeah! Man's sped up quite noticeably.... What a hoot! Outwardly he slowed down so much that a snail looks like a speed freak in comparison, but inwardly he's accelerating like a Formula 1 racer."

Avory broke in: "What exactly triggers these U-turns? Seems an awfully wasteful set-up: to let them run in the wrong direction for so long, only to yank them around at some unforeseen moment."

"There are no right or wrong directions. Humans go through life collecting experiences, but when they get bored with their small I, the centerstage-hogging one they call ego, they start looking for something to really hold their interest. First, though, you have to gain a certain level of personal power. Remember, it takes awhile to get the hang of the goods!"

"Not only the body, but also all these wonderful distractions – fast cars, faster women – keep you busy for quite some time!" Marvin piped in with a wide grin.

"Look who's talking, gigolo! Don't forget the beer and the smokes, bro!"

Before the two could start a "name the most traps" competition, Victoria cut them off. "You're right, of course; the journey inward is also a journey through the four states of matter. The 'I' identity is guided step-by-step through each level, with the goal of integrating each one and finally being liberated from all attachment. And that, my impatient Marvin, just takes time. However, time is of no consequence. There are plenty of lifetimes for each soul to reach its destination."

◆

Ali greeted the early morning light stealing over the eastern horizon. He was sitting on a rocky outcrop, about a mile from the lodge. Before daybreak he had walked over on the cool, forgiving sand – the identity question still foremost on his mind. This 'who' he was, or 'what' he could identify with, just wouldn't let him alone. Millions gained a secure identity from their religious faith. "I am a Muslim, a Jew, a Christian..." they said proudly, but what did they really mean? Could he find his true identity in the way he related to the creator of the universe? No, this path was definitely closed to him. He could not define himself by following one course to the exclusion of all others. Wasn't it enough to be a decent human being? He put more faith in that, than in any of the hundreds of different sects, creeds and religious convictions battling to be the exclusive interpreter of the divine – all claiming to own the exclusive truth. How could a critical mind take any of them seriously?

Ali's train of thought advanced another notch. Apart from numerous religious divisions, there were around 200 different states and territories claiming a piece of the Earth – sharing or rather battling for its limited resources. Now there was another strong factor for identity! Like religious identification, territorial identification was plenty strong enough to make people bash each other's heads in.

During many hundreds of hours in airplanes, Ali had loved to look at the Earth. So precious, like a piece of lapis: deep blues, streaks of gray-green and brown, flecked with brilliant white. There were no visible borders denying access in – or even sometimes out. Borders mostly drawn on far away desks, bargained for in peace agreements, or decided arbitrarily by those wanting to harvest power from national identity – and have as fat a slice of the planetary pie as possible. What may have made sense centuries ago was becoming obsolete. The cost of maintaining this antiquated system was staggering – in money and human life. In a world ever more intricately connected by trade and communication, this fragmentation was archaic. Could he identify with being an Egyptian? Or, expanding on that thought ... an Arab? Wasn't he more, so much more: a member of humanity, each with almost identical DNA and all sharing this heartbreakingly beautiful planet?

◆

"Judging by the vibrancy of his particle pattern, I would say his perception has already expanded beyond himself. He will be looking at the man Ali in the context of the whole planet by now. I'm really quite pleased with the results of this upgrade. We'd hoped the interconnectedness thing would load quickly." Victoria picked up a handful of sun-warmed sand and let it trickle through her fingers. "The next part should clinch it. He will be seeing his life as a movie: to make him understand that he has come to this moment not because he did something wrong or right, or made good or bad choices. He will understand his life is his life is his life...."

"Don't go esoteric on us, Vick! I suppose you are trying to say that suffering is not punishment for misconduct, but just another station on the journey. OK, maybe it's one of the main stations." Marvin was satisfied with Victoria's slight nod. He too picked up a handful of sand, letting it dance and swirl in graceful patterns against the backdrop of an almost painfully blue sky.

◆

Comfortably installed in his favorite deckchair beneath the palms, Ali is embarking on an inner journey. Soon he is lost in images projected from his archive of feelings, from deeply hidden inner records. The scenes are charged with emotion: the picture of his mother – resting on a mountain of pillows, gazing down at the newborn Lailah in her arms – suffuses his whole system with deep joy. The piercing scream of his mother, finding her husband at his desk, dead from a heart attack, sends keen sadness ripping through him. Scene after scene elicits delight, sorrow, grief, elation and fierce regret. Ali watches as if in a movie theater, letting the emotions rise and fall, flow and ebb. But he is no movie critic. He need not vent an opinion. He is like a neutral observer just watching his physiological reactions to the ever-changing content. Once he relives these emotions, they are deactivated and just fade away, like putting down baggage you no longer need. He would travel more lightly from now on.

On the third day of his life-review, Ali is just waiting for "The End." With a deeper understanding of and complete reconciliation with whatever has been, he decides to celebrate the occasion with a particularly juicy Siwa date. There is a new spring in his step when he ventures once more into the desert. He is filled with lightness and an inner strength he didn't have before. He looks to the future with a newfound confidence and curiosity. But he is still one answer short.

Dawn has not yet broken by the time Ali reclaims his post by the desert rocks. Hours pass, and suddenly his half-closed eyes are trained towards his nose, as if by some force. In this weird position, the images he now sees are very different than the last days' movie. They appear to be painted on air, like a perfect mirage. Ali has lost all awareness of his physical presence and his surroundings. He is fully concentrated on what unfolds before his inner eye: in crazy fast-forward, an ant-like Ali-person is speeding around, zipping to and fro with no obvious purpose. Suddenly, it collapses, lies there dazed and confused, until it gathers its wits, picks itself up and slowly, slowly starts moving again. The change is obvious. Now it is an Ali who has gained definition, contours – his movements are filled with purpose. He is more ... more there, somehow more real.

When Ali came out of his vision, he was overjoyed, amazed by what he had seen: an Ali-puppet on a string – twitching wildly – a human outline going through lots of senseless motions. It then morphed into an Ali full of purpose and calm – acutely aware of his actions. Was that the big secret? The answer he had come for? Could it be so simple? He needn't throw out his everyday existence, didn't have to commit to a singular spiritual path and perform specific rituals. He could simply continue what he had been doing before – but less of it, more calmly and with full awareness.

Ali pumped his fist in the clear desert air. Yesssssss! That's exactly how he would try to live his life. Fascinating, how his mind had provided the answers he had been looking for, much as if the brain was loaded with a software that projected a visual lesson on a virtual screen. Did his individual DNA trigger impulses in the brain, which he then felt as emotions? If so, who was in charge of that visual and emotional magical mystery tour he had been taken on? After all, he had not asked for a specific line-up, yet what he had seen had obviously been a private viewing, a program selected exclusively for him. He had not willingly projected the images; how could he have done so?

The Ali-'I' was the observer, that much was clear. So, who or what was this other 'I'? The one who functioned during deep sleep or while he dreamed? Who was the 'I' acting in the inner movie? Ali can only shake his head in wonder. He – and probably most of humanity – encountered these different 'I's without giving it much thought. For all their pride at being the only species outfitted with the capacity to think abstractly – claiming a free will – most people just reeled off their program. Not much different from an ant really.

One thing was certain: neither his abstract thinking nor his free will had been the source of his experiences in these last few days. Besides, hadn't he read some time ago that brain researchers had now shown that fractionally before a person makes the conscious decision to do this or that, the brain has already triggered the correlative impulse?

The implications were staggering: humanity would definitely have to put a big question mark behind the adjective 'free' in connection with 'will'. Matter of fact, humans might lose status as Masters of the Universe! While the mind was convinced of calling the shots, it was actually something else that ruled and was inducing consciousness to do its bidding. When Ali initially read the article, he was not surprised that the German scientist who authored it had concluded that humanity was probably not quite ready for his findings. Maybe so, but he, Ali, was ready!

He was keen to find an answer to one burning question. Was the act of sitting still and holding the mind in one place – watching the images projected by whatever source – a way to reach the core of one's identity? Was the conscious 'I' simply an observer of life unfolding? Was that philosophy? Now there was a stumbling block. Ali wasn't really into philosophy, too many long words, too many convoluted thoughts. He'd much rather apply his mind to technical problems: quick analysis and quick solution. What if he thought of this identity and free will puzzle as a technical challenge, an interaction between hard- and software?

With new energy and vigor Ali started packing. The desert had richly rewarded him. It taught him that keeping oneself company, without distraction or disruption, could be utterly fulfilling, something he had never appreciated. Sitting still had never been an option in his life. Nasrin was right – like some sharks, he was afraid of drowning if he stopped moving. And now this! What the stillness allowed him to see and experience had launched him on a new and exciting identity quest. But he doubted he could share his experience with others. Most of them would probably think he had lost his marbles playing in the sand – severe sunstroke perhaps....

But he might get in touch with Barb, maybe even with the others. How many years had it been? Almost ten? Had it really taken him so long to find a possible answer to Ethan's question? And would he dare tell them? He'd say perhaps: "It was like coming up with the right password. You key it in and gain direct access to the mainframe." Direct access. Whatever code he had hit on – and after some time it would occur to Ali that this in itself might also have been a gift – it had opened a secret inner chamber where the ultimate treasure was hidden. Direct access indeed.

For a ceremonial good-bye, Ali headed over to the hot spring of Bir Wahid at first light – just as the monochrome desert of the night took on the first colors of the new day. At this time he'd surely have the enchanted place to himself. But as he left his vehicle to approach on foot, he made out a lone figure walking his way. The man was dressed in traditional Berber style: cloth turban and haik over chalwar pants. When they came close to one another, Ali noticed the man's eyes. They were filled with an almost tangible kindness. Ali was unable to break eye contact, his awareness drawn into the other man's eyes, and he suddenly saw himself approaching, slowly. He did not feel anything. He just looked at this Ali through the other man's eyes for a few seconds. Then they passed each other, and Ali was back inside himself.

He sat down by the spring, completely thrown by what just happened. Looking at yourself through someone else's eyes took the question of what or who the 'I' was, to another level. There is but one consciousness. Is that it? On the level of biology and chemistry we are locked into our bodies, but on the level of very fine physical structures or waves, we can apparently transcend the confinement of the body. That was quite a stretch for a guy who never really thought about consciousness, could barely spell the word in English. He wouldn't let it freak him out though. The new cool, calm and collected Ali grinned at his reflection in the spring water. This weirdness felt great; as he pondered it, excitement spread through his body. Did this guy have the same source code as he? Or was this direct access stuff perhaps true for others as well, a possible remote access through something like an open Wi-Fi network? It hadn't felt like his identity had been hacked – there were no emotions involved. His experience had been purely on the visionary level. Was consciousness perhaps the web on which one's I-identity traveled? A universal web? As a high-tech guy he definitely could make some sense of this. After all, the brain is an electro-chemical organ from which the impulses of the thought process could be harvested to steer computers, even cars. Whatever – he'd take this experience as a logical sequel to what he had gone through in the desert – definitely a step up from watching inner projections of Ali-ant scurrying through life.

The wireless communication idea, from one brain to another, was electrifying. Ali knew the brain was a marvel at computing myriad different signals it constantly received from the body – probably a few hundred megabytes per second. He had read about futuristic experience beamers, where a person's sensory experiences or emotional reactions could be stored and made accessible to others – on the Web for instance. By plugging into someone else's sensory-emotional beam, you could actually experience what it meant to be another human being. Nanobots was the key word here. They would also one day be used to augment interneuronal connections, boosting human thinking capacity to unimaginable levels. This technology would eventually enable wireless communication from brain to brain.

Fine, so he knew all that. He could even fathom it. But what he had just experienced did not involve nanobots or science of the future. No technological gadgets of any kind. But wasn't that just it with human inventions? Since they were projections of the brain, the gadgets scientists and technicians came up with would mechanically or electronically do what the mind already knew how. Ali grinned to himself. He would not only be an expert in hard- and software from now on, but also in what some geeks called wetware, the human in-built information system.

Ali looked back over the endless sea of sand, constantly shifting, moving, changing shape. What a perfect environment to discover that there seems to be a single conscious- ness shaping all and holding all together. The age-old oracle of Siwa had worked its magic again.

Reto on the mountain

"Belay-off," Gian shouts to Reto, who is eagerly charting the route from his stance farther up the near-vertical face. He is exhilarated by the challenge of conquering this damned rock via one of its rarely attempted routes. It's only the second time Gian and he have set out to show this mountain, in Reto's mind at least, who's boss. Gian had insisted they take it slow. It was a tricky route, with few easy holds and almost no belay ledges. They had to muster all their skill to crack this overhang, but Reto insisted on going a bit faster. He feels the elation of using perfect balance – of knowing his body and how to reposition it in space. He loves how climbing demands his whole being, his total concentration vanquishing the primal fear of the void. On hearing Gian's call, Reto relaxes his hold. But as his weight bears down on his last anchor, suddenly the stopper blows out from the rock face ... and the void takes him.

Coming to – precariously supported by a narrow ledge – Reto immediately knows something is wrong – very wrong. He doesn't feel any pain just yet, and he tries to signal to Gian that he is OK. But nothing is OK. For one, Reto can't move his legs. He cannot even feel his legs. Then the pain starts: like a thousand red-hot needles being stabbed and twisted into his lower back. The needles turn into blades, searing hot blades slashing deep into his flesh.

Through the fiery pain his mind starts flashing pictures at him: people in wheel chairs, mutilated soldiers – limbs blown off on some killing field or other, victims of suicide bombings.... Then one single thought obliterates all else, even the excruciating throbbing in his body: what if I never walk again?

His life would be over. That was it. He would find a way to end what was left of him. He knows with absolute certainty that he could not live in half a body – all his power gone. Neither all the money in the world nor any top-shot position would suffice. His power is allied with his body. He is not cut out to be a victim, another casualty of life. And that is that!

The images of broken and abused bodies flash back into view. But they are now distinctly different. Formerly helpless, weak and defective, they now radiate power – power that in Reto's world belong only to the wealthy and influential. But when those figures swirl into focus, they are no more than empty husks. Before he can grab the thought forming in his brain, Reto passes out once more.

◆

"Wow! Who did that? C'mon admit it! Somebody! Come clean. Who plucked that poor sucker from the rock? You are a monster, you know that?" Marvin's tone was half shocked, half admiring. "That takes some balls."

"Yes. Gravity is a strange and sometimes frightening thing, isn't it?" Big G was careful to keep his tone neutral, neither admitting nor denying anything.

"Reto is a tough nut to crack. You have to admit that, Marv." Avory's eyes were glued to the Plasma Cube showing Reto lying helplessly on the narrow ledge.

"Yes, he is iron-willed, convictions set in granite. So, I'm afraid it takes quite drastic measures to shake that stuff loose in his mind. But watch! He is about to learn something most valuable. That upgrade: I must say I am most pleased with it. It's loading really clean and fast." Victoria tapped the Cube focusing it on the images in Reto's mind, as he spiraled down into the black void.

◆

Later, he would regret sleeping through the complex helicopter rescue. He'd have gotten a kick out of the cool equipment and admired the competent team. But Reto had been deeply unconscious all the way, something he now wished for again and again. He couldn't wrap his mind around what had happened to him. He had started the day as a perfectly healthy, strong and successful man in his early forties, and was now confined to a hospital bed in Zürich: helpless, dependent, and adrift in a sea of pain whenever the medication wore off. Something in his back was ruptured, they said. They would try to fix it, they said – sounding deliberately optimistic and reassuring, while making him sign a release form agreeing to risk never being able to walk again.

Despite what he had understood on the ledge, in that short revelation before descending into darkness, there was no way he would attempt a life in a broken body. For the first time in his adult life Reto felt real fear. He had to admit he was a pale shadow of this major-winning golf pro, who had said of the debilitating illness that shackled him to a wheelchair in later life: "I play the ball as it lies...." Now that guy had serious power! Compared to him, Reto was a wimp, a gutless, spineless chicken. OK, OK, no need to beat himself up too much. Maybe he just wasn't there yet.

But then he thought about how he, Reto tough-guy Ritter, would be pitied and scorned by the strong and mighty – and he crashed again.

The fall off the mountain had been a fall from grace. "Return to Go," he thought, just like in the game he played with Nona, forcing her into early bankruptcy every time. "Return to Go, do not collect $200." Now he desperately needed the 'Get Out of Jail Free' card.

◆

"Now watch closely, another insight is forming! Note what it does to the vibratory pattern of his molecular body/ mind structure." Even Victoria seemed excited – her preternatural calm just a tad agitated. "Again you will see how his awareness rises up through the different states of matter to attain a higher understanding of human nature."

◆

Reto's mind snapped into what he would later call 'hero mode.' In his mind's eye, pitiful losers, weaklings and damaged bodies morphed into individuals radiating power from an invisible inner source. He saw legions of unsung heroes – men and women outside the spotlight – who in the face of the worst atrocities had carried on with great dignity. Could he join their ranks? He had not even been aware of them till now. He had, if he was honest, rather looked down on such individuals, pitied some for their disabilities, disdained others for their weakness. But now he saw each of these people recast as heroes. True heroism didn't need public attention, he suddenly understood, didn't crave applause. True heroism was about living with quiet dignity, with empathy for life and the living. To pity these people was sheer arrogance.

Could he do it too? Live life without being able to stand on his own two feet? Could he play the ball as it lay? A voice came from the depths of his desolation: "Can you handle this, mighty Ritter? Are you man enough?" It was a compassionate challenge, not mean. The voice sounded a bit like Gian, so much so that Reto looked around his hospital room to see whether his old friend was sitting quietly somewhere. But Reto was quite alone ... alone with his thoughts, his fears and his anguish – and without an answer.

The bruises faded, teeth were replaced, the broken wrist still a little stiff – but in halfway working order. The surgeons had done a fantastic job; even his back had healed – after several operations and the fusing of three vertebrae. He'd been in a brace for some time, but now with plenty of prescribed exercise and a very stiff bandage – what he jokingly called his slimming girdle – Reto was finally and carefully moving about his chalet. He didn't venture out much. The fall had broken more than bones. It had shattered the secure anchor to his reality. He had faced many a challenge in his life. In fact, he was hooked on them, daring life time and again to "bring it on" so he could prove himself. But this time Reto found it a bit more difficult to pick up the gauntlet life had thrown down, and not because he could hardly bend over.

His whole thinking circled around a simple question, to which a satisfying answer had so far eluded him. His mind kept gnawing at the question, "Who am I when my ability, my strength are gone?" as well as at the great mystery, "What the hell is suffering for?" Because suffer he did. The hot needles were still there. They kept poking and jabbing him from time to time, literally stabbing him in the back. Physical work was almost impossible, since the attacks were totally unpredictable. He couldn't do any of the sports that had always helped him keep a clear and balanced mind. In fact, there was precious little to distract him from the hell his body was causing. Gian and Annina would visit regularly, but he got tired of their solicitousness and sympathy, however subtly and discreetly it was offered. He didn't want to talk about his pain. He hated to be weak, dependent and needy – in spite of what he had seen. What had happened to him was an outrage, a personal affront. And he was not willing to forgive.

With increasing concern, Gian watched his young friend struggle from within a web of anger, pain and self-pity, seemingly incapable of accepting his fate. He knew Reto wouldn't find consolation in talking to some god or other, even less to someone from ground control. But Gian had to steer the guy away from his obsession with physical discomfort – from this futile wrestling with fate.

It was one of those crisp, late summer days hinting at autumn's coming with its golden larches and indigo skies. The two of them sat on their usual bench by the lake, Gian puffing on his pipe, Reto gazing into the calm water at a perfect mirror image of the mountains.

"I know you suffer, my boy. And I think it's time you used it to your advantage. Show your pain some gratitude."

Reto's head came up like a snake ready to strike. "What the hell are you...?"

But Gian's look cut him off in mid sentence. There was so much compassion, so much love and warmth in the old man's eyes that Reto went quiet. He let the gaze hold and comfort him.

"Through the awful grace of god comes wisdom, said a Greek philosopher, and he knew something most people have to find out the hard way. Remember the fairy tales your Nona used to read to you? They all have something in common, don't they?"

"What are you talking about? You into peddling philosophy and fables now?" Reto sounded gruff.

"They all have a similar structure, I'm sure you have noticed that. Heroes and heroines sent out on all kinds of adventures, having to pass all manner of difficult tests. They encounter dragons and witches and fairies.... These mythological tales and figures are but descriptions of the human path, the challenges an individual faces on the road towards understanding and knowledge."

"Fine, Gian, fine. You know, even I have heard of the psychological interpretation of Little Red Riding hood and her cohorts. What does all this have to do with anything?"

"What do you think pain and suffering are, dear boy?"

After the excursion and the talk with Gian, Reto was beat, happy to sink into the embrace of his large and comfortable sofa. He was no longer a boy, even though Gian still called him that on occasion. After all, he was on the road towards the big Five-0. But Gian was right of course about the fairy tales, myths and great sagas Reto had eagerly devoured as a boy. He just hated to admit it. What was suffering for? For the foxes, if you asked him. Then again, what use was fighting the pain? It was part of his life now; he may as well learn to live with it and not waste all his energy fighting back. Reto's laugh was more like a groan. Might as well ask a tiger to change his stripes.

But wait, wasn't that what this meditation thing was trying to teach him? It really had helped relax the mind so it didn't cling to the pain so much. God, if his buddies could see him: the mighty Ritter, plugged into his smartphone, cruising through a Tibetan meditation! On a suggestion from Annina, and after an extensive search on the Net, he had downloaded this app and dutifully practiced every morning for an hour or so – feeling like a complete idiot in the beginning. After a few weeks, the idiot bit had just faded away and he had come out of these sessions feeling relaxed and refreshed.

Why not do some now, seeing it was on his mind? Reto started with the breathing technique. After a while, he felt himself sinking into and through the throbbing jabs in his back. He was withdrawing from the pain and leaving it where it belonged, to his physical body. Now Reto's awareness was no longer attached to his solid form. So there was clearly a state beyond pain – reachable with the right kind of concentration – but getting there wasn't easy. Climbing the Eiger north face would probably be a Sunday stroll by comparison. It would be work, hard work, require strict discipline and determination. Reto smiled. Right up his alley.

... There were images from this altered state flowing into his brain. He and Gian were back on the rock face, but there were no sharp edges. Everything seemed to shift ever so slightly. The closer he looked, the more the solid forms seemed to come apart, like a computer image dissolving into pixels. He saw a universe of particles moving at different speeds, creating the myriad forms visible to the human eye – Gian and himself and the mountain included. And he knew in that moment, if he maintained that state of mind and kept that degree of focus, he would rise above the pain that was dragging him down – vying for his attention. He knew he would be able to live with pain and eventually even overcome it.

With a sigh that seemed to come from the center of the earth, Reto returned to the solid world, to the soft leather of the dark blue sofa. In his back the needles were still stabbing away, but he felt a new kind of detachment – as if he didn't have to take it so personally anymore.

Maybe now he could tell Gian that he understood, or at least had an inkling of what this ancient Greek had meant by the suffering and wisdom bit. This glimpse of another plane had made it clear that pain and suffering were diabolically effective tools which life wielded to pry you from your daily routine – so you'd begin living life rather than just go through the motions. Now he could even appreciate what Gian had meant by being grateful. One thing was for sure: this pain, which an awful grace had bestowed upon him, had shaken loose his rigid concepts of the mind, his tried-and-true living patterns, his routines and pet prejudices.

He would not pity people anymore; no one, least of all himself. Pity was a feeble concept, and self-pity was no more than feeding yourself weakness. The power lay in understanding, empathy and compassion. But these didn't come without effort. A broad spectrum of experience helped: to have lived in a variety of different circumstances. Walking in another man's shoes for a while or – as his Nona used to recommend – "Take my eyes and look." It made you see things from a new perspective. True understanding meant you really connected to others. And this kind of understanding lead to empathy not pity.

If you looked at things from this perspective it became apparent all humans were on a hero's path, just like in Gian's fairy tales. Reto would be careful passing judgment again, knowing it was next to impossible to see what others were really going through – what inner challenges they faced. He might even be tempted to tell those so impressed by wealth, that real gold could only be discovered when you started digging within.

Another deep sigh rose from his chest. He felt exhausted by these insights. How could thinking be such a physically draining act? Another new experience for the man who thought he knew pretty much all there was to know about anything of importance. Reto smiled. Matter of fact, there was a huge grin spreading on his face. Understanding was great. It was a buzz – just as good as jumping off a 9,000 ft peak with nothing but a flimsy paraglider. Insights made you high, really high. As Reto carefully lifted his legs from the sofa to get into an upright position, he muttered to himself: "Now all that remains is the successful implementation...." He looked at his reflection in the glass facade that lead out onto the terrace and gave himself a smart salute. "We'll get there, buddy. Implementing new strategies is, after all, one of our core competences."

Perhaps buddy was not the right expression. Wasn't he rather a soldier on a bloodless battlefield? The decisive battles were not fought in foreign lands or in courtrooms. They were waged within, on home soil. That's also where the glory lay and the medals were awarded. Reto smacked his forehead. Now he understood what was meant by that cryptic quote Gian had dropped a while back: 'He who has conquered all the world is for sure a great man, but he who conquers his own self is the greatest of them all.' Where did this guy get stuff like that? He had barely ever left his hometown! He was right with his damn fairy tales too. He, the mighty Ritter, was now on the only worthy warpath, en route to conquering his inner kingdom. Whatever lay there, he was willing to find out.

As he selected a bottle of 1997 Tuscan Sangiovese, he recalled the night, years ago, when he had shared wine with strangers. Now he was surprised by an urge to share what he had learned – but with whom? Neither his sports buddies nor business associates were exactly the types you could talk to about complex and personal issues. Annina would listen as she always did – sympathetically of course – but her mind would be running through her packed schedule ... busy with a thousand things.

No surprise then that the faces of Barb, Shiv, Haki and Ali emerged from the darkness that had fallen over the village and the mountains. While sitting by the lake or wandering shadowy paths, Reto's thoughts had more than once returned to the little gazebo across the ocean; where he had first encountered the strangers he still felt so close to, and most importantly heard 'The Question' – Ethan's parting gift to them all. It would be cool to find out what progress the others had made towards a dependable answer. In fact this random wish to reunite, to pool experiences and insights, was slowly shaping up into a serious plan. Had his companions understood Ethan's gift in the same way: an assignment it was their duty to fulfill?

Mrs. Gyger did a fine job of greeting Reto on his return to the world of the working. She had baked a sumptuous chocolate cake with a "Welcome Back" written in white over glossy dark chocolate icing. They were all assembled in the meeting room, where Mrs. Gyger had put up some discreet garlands and balloons. The atmosphere was somewhere between office and children's birthday party. Reto didn't mind. In fact, he was quite touched that his staff would make the effort. Just as he was sinking his teeth into the fluffy cake, there was a timid knock on the open door.

"Professore," Reto smiled at the elegant old man he hadn't seen in years. "Please join us! How about some of Mrs. Gyger's world famous chocolate torte?"

His secretary blushed from joy.

"Oh, thank you, but I don't want to interrupt. If I could just have a short word, Avvocato. I'll be quickly on my way again," Roberto Benedetti said with an apologetic shrug.

Reto wiped the smudges of chocolate from his mouth and hands and led the Professore into his office. With a stifled moan he sat down in his orthopedic chair. The fused vertebrae still caused his back to stiffen and hurt. But the breathing technique – second nature by now – not only helped him through the pain but had also become his power source.

Roberto Benedetti, the world-renowned linguistics expert from the University of Padua (Reto had only learned of his eminence after the first mysterious visit several years before), seemed even more fragile than the expected toll the passing years might have taken. But his dark suit was just as impeccable, his white shirt with the starched collar just as spotless. He adjusted his steel framed glasses and asked, "Are you in pain, Avvocato? What happened?"

As Reto related his story, he was surprised at how easy it was to open up to this old gentleman. There was a rare understanding in his repartee, an openness that did not rush to judge or put a label on things. The old eyes were calm and full of warmth. When Reto ended his tale of woe, Benedetti let the silence spread for a moment, then quoted in a voice surprisingly resonant for such a delicate frame:

"If you knew how to suffer
You would be able to keep from suffering.
Learn how to suffer
And you will be free of suffering."

Now Reto let the silence stretch. "Is this from a text you have been translating?" he finally asked in wonder. This quote matched, in a minimum of words, precisely the conclusions he had drawn from dealing with the pain his body caused him.

"These are words from an expert in suffering, one who is probably well known to you too, Jesus of Nazareth, as found in texts from the second century. Jesus explains to his closest companions that man has to lift his awareness beyond pain and sorrow if he wants to find wisdom."

"You don't know how great a gift you have given me with this quote, Professore. This is the first sensible explanation of the concept of suffering I have ever heard. And it expresses perfectly what I have learned during my own fall from grace."

Again he remained silent for a while then shook his head. "Or perhaps I should say, my personal fall into grace. Here we are, 2,000 years after this enlightened man told us not to stick to our suffering, but we still don't have a clue why we all suffer so much. I had to learn to live with my pain without knowing why or what for. OK, after a while I began to gather some clues...."

Reto looked at the trim figure perched on the visitor's chair. "Had I known suffering was some kind of entrance test to seeing the bigger picture, I would have approached it quite differently." He smiled and stretched his arms: "I might have faced it as a worthy opponent I needed to overcome... or maybe embrace. Well, in the end that's what I did, but always with this nagging thought at the back of my mind: "Why me? Why do I have to deal with this?""

Benedetti nodded and opened his hands in that typical Italian gesture of "Oh well."

"Have your translations revealed any more of these extremely helpful clues on how to go about life?"

"Oh yes, indeed. The Gnostic texts dating between the first and third century after the death of the Nazarene are extremely rich in these kinds of insight. You know gnosis is the Greek word for knowledge? I have dedicated my whole life to translating these texts. They were written by those experienced in things which others only talked about, by people with a higher knowledge – an inner knowledge. This is why these texts give great insight into the purpose and goal of human life."

While Benedetti talked, Reto got up from his chair, suddenly a much younger man, full of enthusiasm and glowing with joy.

"So why don't you go ahead and publish? Why wait? Wouldn't it be useful for the world to learn why humans are on this particular planet? Look around you. If we go on as we have, soon there won't be anything left."

Benedetti gave Reto a cunning smile. "I don't want to deal with the controversy; it's that simple. Why fight about something that will be understood by the few capable of understanding, and misinterpreted then fought over by hordes of others. My translations will not be published until after my death. Basta." Then, a spark of mischief broke through the dark clouds like a ray of sun. "Don't worry, that will be soon enough. I can assure you, dear Signore Ritter, what I have found in these writings is extremely controversial and will have enormous consequences."

Reto wanted to shout "consequences for whom?" How could something so insightful and practical be at the same time controversial – even dangerous? But he was after all a professional, and discretion was one of his most valuable assets. So he let it go.

Like during his first visit to Reto's office, Benedetti handed over another fat folder filled with papers into his safekeeping – as well as detailed instructions about the disposition of these papers should death take the Professore unexpectedly. Then Reto accompanied Benedetti to the door, grateful for the gift of the quote about suffering. He would not forget it. It may have been uttered 2,000 years ago, but it shed a new, a clear light...and not only on his personal situation.

Barb descends into darkness

Barb considered what her father had left her – left the five who had heard him phrase this question – to be a demanding legacy, even an obligation. It was as if his dying wish was to send her on some sort of vision quest, in the tradition of Native American cultures, to search for her own answer to the eternal question of "Who am I?"

So far she had failed miserably.

At least she had pursued her educational project in Peru – the only thing for which she could muster any energy. The collaboration with Ali on content, software and practical implementation had been the only ray of light that penetrated the gathering murk. Mercedes had hoped and prayed the handsome Arab could prevent Barb from falling into the abyss. But like the prince in the fairy tale who could not get through the thorny hedge on the first try, Ali had faded out of the picture. Once the Peru project was up and running and Haki, a close friend by then, returned to Africa with an excellent Business Admin. degree in her pocket, Barb had gone down.

Instead of venturing into the wilderness – up on a mountaintop or deep into a cave – to gain the answer, she had buried herself in her father's house in Indian Wells. She really had gone underground, sliding into a deep depression, until she was finally unable to move. Not even Lucy could rouse her from her brooding. And Mercedes' valiant efforts to pull her out of the swamp all came to naught. Barb would not, could not grab a lifeline. Even Dr Mader, her trusted therapist for so many years, had failed to sway Barb's stubborn refusal to see anyone.

She was neither a mother nor a daughter, and she couldn't accept it. She was in a limbo of loss, unable to get a handle on the new Barb Bernstein. No family ties, no Daddy on whom to offload unwanted tasks, no son to wrap her arms around and envelop in her love. Gone, both of them gone. Out of her reach. There was just this carrousel going around and around in her mind, flashing the same message: that she wasn't worth being with. She had nothing to offer anyone. She deserved to be abandoned. She felt like both an incompetent mother who couldn't protect her young and a demanding, clinging daughter unable to stand on her own two feet.

"Who am I?" her father had begged to know. Hadn't it been enough for him to be her Daddy, her hero, the strongest pillar in her life? And who the hell was this crumpled heap of flesh and bones, this miserable woman left to fend for herself by all those who really, really meant something to her – who had given her an identity and provided a haven in stormy weather?

So Barb stayed in. It had started gradually. She ventured out less and less until one day – years after the traumatic event – she stayed home for good. Mercedes ensured there was food, the house was cleaned, plants watered, gardens tended. Left in the care of Miz B. in her current state, even an artificial plant would have withered... It tore at Mercedes' heart to see her boss, her friend and charge, sliding back into hell, just when she had worked so hard to haul herself halfway out of it. Now that her dad – the one person Barb could always turn to no matter how big the mess she had got herself into – had followed her son off stage, Barb had no-one to turn to but herself.

They had gone to Peru, twice actually. Mercedes had enjoyed it tremendously, in spite of her misgivings. Since then? Nada. They had not gone anywhere in years. Mercedes was not sure it was a good thing that Barb didn't need to work for money. Maybe being forced to be productive would have helped. But just as likely, she could have ended up living in some cheap dump, strung out on who knows what. The inheritance, bolstered by her own considerable funds, enabled her to keep her place in the hills and her offices as well as hang on to Mercedes; now more nurse than office assistant. She kept her father's house too. There she hung out – staring at water falling into the pool, golfers moving along fairways, mountains turning from dark to light, from light to dark.

◆

"Are we just going to leave her in that swamp? Beats me what good this can do." Avory felt for the pretty female. It seemed the longer they stayed on assignment, the more they were infused with these intensive emotions. Not altogether unpleasant, as long as you knew exactly what it was and how to handle it. The Forces had returned to Mission Base, where they huddled around the Plasma Cube.

"You are feeling empathy, Avory. For humans that is a good thing. Our self-made mission cloaks, however, do not register these physiological impulses. Perhaps you are a touch more susceptible to these kinds of vibrations, while dear Marvin is more in tune with the callous vibes."

Marvin just snorted at Victoria's comment. "Ave's right, though, this down-in-the-dumps groove is getting kind of boring. It's a bit like watching quarks at absolute zero."

"You remember that Barb is associated with earth – with solid form – and her traits are emotion and drama? Even with the upgrade, it'll take months for insights to filter down into denser matter. However, time is not an issue, and looking at her brain's vibratory pattern I'd say something is bound to happen – change is coming." She pointed at the Cube.

"Ok, I do see it now. All her life she has ridden tidal waves of emotion. Too bad she's such a poor surfer and gets constantly dumped. Now she's drowning.... She's been so focused on appearances, on performing on the world's stage, that it's a giant leap for her to check out her inner stage. I'd say she needs a kick in the butt!" Marv made as if to carry out his proposal.

◆

The next morning, over tea on the terrace, Mercedes took the plunge. "Listen up, Missy, I think you've moped around enough now. It's time to get moving."

Barb just glanced at her, not even mildly interested.

"You know, ever since that mule ride in Peru, I've been looking forward to going again. Now I'm not getting any younger, see." She pointed at the broad silver bands streaking her dark hair. "And I'll be damned if I'm going to my grave without having ridden on them animals through them Andes again."

Barb gave her a wan smile and a dismissive wave: "Go, for god's sake. Just go. Book a ticket, rent a mule. I'll pay for it. Have fun." She turned away to stare at the cascading water once more – something she could do for hours.

Mercedes changed tack. Softly she said, "I met a good friend of your father's yesterday, guapa. He sends his love. We had an interesting talk, he and I. And he would be really happy to talk to you too."

The two women faced each other across the low table set with teacups and Barb's favorite cookies Mercedes' mother had baked for her. Mercedes face expressed her deep concern with the frail looking woman, whose once fiery hair now hung limp around a face that had lost its expressiveness. Barb's delicate frame was invisible under her uniform of bulky shirts and cut-offs. She didn't look at her friend. "You talkin' about me behind my back? With friends of Daddy's?" Barb sounded heartbroken. Mercedes had rather hoped for one of those infamous volcanic eruptions Barb used to produce at regular intervals. She would have happily cleaned up after a Miz B. storming once more through the office like a hurricane, yelling and hurling things. But Barb just sounded teary and broken.

"Nathan David is a professor at UCLA, director of the department of brain research. They do really exciting stuff, ground-breaking work helping those with depression."

"Great, you want me to be their guinea pig? What do they do? Show you funny movies and measure your brainwaves?

Give you electroshocks to jumpstart your happy sector? C'mon Merc, leave me alone with this stuff."

Mercedes stifled her sigh. She had to find an angle to pique Barb's curiosity; after all, it was this trait had made her such a terrific documentary producer – curiosity, coupled with her talent for telling stories that touched people's hearts and minds.

"No fear, girl. None of that Dr. Frankenstein stuff. You won't be hooked up to a generator waiting for lightning to strike! No, in fact their research ties in to one of your fields of expertise."

"What do you mean ... moping? That's the only thing I'm a certified expert in."

Mercedes smiled at the weak joke. "I'm talking about a fascinating topic – cutting-edge research in a field you are uniquely suited for, thanks to your professional experience. And besides, it might be really important for society. You always had the knack for putting your finger on what was wrong with the system. Remember? This quality appears to be in serious demand nowadays. That's all I'm saying."

"So, and how do they work all these miracles?"

"Again, it ties in with what you know a lot about: drugs and what they do to individuals and society. Dr. David and his colleagues are studying how mind-enhancing substances can guide a person towards deep insights. It would be a great topic for you – to show another side to the issue, maybe even a beneficial one."

"You seriously want me to take drugs, Merc? How very very sensitive of you. Besides, why the hell should I do anything? Why work, why rip out my guts to enlighten the masses, trying to make them see, make them think? Has any of my work ever changed anything? The world is going to hell in a Hummer and my life has gone down the tubes, so why should I care?"

Mercedes was pleased with the response. It had been a while since Barb had strung so many sentences together.

"Why don't you talk to the professor, sweetie? Just listen to what he has to say. We'll invite him over so you won't have to go anywhere. Perhaps for breakfast tomorrow, what do you say? Just listen to him. You don't have to do anything if you don't want to."

Barb just nodded. "Fine, do what you want, I'm not going anywhere. But just leave me in peace right now, ok?"

Mercedes immediately got up, grinning widely. The bait was taken, now it was up to Professor Nathan David to reel her in.

Since the man was an old friend of Dad's, Barb had at least bothered to change out of her standard ragged cut-offs topped by one of her father's dress shirts. She greeted him in a pair of khaki shorts and a simple black T. Over coffee they had talked golf and the heat, Barb keeping to monosyllabics. Professor Nathan David – "call me Dave" – regaled them with stories of wild days spent with Ethan at college, before gradually steering the conversation where he really wanted to go. He had, after a long phone call with Mercedes, thought carefully about how to broach the subject. He would shamelessly call upon the help of both Ethan senior and junior.

"You know, Barb, I really admire the work you did on the destruction illegal drugs leave in their wake. It was really bold, as were your conclusions. Matter of fact, there are first steps being taken in a couple of European countries toward legalizing drugs in order to gain control over this dirty and lethal business. Your father was very, very proud of you. We used to talk a lot about what might be the most sensible approach to drug use in a civilized society. It was clear to us that humans will always search for ways to alter their everyday consciousness. After all, they have done so since the beginning of time."

"Dad was into that topic? I never knew ... I mean he told me how proud he was of my work, but we never really discussed the subject of drugs."

Encouraged by this direct response, Dave ploughed on. "Oh yes, he was convinced there were beneficial sides to certain new mind-enhancing substances. After his grandson died – you know how much he adored your son – he really dug into this research. He did a lot of reading about what these substances can do, and we had many interesting discussions. Actually, he was a major funder of our Mental Trauma Integration Research program. Without him, I don't know how we could have got it off the ground. Government sure as hell doesn't give any money for this kind of research, however much society might benefit from it. You know full well from your own work that government drug regulations are guided more by fixed ideas than by scientific fact."

Dave's obvious frustration – anger even – touched off a familiar emotion in Barb. She vaguely remembered feeling this same passion for her work. The conviction of doing something important that would benefit society, only to be hindered by bureaucracy, disinterest, jealousy and plain stupidity. It was so typical of Dad to put his money into something like this. Perhaps she should listen to this man Dave. If Dad had believed in him and his work, then maybe she should at least take an interest.

"Anyway, to get back to our research, our goal is to help people integrate traumatic life experiences, and extract so-called core lessons through artificially induced states of consciousness. The question we try to answer is: do humans suffer in order to learn specific things, and can these things be named?"

"You want to make a list of all kinds of human suffering, and then tell people what it's good for?"

Dave smiled. "They needn't be told, they'll find out for themselves...."

"Ok, so what core lesson do I learn, when I check under 'losing only son and father within a year?"

Dave didn't smile since he knew the abyss these losses had pushed Barb into. He briefly touched her hand and said,

"We're not quite there yet. But one reason for my work is that I was aware of all this human suffering – and frustrated by not knowing what lessons or insights were gained through suffering."

"Is it really good for anything? Are you sure these core lessons exist?"

"That, my dear Barb, is what we are trying to discover through our work."

Dave shared with her much of what he had told Mercedes, who contacted him after reading his article on the subject in a journal Barb subscribed to. The piece had stirred up quite some controversy. He had cited the staggering numbers of those damaged by wars: a shadowy army of men and women who mentally did not find their way back from foreign battlefields. They carried their memories and trauma into their families and communities, where they kept festering and bleeding. He talked about the multitudes discharged from mental institutions and hospitals because of lack of funding and capacity; people who could not be lead back to a self-determined life, who could not be integrated back into society. He said severe burnouts, depressions and addictions of all kinds were increasing exponentially, especially among the young.... And Barb listened, listened and nodded. She even voiced loud agreement when Dave talked about society's general ignorance about certain substances – how research was unfairly restricted – how they were prevented from alleviating the suffering of so many.

"It is so absurd that the legality of substances is decided by politicians. Most of them have no personal experience with any kind of drugs, except booze and nicotine of course, and possibly a few white lines here and there. You know, some time ago I talked to Dennis Naught, an eminent British research scientist. He had been fired from his post as a government-appointed drug advisor for stating that some of the substances government perceived as evil were about as dangerous as riding a horse", Barb said, shaking her head.

"Yes, I've heard of him. And I know his research, very thorough and totally serious. But many governmental decisions are not primarily based on scientific facts. Now I'll tell you something else: the substances we are researching have the potential to break dependence on destructive drugs, to get people off heroin or alcohol." Dave saw that he had Barb's full attention now and started gently reeling in the line. "We might also be able to help those suffering from serious fears and phobias, and we have achieved great results with severe depression."

The silence spread. Barb's eyes sought refuge in the falling water; she felt like a snail that had dared to put out its feelers, only to have them hacked off. She just wanted to withdraw, slide far back into her shell. But something had hooked her and prevented her escape. Dave did not break the silence ... he knew enough about human nature not to hurry these things. He was good at waiting and letting space open up.

"Years ago, when my son died, part of me died too." Barb's voice was no more than a whisper. "I did get help then – a wonderful woman helped me survive. I learned a lot about suffering, about the suffering that comes from attachment and how it would make me grow stronger. But then Dad died and everything became pointless. Why should I do anything? Why should I live when annihilation is just waiting around the corner? Why should I love or take an interest in anything, when it could be over any minute? Why feel, why do, why even think? And this is where I am now. I just can't get out of this hole and – frankly – I am not even sure I want to."

Dave was far too intelligent to feed Barb platitudes about life always being worth living, full of wonders and excitement, so much to learn yet, so much to discover. All he said was: "Why don't you join our research group? See for yourself what these substances can help you discover, especially concerning attachment. That's actually one of the most fascinating aspects of our work. These substances allow you a very detached, dispassionate look at your situation. You observe what you have lost, what you have experienced. But there is no pain or heartache, just one big 'aha!' after another. My invitation stands: participate and document. I'll allow you full access to our research and support you in any way I can, should you one day want to go public with what you uncover."

Dave then went on to explain the different kinds of substances – those boosting the ego and those allowing a glimpse of the individual in a broader context. "It's the first group that are dangerous, often leading to addiction and abuse, because for the ego enough is never enough. The ego doesn't know the word or the condition of 'enough'. The second group, however, takes a person to a level where she can take a detached look at her position in life, examine the context of that position and make sense of it. It's like taking an internal journey through which you gain insight, understanding and strength; often enough strength to take the next decisive step towards a more fulfilling life."

Barb sighed and for the first time looked directly at Dave. "You knew my father and he trusted you. But before I decide, let me ask you one thing. You know that addictive drugs were the death sentence for my son. I have many friends with long histories of drug use ... and abuse; man-made substances as well as the bio-organic kind Mother Nature provides. I also have a bit of experience myself. But when little Ethan died I swore never to touch the stuff again as long as I am damned to live. Now, I could perhaps view what you are proposing as medication. What do you know about the possibility of dependency on this stuff?"

"To be quite honest, anything can create dependency in the wider sense. You should know that sugar is the worst addictive drug in our society. Probably wouldn't even be given FDA approval anymore.... But as to what we are working with, the danger of dependency is less than with alcohol or nicotine. You're right; instead of seeing this as a drug, look at it as a remedy, as a pharmaceutical. Even more so since it is purely synthetic."

Dave looked at her with a serious expression: "A word of caution, however. You might feel a bout of sadness coming on after the sessions, when this higher self starts to fade away and leaves you with your everyday self. It's up to you not to give in to that sadness. The best way to gain the strength to do that is through physical exercise. Go to the gym, go jogging or walking."

With a frown Barb said, "How could I do that? I've been in the seriously deep dumps for so long, I don't think I can deal with any more pain."

"Look, I chose you for your inner strength. That was the first thing I noticed when we met. Even though you are in a deep depression, I feel there is solid ground there, power and a strong will. The experiment sessions are giving you a visual account of your mental state, but it is you who has to translate this knowledge into action patterns. It will give you the necessary tools and insights – if you so wish – to understand and reconcile yourself with your life, with who you really are. This in turn will help you fight the gravitational pull, and conquer that inner ground. You will need determination, the right food, exercise, and no self-pity." Dave smiled to soften the last words.

But Barb still looked stung. She didn't feel like flaring up at him, though, or accusing him of thinking her a sissy. Instead she surprised them both by softly whistling "unchain my heart."

Barb reluctantly slips into the lightweight black sleeping bag, adjusts the black eye mask and inserts silicon earplugs. All she hears now is her own heartbeat and the blood coursing through her head. She is scared, really and truly frightened. She has never been so totally cut off from the world, and after a short time she pulls out the earplugs and shoves the mask up on her forehead. But she resists touching the small bell Dave had told her to ring if she felt like company.

When she had asked him earlier for earphones with music instead of earplugs, he had explained that music affected the mind, pulling it in different directions and inducing a variety of emotions – depending on the style and the context. His goal was to find out what her mind produced when not influenced by any outside source.

Sighing softly, Barb puts the earplugs back in and pulls down her mask. In the adjacent room, Dr. David is pleased to see Barb participating. Before they started, she had voiced her fear of what she might encounter on these journeys and had realized, with quite a surprise, that her fear released new energy within her body. Something she hadn't felt for months, even years. She described it to him as a rushing stream washing away any obstacle in its path.

Now, Barb swallows the capsule Dave has given her and, after about ten minutes, she begins to breathe deeper. She feels her body, her cheeks flushing, as the increased breath warms up her body. The sensation is like exercising on a stairmaster without having to move. There is a pleasant feeling of calm and contentment spreading through her. She is completely taken with this wonderful feeling of just being and breathing. She feels her lungs working, her heart area expanding. Into this sense of physical wellbeing drift images of her son and her dad. Barb just keeps breathing, looks at their faces, breathes deeper and deeper. When Dave gently touches her shoulder, she takes off the mask, pulls out the earplugs, and cannot believe that two hours have passed. Time shrinks – she learns – when a person concentrates fully.

When relating what she has experienced, she is astonished at how calmly she can talk about her lost loves. "Till now I could not even look at their photos without it ripping my heart apart. And now I encountered them in my mind, saw them real as life. I felt no pain, no joy either, just somehow ... neutral, maybe? I was just an observer watching their familiar faces."

Dave gently touches her hand. "Pain makes the heart muscle contract, the breathing pattern becomes very shallow. Your breathing deeply throughout this whole experience made the difference. Breath is a powerful tool to fight and neutralize undesirable emotions."

The second session brings on father and son again. Barb keeps breathing, while she watches the two figures moving around, going about some business or other. When she goes back the third time, she comes into the picture herself. She sees herself interacting with her son, with her father, as if she were watching a movie. She notices that the mental image of her own self is incomplete. There are two holes around her heart area, one larger than the other. She understands this is the space son and father had taken up. She turns towards her son, and sees how she is connected to him with some sort of chain. When despair is just about to wash over her, she takes even deeper breaths, hard breaths, as if she were forced to carry a heavy load up a steep hill. Then the images fade and she keeps breathing.

"You have done tremendous work, Barb. Just by looking at your patterns I can see you shouldered a heavy load today." Dave's voice is calm, soothing, as he shows her the printout of her brain waves.

Barb had needed his help to rise from the bed and to move over to the 'chill out room,' where they discussed these journeys into her inner self. She feels exhausted. The realization of what she has seen is almost too much to bear. "I have seen the enormous energy, the immense need I have always projected onto my father, and even more so onto my son. How can that be? I have always thought of myself as strong, successful, independent. But now I have seen what lies beneath the glossy surface." Then she adds with great conviction: "The truth about our lives is to be found within."

Dave looks at her with a broad smile. "You truly are on the right path, I can see that. Now about that projection: you must realize most of us live with great inner voids. That is nothing to be ashamed of, or cause for guilt. Most of us offload the burden of filling these voids onto those we love most. Life is, aside from many other things, a game of energy exchange. We still are pretty clueless about life. But now, through new techniques and increased knowledge we begin to understand some things. Once we access the underlying mental patterns of human existence, we will live more fulfilled and independent lives. People like you, Barb, are helping us on this path; through your courage to explore yourself and by sharing what you learn on your mental voyages."

Barb listens closely. She is keen on understanding what happens to her when the mind enhancer affects her normal perception. "I still feel a bit uncomfortable taking a drug, you know. Somehow it just doesn't feel right... Aren't there natural ways to gain these insights?"

"Oh there might be certain physical and mental disciplines, but they usually require years of diligent practice. My research has led me down this path; one that I am convinced is the future. This substance is stimulating a higher self, through observation of the everyday self. You could call it an inner therapist, an unerring authority, that guides you from ignorance to knowledge."

Mercedes had called Dave after Barb's first session. She wanted to know whether she should watch out for something specific, do anything in particular. He'd put her mind at ease, saying all was well. Simply agreeing and taking that first decisive step had set Barb on the road to recovery. And he had been right. She seemed to come back to life little by little. She had moved back to the Hollywood Hills – "Just for the duration of this experiment," she had said – but was quite at home within her own four walls, even asking for Ms. Hound, a veritable antique by now, to move back in with her. Something Lucy had greeted with uncontrollable tail-wagging and copious slobbering over her British racing green sofa.

When Mercedes dropped by on one pretext or another, Barb didn't talk much about the work with Dave. But after this last session, she had looked at Mercedes with bright eyes as they had sat together over fresh juice and flakey croissants. "Life is not only what you see or do or feel in your daily grind, it's much more. There are these undercurrents, these underground streams of energy, that not even the most educated seem to know about. The deep love a mother feels for her child, for instance, could just as well be need or dependency. It's not that selfless emotion we believe it is. Oh no! It's something you lay on the child like a yoke...." Barb had cried as she said that, but it was not the same crying as before. Mercedes did not feel desperation in those tears; more like a coming to terms, a letting go.

It is during her tenth and last session – Dave told her this was the limit, since there was no information yet on longterm effects on the body – that Barb uncovers her innermost treasure. Again she gazes upon her son and her father, sensing the quality of her rapport with them. The scene is pretty much the same it had been, like watching the same movie for the nth time, discovering ever more detail, gaining greater depth of field.

She sees them fall, first the son, then the father. From the lifeless bodies rise two shimmering spheres. In wonder and awe she gazes at what she understands to be the soul leaving the body. Inside the shimmering orb she makes out a blinding white light. With absolute certainty she knows she is looking at the pilot, the driver, the animator – at the subtlest of all forces, the source of creation. She understands that this brilliant white center is to the sphere, what the sphere is to the body. Just as the sphere left the body behind, so the innermost essence would eventually eject from the sphere. Whatever this brilliant essence was, it held the definitive answer to Ethan's question, 'Who am I?"

Death, she understands, is not what has been commonly perceived. Death is not an end, but a mere change of state, a standard move in an eternal game. A body dies, but the emerging essence knows no beginning and no end. And deep inside Barb makes peace with her son's, her father's essence having returned to the source.

"Here we are, a century after the Model T, but only very few really want to know how a motor works. That's how I feel about myself right now. I have been living in this body for 40-odd years, but never really asked what makes Barb run.... This just about blows my mind! Do others see the same things, Dave?" Sitting in his office after this last journey, and after having related her latest experiences, Barb seemed ready to move into documentary mode.

"The images are very individual, but there are similar underlying themes, those elusive core lessons probably. Then again some test subjects don't have any visual images at all; just a change in their breathing patterns and of feeling a lot calmer after the sessions. Our people sample is not yet large enough to draw any significant conclusions."

"When will you go public with your findings?"

"Well, we're looking for at least 500 documented experiments; then we'll work out the common denominators. I'm really excited about this work, because I believe deeply that humanity needs to become more aware, pronto. Just look at the tremendous challenges we are collectively facing! But all the legal substances – as well as those traded on a huge scale by illegal drug cartels – either diminish people's capacity for thinking and insight or actively feed their aggression. So, here is my crusade: I want to provide humanity with substances that increase wisdom and deepen understanding of life."

"Bravo!" Barb was lightly clapping her hands, the smile she bestowed on Professor Nathan David full of light and life. "You know how wary I am of drugs. Most leave nothing but disaster in their wake. But these substances are profoundly different. Perhaps we should put that stuff into the drinking water – like fluoride – to make people more thoughtful, instead of just giving them strong teeth!" Barb giggled like a teenager. Here she was already provoking again.... What a change from the lifeless, pale creature Dave had met just months before on the terrace in Indian Wells! If these substances were capable of lifting patients out of severe depression on a broad scale, the findings would be spectacular.

When she hit the street, looking for a cab to take her home, Barb wanted to call her comrades in the quest instantly. The urge soon gave way to a deep longing to reconnect with Ali, Haki, Reto and Shiv; to see them, touch them and hear what avenues life had led them down – what they had discovered along the way.

◆

Marvin and Avory were also clapping their hands. "What a performance! You think Prof. Dave might get sanctified? You know, for working miracles and stuff?"

"It's certainly been an awesome transformation." Avory was gesturing towards the Plasma Cube which showed Barb comfortably installed in the filigree lounge chair she had hijacked from her dad's house a lifetime ago. Her fingers raced over the laptop keyboard, trying to keep up with the flow of ideas for a script. "I really liked her car-driving analogy."

"I'll give you another one," Marvin piped in. "Electricity! You flip a switch and it's there, you flip it again and it's gone. Where it goes? Nobody really wants to know, as long as it's there when you push the on-button.... Same with a human! When one is conceived, the on-button is pushed. When one dies, the power source goes off. Where does it go? What was it? Where did it come from in the first place?"

"You could take this simile a step further! When they switch off the lamp or the laptop, they don't think all energy has vanished forever," Avory exclaimed. "But when a human goes into off-mode, most are convinced the game is over for good! Just like our human Barb over there. She couldn't fathom that concept. Yet just as there is a power source for the lamp, there's also a power source animating the bodies she was so attached to."

One of the reasons this understanding eluded most humans was a lack of awareness of their innermost shell, Victoria reminded the twins. The upgrade would give them access to their soul, which they called eternal. It certainly was on a human timescale, eternal as a star – which would burn up when its time came. But like anything put together from particles the soul was also finite. The gaseous substance of the soul carried the information code for all lifetimes in the past and in the future. Mind and body were like a single chapter in the book of a human soul – one single story out of thousands. And as there are infinite stars in the skies, so are infinite souls on their journeys.

"The only immortal entity is It. Unmoving, It is beyond time, all-pervading. And all who learn to focus their senses so the fusion-sense is activated, will sense It everywhere, will become aware of its omnipresence." Big G paused, then continued: "Come on, let's move! We're about to witness another spectacular burst of awareness." He was suddenly excited, which didn't do the furniture in the spacious room much good. In an instant the Forces had vanished.

Haki on the road

"We're losing her! Her heart's going!

Dear god in heaven isn't there anything you can do. You must save her. You just must!" Makele was frantic. "Where's the bloody defibrillator? Where the hell is everybody?"

Haki gazed at the chaos below. She saw people dancing around a figure lying immobile on a simple bed. Oh, it's the operating room at her old bush hospital. Isn't that Makele over there? Running around madly, tears on his cheeks? And the woman lying on the bed... why, it's her.

But then, what was she doing up here? There had been a strange sensation at first. As if her heart were expanding somehow, opening up, allowing her to step outside her body. It felt great, so unencumbered, suffused with wellbeing and joy – inside and out. She was light, she was free, she was whole. She had floated gently towards the ceiling – perception fully open – observing everything in the simply furnished room. Without moving her eyes she could take in what is above, below, behind and in front of her: the desperate voices and hectic activity, the familiar rhythmic creaking of the fan – blades moving in strange slow-motion beneath the new ceiling lamp she had brought from the capital just weeks before. She could discern the slightest sounds amid the commotion: the dripping faucet, fat bugs stubbornly clunking their heads against wire mesh, rapid breathing of men and women trying to jump start the body lying on the bed – to bring it back to life.

Now that was downright funny. She was more alive than she'd ever been, she had complete awareness, she was wonder woman – her five senses fused into one super-sense.

♦

The four Forces also hovered. They could make out the ethereal Haki as clearly as the physical. "Now you can watch a truly interesting phenomenon – a human hovering between life and death ... still here, already there, but not totally gone yet. But we have to be careful she doesn't see us in her state of heightened awareness," Victoria pulsed and Marvin fired off a warning: "Yo, Mr. G! Don't twitch. This baby's gonna crash if you so much as hiccup."

"Am I a dodderer, a doter? Just because you call me geezer, doesn't mean I am one! Instead of trying to be funny you should admire my skill in respectful silence! Holding a life in perfect balance – suspended between realms – is a master's skill."

Victoria added her pulses to the heated interchange: "Whatever it is, it's a unique opportunity to observe what happens when the fastest moving particles begin to detach from the slow moving physical body."

"But the software cannot be effective without hardware! And since she's already upgraded, it would be a serious waste. Marvin is right."

"She's not going anywhere. Don't worry, Avory. I'm holding perfect balance here. This is her lesson in detachment. This compassionate heart, so deeply pained by all the ills she sees in the world – by the suffering of her fellow humans – is now allowed a short glimpse of a greater reality."

◆

As Haki hovers and observes, she is engulfed in a rainbow – purer and more brilliant than she's ever seen with her everyday eyes. What's more, the colors have depth, almost body. Green and orange break free and move closer to her, as if wanting to tug her sleeve and tell her something. Or do they want to invite her to dance? Green flows over her, enfolds her. Wrapped in its aura, swaying with it, she hears the sound ha-ha-ha, perceiving it like pulses of energy. When green releases her, orange takes over, the sound changing to ki-ki-ki. But while she could flow into green, orange is more compact and solid. Her name, the colors tell her, represents water and earth.

Now Haki floats through blue – which she experiences as weightless, caressing and airy. Red exudes strength and warmth. She feels as if welcomed into a quartet of sisters and brothers; each defined by a special quality and bound by friendship. She travels on, awed by the magnificent yellow, which comes across as a mysterious distant cousin – a family secret. Finally she dives into a pure brilliant violet – a stern power, bringing to mind a solemn uncle, always bent on testing her strength but also willing to bestow some of his power on those seeking to know him.

♦

"Ahhh, she just grazed my outer layers!" Big G did his utmost to reign in his excitement. After all, he didn't want to upset the delicate balance in which he held Haki.

Marvin pulsed: "What'd you do? Charge her batteries? Sneak a trojan horse into her system? Or did you wipe her hard drive?"

"None of your business. You wouldn't understand how it feels when human awareness penetrates your realm. It's indescribable. But if I have to put it in words, I'd say it's like a power boost. You'd probably get hooked right away...."

"I think it's important for you to understand that human perception is perfectly capable of reaching our level. But only when uncluttered by all that material world stuff the five senses constantly drag in for processing," Victoria added. "Besides, as the mission cloak gets lighter and more transparent, more and more human players will be able to temporarily step outside of it – not dying mind you. What our friend Haki is experiencing right now will become much more commonplace. The diminishing density will also allow the very young to recall their previous roles."

"Don't know if that's a good thing really," Marvin interjected. "What if a boy remembers he's played a king and his father his stableman or, worse, a traitor? Make it difficult for Mr. Dad to force the kid to do homework."

"Yep. Remembering past roles will change the concept of parenthood. It'll all become a bit looser when humans realize they have been mothers and sons and daughters and fathers in all kinds of combinations already. Parents will eventually accept that their job is simply to produce a mission cloak for a soul to don for its next role."

"Could have a great side effect, Big G," Avory pulsed. "Less focus on the abilities of the mission cloak or intellectual capacities – be it in school or sports or pushing one's offspring in a particular direction. Instead, parents might pay more attention to the role this soul has come to play."

◆

Haki is pulled towards the core of the 3D rainbow, towards a brilliant white light. But she is kept at a distance and barely dares look at the mighty ruler the other six colors seem to bow to. "Not yet," it tells her. She is not sad, not disappointed. She is enveloped in a cloud of ecstatic love, inside and out. She understands – with every particle of her being – the inherent rightness in all of creation, and that it is up to her to love, to appreciate and enjoy. Then she feels herself being gently pulled back through the rainbow, taking its blessings with her.

She feels her senses starting to reconnect with her physical form. Slowly she opens her eyes and whispers: "I took the defibrillator to the capital with me to get it fixed! Don't you remember?" Makele stares at her, open-mouthed. Then his hands come up and he staggers a few steps back, as if shielding himself from the attack of a ghost. Repeatedly crossing himself, he stuttered: "What the... How do you... Where on earth...?"

But Haki has already slipped back into a blessed unconsciousness, and Makele slumps into the one chair in the room, face in hands.

Haki had indeed traveled once again to Matadi. It had been a one-off, because she was rarely at Kizu hospital anymore. Since completing her training in the U.S. Hakika Hasina had moved to Kinshasa, where she oversaw the building and staffing of new medical stations throughout the country – as well as the training of qualified personnel. She ran a tight ship – something many big, strong men had to learn the hard way – underestimating the steely resolve beneath her deceptively mild demeanor.

Yes, she had taken the path she had charted with Ethan Bernstein, in what seemed another lifetime. She had studied and worked diligently, not to make her mentor proud – he was long beyond that – but to honor his memory and the trust he had put in her. After Ethan's death, she had redoubled her efforts and completed her studies in record time. Truth is, she reveled in testing her limits.

But it hadn't been all fun and games. Living in the land of plenty had been a trial, a true test of strength. Haki had had difficulty coming to terms with the blatant imbalance, the injustice of it all. What people wasted there could have fed, clothed, housed, educated, occupied and powered probably half her nation. In the first months she had to exercise great restraint not to berate a particularly ungrateful fellow student: a spoiled brat of a youngster with not a shred of awareness.

"There's a good reason gluttony is listed as one of the deadly sins!" she wanted to shout at him. "Gluttony leads to ruthlessness." If only the people from the north could see life from our perspective. There should be many more student programs, where those from the north were shipped south and vice-versa. Living for a while in each other's conditions would do more for world understanding than a hundred summit meetings.

Yes, Haki had to contend with plenty of challenges to her compassion. She knew people often acted ruthlessly because they just didn't know better, but it took many long runs and countless miles to regain her inner balance. She knew coming north was a great opportunity, and all thanks to one man's generous heart. And she would make the most of it, not waste it on useless anger. Whenever her mind was pulled towards anger and outrage, Haki held on to the example of Nelson Mandela. He was a star in the U.S. and an idol to many around the world, thanks to his boundless forgiveness, even for those who had imprisoned him for close to three decades.

Haki knew hate, envy, and the inability to forgive were just different forms of suffering. Not opening up to beauty, the countless miracles all around, ultimately affected the heart. She was quite sure of that. A loving, compassionate heart could expand to take in the whole universe, whereas distrust and hatred constricted the heart, made it small and hard like a pebble. Emotions like anger, greed, jealousy or hatred isolated a human being from his surroundings – a form of self-censorship that cut him off from the fullness of life. Deep down every human being wanted to experience the fullness of the heart.

She had always believed compassion to be the one dependable bridge connecting everything and everyone. It soothed and tamed the ego, whose sole job was to construct a fake identity and thus set the individual apart from all others.

She had read somewhere that compassion was housed in the same brain area as higher understanding. This made perfect sense to her because both led to inner peace and lasting happiness.

Through her work Haki had come to really understand what was meant by 'love thine enemy'. Compassion was not weakness as many proclaimed, and it was not fear of power. What a fallacy! The power of compassion could not be trumped, since it sought a solution that served all parties, thus creating satisfaction and peace. It was what a former U.S.

president had meant, when he said: "We will never fear to negotiate, but we will never negotiate out of fear." Power lay in showing compassion, and in not submitting to bad deals. Quite simply, it was beneficial for every soul to exercise compassion.

With growing horror, Haki had listened to those who spoke in the name of one of the truly non-violent figures in religious history, and turned him into a gun promoter. How could you preach world peace while wielding a nuclear arsenal that could destroy the earth 200 times over? Her intellect was obviously not constructed to grasp this kind of logic. It was logic lacking compassion – and should have been abandoned before Hiroshima. Only people guided by true compassion could influence dangerous minds; minds brainwashed into certain beliefs or frightened out of their wits. Only compassion had the power to lead a mind bent on evil toward a more peaceful path. Compassion knew no borders, doctrines or concepts. Compassion flowed from heart to heart.

But this commodity obviously did not come easy to human beings. Just as opening up to life, throwing yourself into its arms and letting it sweep you up in a wild and wonderful dance seemed impossible for most. Haki had been pondering just those riddles – for the hundredth time – when the truck barreling towards her blew one of its giant tires and rammed her car into a tree trunk.

A broken rib had punctured her lung. Another driver, who had miraculously shown up on this usually deserted dirt road, had saved her life by quickly taking her to the nearby Kizu hospital. There, her staff had done the impossible, staunching the flow of blood and keeping her from slipping away.

After the excitement of her amazing return to the living, Haki had begged for solitude. She had plenty to come to terms with – without people hovering over her, crying and laughing and praying and touching and asking a million questions. She had enough questions of her own.

Coming back from that wondrously free place, where the mind expanded and knowledge seemed to flow gently into all empty spaces, Haki felt as if trapped in a restricting corset. With a jolt she had landed back on the operating table, wondering how she would be able to go on living in this too taut costume. But since there was such boundless happiness greeting her return, she gave them all a tentative smile and tried to arrange herself in this misfit shell.

While recovering, Haki had plenty of time to think, when she wasn't being mothered by the select few her personal guard Makele let through the door. "So this is what dying is all about," she finally dared to think. And it was a pretty big leap she had to take here, since she had been surrounded by tragic deaths since birth. Her mother had pressed her out of an emaciated body that soon wasted away for good. There was no father in the shack the five kids called their home. Missionaries had divided the children up, placing them in whatever facility had a much-coveted opening. Growing up, Haki had seen people dying of violence or of hunger when the rains didn't come. As a nurse she had dealt with the devastation of HIV, which killed almost a whole generation. She knew firsthand about children and adults wounded and violated by warmongers and rebel soldiers. Her continent had been dealt a bad hand in so many respects. It was one of the reasons she had become a nurse, even if she did just spoon mere drops out of the ocean of suffering. How often had she sat at a sickbed and demanded an answer from god as to why there were so many premature, unnecessary deaths.

And now this! Had her question been answered once and for all? Or had she drawn a false conclusion from her experience? The hardship was not in leaving the body, but in coming into and wearing one! How would that new knowledge change her life? Where she had been there was no suffering, not even the idea of suffering. Would this amazing knowledge influence the course of her profession? She didn't believe so, at least not outwardly. She would still try her very best to relieve suffering and pain and make life as bearable as possible for the sick.

But her attitude towards death and dying had been changed dramatically and permanently. She could no longer bewail a person's death, but just silently bid them a heartfelt "farewell". She now knew from her own experience that they were embarking on a fantastic and mysterious voyage. No more would she prolong life at any cost, but rather try to explain to the patients on the threshold – and their loved ones – what she had experienced. She could alleviate the fear of death and help loosen the grip of those who desperately clung to life.

When Haki resumed her work, she was a changed person, as if she had received some kind of energy charge. She felt deeply grateful and blessed for her glimpse into another realm. She had lost all fear – not only of death – but of life too. She was aware that no being is ever alone, abandoned or isolated in this world and that all was well with creation. There was no guilty or innocent, good or evil. There was just life unfolding, all connected and interrelated. She had seen the different levels of moving particles, visible to her as brilliant colors, dancing with each other, revealing this whole visible world of form. This act of grace shone through Haki's whole being, radiating outward as compassion, love and understanding. When people asked in desperation, 'but who am I?' she now had an answer. She knew the essence of a human being – the soul – lives on when it leaves the body. Her deep conviction brought comfort to those who have to let go.

Not surprisingly, Haki thought about Ethan and his last question. Then she thought about getting in touch with Barb, Shiv, Ali and Reto. Should she write them and tell them she'd been successful in her quest for an answer to Ethan's question? Haki was still wavering. On one hand, she wanted to let this life-changing experience settle – to see whether it would endure – while on the other hand, convinced of its healing power, she wanted to share her new-found knowledge with the world. At least she knew now how she would word her message. She would say: "The body is but a vehicle you use for one lifetime, like a car we use to get around. The essence of a human being is beyond the body. It is something that moves on after you step out of the car. And for myself I know that my body is the vehicle I use to spread love and compassion in this lifetime, to relieve pain and ease the fear of death."

Shiv up in the air

Suffering did not come easy to Shiv. He just wasn't the type. He might suffer short-term setbacks in his work or bouts of frustration with the dimness of his fellow man. But that kind of suffering did not go deep and was annoying at worst. Delving ever deeper into the mysteries of the particle world, and collaborating globally with like-minded specialists absorbed most of his time, mental capacity, and whatever emotions he could muster.

There was still this one major stumbling block, though. It was his mother, not surprisingly, who had pointed it out. They had talked about religion and faith yet again and what these meant to different people. As was his custom, Shiv had made a clear and convincing case for science being the religion of the 21st century. While both disciplines were trying to solve the mysteries of the universe and of man, science strove for understanding through analysis – uncovering structures, connectivity and such – and making the results available to anyone who was interested. But religion, in his very informed opinion, contented itself with repeating outdated moral concepts, endlessly recycling incomprehensible myths that always needed interpretation. Science was not only evolving with time, but was also deeply democratic. Anyone, regardless of background, gender or religion, could contribute new findings to expand old concepts. Religion, on the other hand, was by and large hierarchically structured, unique in significance and – as he had pointed out repeatedly frozen in time.

"Oh, I do agree with you completely," Devi had smiled, touching his elegant, long fingered hand. "But I ask you: where is the human in scientific concepts? Why do so many scientists exclude themselves from their observations? Isn't this bundle of particles that form a human being the most fascinating of all objects in the universe?"

That had put a stop to their argument right then and there. Shiv had to admit, his mother was right. Even though scientists knew everything in the universe was in constant motion and intricately connected, many did not include themselves in this moving, vibrating stuff. There was a very good reason for staying on the outside, looking in. At the root of this inability or unwillingness to integrate man into their concepts lay something very banal, even with the latest results from the Large Hadron Collider at CERN, no one really understood the force that brought all these marvels about and set the universe in motion so to speak.

"How about developing a scientifically acceptable concept shedding light onto what body, mind and soul truly are?" his mother had challenged him then, not knowing how deeply her playfully uttered words would affect her son's course through life. Shiv realized that however much this human trinity was cited, even in ads for specialty foods or douche gels for goodness sake, no one really bothered to dig deep and produce a scientific concept of body, mind and soul.

With her simple question Devi had unwittingly pushed her son beyond the scientific comfort zone. Perhaps he could follow in the footsteps of those scientists of the mind, the great rishis – seers of the past – returning from their mind journeys to create the timeless Vedas. They had turned their perception inwards, away from the illusion of being surrounded by myriad material objects, inward to where they found but one underlying substance.

With the single-mindedness he applied to everything catching his imagination, Shiv had set out on an inner journey. He had taken the first tentative steps shortly after returning from California. But then his scientific work had so completely absorbed his intellectual and creative capacity – greatly stimulated by frequent exchanges with his Princeton professor friend – that he never found enough quiet time.

Under Devi's gentle but persistent nudging, Shiv began regular meditation. With surprising ease, he had mastered the technique of tuning the five senses to the subtler realities of his inner being. The impact was far greater than he cared to admit. Initially it just helped to still and focus his mind, but after a few years it opened up a whole new universe. Truth be told, he was now at a point where he treasured the early morning 90 minute sessions more than his entire day at the lab.

Shiv wouldn't be Shiv if he hadn't also done a lot of research on the topic. He was fascinated how experienced meditators produced a lot of gamma brainwave activity. The amount and amplitude increased the deeper an individual went into meditation. He learned that these gamma waves allowed a person to experience connectivity. They led your perception to a place where the vibrations of the mind were so minute as to be non-existent.

He knew meditation created stillness, in which one could observe the brain-induced chain reaction people call life. He could watch how brain activity triggered emotional and physiological responses, making a person move or feel. As the scientist of introspection he had become, Shiv was naturally most interested in locating the source of these chain reactions, the subtlest of energies that set denser matter in motion. And he wanted to attain this goal without having to build a Large Hadron Collider – circumference more than 26 kilometers – where they strove, deep under Swiss and French soil, to uncover the secrets of particle physics. He wanted to achieve this with nothing but the power of his mind. Concentration was the key word here. In order to track down the smallest particles, he needed to focus his five senses inward, toward the minutest movements of his brain waves.

Just as in classical science, the path towards insight led from the coarse to the refined. Both were targeting the most elusive, the minutest particle. On the introspective path you could experience these tiny particles – you actually became them – whereas trying to detect them with the use of technology was an intellectual concept.

Shiv likened meditation to looking at an empty screen. It induced calmness and a limitless happiness. It was wholly unspectacular yet more desirable than anything his five senses could drag in. In time, his meditation had taken him to the realm his mother had been so insistent about. A place where nothing was separate, where he felt he could touch the fabric of life, make out the individual threads, and even sense the weaver.

When the view cleared even more, Shiv realized he had developed something like a super sense. He dove into a swirling world of particles, of which his own body, mind and soul – every body, mind and soul in the universe – were part and parcel. These particles moved at different speeds, making up the four states of matter, from solid to plasma. In this world of form, every subatomic particle was animated by the subtlest of energies. He was not overawed by what he had experienced, for he had known this to be a scientific fact since childhood. But he was overwhelmed by the gulf between intellectually understanding and truly knowing.

Instead of basking in the world's gratitude and admiration for solving the planet's energy famine through nuclear fusion, Shiv had undergone fusion himself. In the depth of meditation, he had expanded beyond his physical limits, broken free of mental boundaries, and merged with what he called – for lack of a better word – 'it'. It was the finest, the most ethereal of substances. The mind could perceive it, but not become it. If you wanted to merge with it you had to let mind and body go.

Once Shiv had overcome the fear of quite literally losing his mind, he considered what he had experienced as the ultimate gift. Was this perhaps 'the message' the astrologer had burdened him with close to half a century ago? Was this what he had to convey to the world? Not as a guru or a shaman or a monk from a Tibetan monastery, but as a globally renowned fusion scientist.

He would tell them there is no duality – no birth or death – just a single life-sustaining energy in billions upon billions of different forms. All energies, all material things ultimately come from this one source, and all return to it. This substance animates the universe just as it animated Shiv and all his fellow travelers on Earth.

This knowledge gave him a definitive answer to his father's decade-old question, first posed at the golf club bar: how do you make a thought? They had been playful, and Shiv had laughed then. Now he wished he could tell his father, who had left his body behind some years ago: "It is not the 'I' that makes a thought. If there is no duality, then there is only one energy making hearts beat and thoughts project." And he would look at his father's loving face and tell him there is no beginning and no end. But perhaps his father had known that anyway, given how serenely he had moved to the next plane. When his time came to die, he had been unafraid, even eager to find what lay beyond the physical.

"I know you're aware that this beginning and end stuff, this linear thinking, is created by the human mind. And since the mind has a beginning and an end, it projects the same concept onto everything else, including the universe. It creates a Big Bang, because it desperately wants to pinpoint a beginning. But you and I, Dad, we know now that this is just nice theory. Reality is beyond movement, and since no motion means no time, then reality is eternity."

You have to experience it to understand it, his father might say, and talk about the seers who since time immemorial had reached those heights of knowledge. They went where particles ceased to move, catching a glimpse of the all-pervading substance they called Brahman, Father, Yahweh, Allah, Ishvara, Qi... and to which Shiv had given the name 'it'.

It was not only the answer to Ethan's question, It was the cause of everything. Everything! Shiv smiled, anticipating his father's objection. Of course, you could also say 'nothingness'. That would make sense to all those who did not believe in any kind of creator. The Chinese with their official atheism would have a definite advantage grasping this concept. Scientists could probably agree on calling 'it' zero. This was all the more appropriate since zero meant different things to different people. For some, 0 meant nothing, while to others, to the money people or the digital crowd for instance, 0 was everything. What an elegant concept. The 0 alone represented nothingness, but multiplied the value of every other number standing in front of it.

While deep in discussion with his dead father, Shiv suddenly thought of his professor friend in the U.S. Right after that memorable visit, which ended in such a dramatic way, Shiv had immersed himself even deeper in the "Theory of Everything." He had admired the intellectual framework, the boldness of thought and the mathematical beauty of it. He had enjoyed wrapping his mind around such a complex concept. But actually experiencing the physiological consequences of this theory literally blew his mind. Shiv caught himself grinning widely. Had perhaps the sly professor come up with his elegant framework through a similar experience?

And what about Ali, Reto, Barb and Haki? Had they come up with answers to "Who am I?" He was particularly curious about Reto, this very decent Swiss guy, whom Shiv liked so much for his down-to-earth manner. The man was really rock-solid, just like the mountains he stemmed from. Yet he had an openness of mind that freed him from being too earth-bound, a willingness to change his point of view when so convinced. Wasn't this all it really took? No matter what your character – if you kept an open mind then you could fly!

Now there was an experience Shiv would most certainly keep to himself. He would never forget it as long as he lived, and he had no wish to repeat it. It had felt like flying, well like floating at least. And it had happened just a few weeks ago. He had just attained full concentration in meditation when his self-awareness began to melt away. What happened then was difficult to put into words. While in a deep state of meditation his body had lifted off the ground – not mentally – physically.

How would you relate this fact to anyone? Over coffee with your colleagues at the lab, saying, "Hey, and by the way, I did a bit of flying last night!" But that's exactly what had happened. He had literally levitated, just like those Tibetan monks he had read about, or some of the Christian spiritual masters. He had actually overcome gravity, or gravity had momentarily withdrawn from him – letting him experience weightlessness. He had come to the end of his existence as Shiv Singh Sitaram, his consciousness, his identity completely dissolved in this substance he could not name.

When suddenly gravity grabbed hold of him once more – gently tugging him into substance and consciousness, and his I-identity returned – his mind brought back what he later called a formula of truth or what in his culture went under the name of mantra:

I am the eternal – the immortal – the all pervading. I am 'it'.

Upon regaining full consciousness, his lips were repeating this formula. He felt deeply satisfied mouthing this code as proof of having reached that elusive place described in many Eastern scriptures.

Shiv was extremely reluctant to talk about this. But he wanted to share it with his mother at least, as a gift. Devi, true to form, had once again completely thrown him. She had actually sunk to her knees, trying to kiss his 'lotus feet,' as if he were a guru! He had quickly helped her rise from her knees, sat her down in a chair, and told her in no uncertain words to come to her senses. "This guru stuff is the opposite of what this experience has taught me! Everybody can have it. Every human being is fully equipped for it. And instead of eating up what someone else has experienced, people should apply themselves. The only guru worth following is your inner reality. Instead of listening to masters or teachers, humans should think for themselves, use what nature has given them. So, please accept the fact that I am a scientist, and I will die a scientist!"

"Yes, of course you are, my exceptional son, but an average person cannot understand science or creation at your level. They need spiritual uplifting and guidance, that's why they need gods and gurus."

Shiv conceded the point. "I have to admit that in my scientific arrogance I long considered gurus, holy men and the whole assortment of gods as so many fools. But my view has altered. Inner vision is a fact. The tricky question is how do you pass it on? Should you even pass it on? OK, you can formulate it in numbers like Pythagoras; clothe it in words like Plato; compose it in sounds like Beethoven in his 9th; in paintings like Leonardo da Vinci; or in songs like Guru Nanak. You can wrap it in stories and give your experiences identities like in the Mahabharata for instance. Now for me, personally, mathematics is the purest of all these forms...."

Devi had smiled at that, her composure regained, dark eyes even more hooded by age, but still glowing with love for the son who had been entrusted to her. Looking at him now, a man who had delved far deeper into the secrets of life than they could ever imagine, Devi thought about a story from the Vedas. It said the mind is like a magnet causing the soul to reincarnate as long as there is unfinished business. Depending on the mind material, the soul incarnates at a certain place with certain parents. She and Gopal had obviously needed to keep room for this particular soul. With deep gratitude she bowed to the gods who had given this shivan mukta, this liberated soul, into their care.

"No matter how you feel about these things, you are a Buddha now."

The answer came in a tone of exasperation: "You just can't leave it alone, can you?"

"There's nothing otherworldly or esoteric about this, Shiv. Think about it. Buddhi is the Sanskrit word for intellect. And someone who discovers the unity of all things within himself, has activated the inner intellect, the buddhi, and is therefore called a Buddha."

"So Buddha is some kind of technical term?"

"Yes, you could say that. Or you could call it a job title, like bookkeeper or physicist," Devi smiled, knowing full well that giving the statement a technical twist would not raise her son's hackles.

"So, a Buddhist is a student of the inner intellect...." And as if to test her, he asked: "But how would you describe this inner intellect more precisely?"

"Buddhi conveys a holistic vision of whatever is in and around you. We usually call these experiences insights, while what most people call intellect is nothing more than an aptitude to learn stuff easily by heart, coupled with an excellent memory...."

Not for the first time, Shiv marveled at his mother's eclectic knowledge. And when he told her so, she smiled, her obvious pleasure tinged with shyness.

Shiv didn't let on how thankful and happy he was. It's like he wanted to conserve these feelings inside. While still slightly embarrassed by this levitation thing, he was deeply pleased he had fused science and religion for himself. What he experienced, what others before him had experienced and clothed in religious stories, was scientifically fathomable. There was nothing miraculous about such occurrences, not even about the guy over there in the Middle East supposedly taking a hike across the lake a couple of thousand years ago. People called them miracles because they could not rationally explain them yet, due to a simple lack of scientific discoveries and knowledge. Understanding the laws of the universe will eventually allow rational and calm explanations of these phenomena.

Shiv – body, mind and soul – is very much at peace.

13

The Declaration

Sprawled in his swivel chair, Marvin stared at a transparent screen in their control station. With a magician's flair, he'd conjured up part of the Antarctic coastline. Earth's coldest and windiest continent – cloaked in up to two miles of ice – was definitely coming out of hibernation. He watched fascinated as building-sized chunks of ice sheared off and thundered into the water.

A slight increase in temperature was all it took to change this seemingly eternal ice from solid to liquid. Marvin was satisfied. Temperature was nothing more than a measure of particle speed. And if this speed was to be increased – mission cloak particles included – the average planetary temperature needed to rise. Higher speed allowed particles more freedom of movement, a prerequisite for the upgrade to load properly. If the Forces did their job right, they'd be the unsung heroes – steering Mother Earth into the next phase without too much damage. OK, a hundred or so million people living in low-lying coastal areas might get wet feet. That was inevitable. But most probably, they would have enough time to prepare and relocate. Others wouldn't be so lucky; when Ave and he had charted the way forward, they noticed an unavoidable increase in so-called natural disasters. And not just the standard flood and fire, but also some of the big-ticket items like earthquakes and volcanoes. The upside was – hopefully – that the mayhem might wean humans off their strange urge to acquire and hoard possessions ... not a useful trait when mobility would be key.

Ave and he would turn this planet into one giant learning arena with a single goal: collaboration based on radically new ideas. There would be climate change in more ways than one! It would spur the global community into coordinated action: plenty of opportunities for all these souls coming to this planet to gain experience. Marvin smiled at the image. Souls, keen on getting to work, rolling up the sleeves of their mission cloaks to do the job called life. And there'd be plenty for these eager souls to do – no sitting around whining or getting in each other's way, but preparing the planet for the billions more job seekers to arrive.

"How's it going with the shakes, bro? Things calming down?" Avory interrupted his musings.

"Well ... the indicators are unsteady – rotational speed is very variable. If it doesn't stabilize, we could go into a serious wobble. Don't want to think about what happens then. I have another little scenario keeping me on my toes: if excessive melt from the Greenland ice cap messes with the Great Ocean Conveyor – Gulf Stream included – we might get our butts frozen."

"Not very conducive to our upgrade! We don't want ice cubes chilling the general particle acceleration."

"Whole thing's pretty tricky, my man. Maybe you could give me a hand, if your species update leaves you any time?" Victoria broke up their banter by informing Marvin that the global surface was slightly over-cooking. Perhaps he should stay focused on what was happening in Antarctica. "Oh dear me, Miz V., I had so much fun watching that big sucker break up, I forgot to monitor the temperature. No biggie, I'll get to it right now." But Marvin's nonchalance was unconvincing. He knew how important it was to be meticulous. The planet must remain tolerably stable during transformation. "Before I go. Any news from our... no, I won't call them lab rats... our five specimens? Our shining stars?"

"Should you by any chance be referring to our five human friends who have shouldered the major task of heralding the age of inner independence? Yes, as a matter of fact, we'll soon be catching up with them."

"Pray tell, Victoria dear," Marvin said with mock servility. "To what good fortune do we owe this pleasure?"

"Your Victorian phrasing is not convincing, Marvin! It's getting time to wrap up our assignment here on Earth. When the five gather in Indian Wells, they'll do what's necessary to trigger the new programs in all humans." Victoria gave Marvin and Avory an affectionate look.

"Do you think they will finally get what's been in their myths for almost as long as there have been humans? Will they understand the big picture? Like the few who could think beyond catching a woolly mammoth, or turning plants into alcohol, or ensuring survival of the species by distributing their sperm as widely as possible."

Avory grinned at Marvin's description of humanity's major preoccupations. "Will they finally realize they are never alone – that we and Big G are always active within their mission cloaks and in all that surrounds them?" After a moment he added "and that their ultimate guide is within?"

"I'm sure ... in time. They will understand that whatever they encounter is just another opportunity to increase personal power, gain deeper understanding and compassion. They'll realize they don't need saving..."

"... Because they have always been in a state of grace. They simply forget this when they don the mission cloak!" Marvin shook his head. "What a hideous set-up, what a devilishly clever trap humans have set each other with all this sinner and savior stuff!"

"Just think about it for a moment, Marvin. It would be quite a shock to accept that all particles are a projection of one single force. This is really at the heart of all mysteries. Remember how eons ago, we four Forces also had to concede that we were nothing but expressions of 'it'? I recall one particular force had great difficulty accepting this."

Marvin was suddenly very busy inspecting one of the screens.

"We accepted that we would never fully understand, and so now we are content to play our role in the pre-determined game. It's the same for our human friends. The upgrade allows for deeper understanding, lifting the veil from so-called secret knowledge."

When Victoria headed upstairs again, Marvin turned to look at Avory. "Realizing the truth about human identity will come as quite a shock to most..."

"...yeah, lots of humans might be thrown off track, when they realize they are just a player in a pre-determined game. But it's a beneficial shock. Offloading the burden of ego can be a tremendous relief. Now I'm even more curious to see what our five friends are up to, how well they've recovered from their lessons in detachment! Pretty grueling stuff they experienced. Sure hope they broke through."

Marvin had the last word. "Well, all that suffering would have been pointless if they are just as unknowing as before."

◆

Renato Ritter put down his glass very carefully. He was ready for the meeting of minds and hearts he had pondered for many months and finally arranged on the spur of the moment. He had felt an increasing urge to see the four women and men again whom fate hat thrown together a decade ago – Haki, who had gone back to her homeland in Africa, vivacious Barb, whom they had accompanied through such dramatic times in Indian Wells, Shiv, the man with the awesome mind, probably still trying to bring the sun to earth, attempting fusion, and cool Ali Ben Calif, the lively Arab, whom Reto thought of as a true friend. He wanted to share his experiences and, Reto wouldn't have been Reto, if he didn't want to compare results, convinced that this would afford them all a wider view, an understanding of some grander truth. Knowing how risky it was to bring four busy, independent individuals together at short notice, he had sent out invitations anyway. "Let's ring in the New Year together in Indian Wells. Villas at the best hotel – butler service and golf facilities included – first-class plane tickets arranged!" The rest he left to fate.

He'd been sitting and reading by the villa pool for half an hour, when he became aware of someone doing their best not to be heard. He turned with a big smile, and Barb literally jumped into his arms. "I figured I'd be first, since I didn't have far to come. But I also wanted to have you to myself for a moment!" Barb pulled over a rattan lounge chair and fell into it with a dramatic sigh. "You look great, Reto, different."

"Yes, the ageing process has obviously not passed me by ... quite in contrast to you, I might add!"

"No, no, no, that's not it at all. You look better! Much better. But also distinctly different." Barb frowned in concentration for a moment. "You were like the cocky type, you know, very self-assured, almost a touch showy. That's all gone, I see that immediately." She bit her lower lip for a moment. Reto noticed the still very alluring mouth, now bracketed by fine lines. "You appear much more fluid somehow, warmer too, accessible...."

They looked at one another with surprise, realizing how easily they had bridged the years.

"I could sure do with one of these ice-cold Cokes you guys are hogging!" Ali grinned sheepishly at the man and woman on the terrace. "Hope I'm not intruding?"

Contrary to how she had greeted Reto, it was a much more subdued Barb who held out a hand to greet Ali. The angular lines age had chiseled into his features only added to his handsomeness. When she dared look into his bottomless dark eyes, she felt butterflies in her belly, and also a twinge of fear.

"Ali, how wonderful to see you again," she said politely before feeling weak in the knees as the fabulous looking Arab pulled her into a warm embrace. "Time has only added to your beauty, Barb. What kind of magic do you know? You could make billions with it." She had never been able to resist flattery, especially when bestowed like a precious gift.

Only Reto heard the light tread on the flagstones. He'd gotten quite a kick out of seeing the sparks flying between Ali and Barb the moment they had become aware of each other.

Wow. Would be interesting to see how that developed. But then all such thoughts vanished. A figure walked between the palms like a head of state passing an honor guard. Head held high on a long and graceful neck, her tall and slender body in fluid motion. Reto had flashbacks to the party where Haki had made heads turn. Now he saw a woman in her prime, a queen.

"Seems to be my destiny to be last." His lilting English was unmistakable. All four turned in unison to greet the lanky Indian, to whom the years had not added an ounce. Reto squinted and stared. Was it a trick of the sun playing on the water? Somehow Shiv's slim frame seemed enveloped in a weird shimmering light.

When they were all properly greeted and settled, an amicable silence descended. It felt as if they needn't talk just yet, but get the feel of each other – literally.

"We are gathered here today..." Barb began with syrupy pathos, then grinned and added, "That's the question, isn't it? Anyone care to answer?"

"Since I arranged this get-together," Reto said, "I'd better do some explaining. First of all, I'm so happy you are all here ... at such short notice and without asking for explanations. Shows I still have the touch." Reto laughed at himself.

"An uncanny knack for timing, I agree. Typical lawyer," Ali quipped.

"It's been ten years since we met. Years that have been the most interesting and rewarding of my life." Reto looked at his friends, who nodded and smiled in understanding when he added, "and the hardest, too." He turned to Barb. "It was actually your father's last question, the one he left us with at the fateful party where we first met, that set me on a journey to find an answer, my own answer. Much as I tried, I couldn't ignore his question. It just wouldn't go away." Reto smiled as the others nodded again or muttered "same here" and "don't I know it."

"I'm not prone to esoterics, none of that stuff. I consider myself quite sober and levelheaded. But I realized what has happened to us was no coincidence. It is much more. I'm just not sure what the more is...." Grinning sheepishly Reto looked at the others, worried he had just made a fool of himself.

Ali came to his rescue. "I know what you're saying, Reto. Look, I don't talk much about myself either – don't really see the purpose or benefit. But when I got your invitation, it was like a summons. I couldn't ignore or refuse it. I just knew I had to come, wanted to come. I still feel it's the right moment to be here – because we do have an assignment together." Ali's voice had lost all hesitancy and taken on a quiet conviction.

A smile twitched at the corners of his mouth as Barb grabbed his arm and cut in excitedly. "A quest, it's like Dad sent us on a quest, to answer probably the most important question a human being could or should ask. And he didn't want just one answer, but five. And I tell you what, I can't wait to hear about your particular journey, and whether the essence of your discovery is similar to mine."

Shiv didn't say anything. He agreed with what was said. He was convinced they had, for whatever reason, been sent out to procure answers – and were supposed to act on them. But how could he relate his experiences without feeling like a complete freak? It had been difficult enough to talk to his mother about it, let alone four people he'd met just once – ten years ago.

Haki also kept quiet. She felt completely at ease. That was the first surprise. She felt a sense of belonging, maybe even of destiny. That was exactly what Ethan would have wished for, she mused. That we come together again, share our thoughts and innermost feelings, and find an answer to who and what we are. If we can figure it out, and dare to believe the answer, then the universe would – Haki had no doubt – reverberate with joy. But was she the only one who thought so? Perhaps the others had come to completely different conclusions? Haki was reassured by a glance at Reto. He radiated such quiet strength and confidence. As long as he was with this group, she would feel safe.

◆

When Marvin complained that the five friends were just hanging out jibber jabbering and he couldn't make out any sign of upgrade – only that their mission cloaks were a bit worse for wear – Big G commented that Marvin greatly lacked patience and depth of observation. Instead of focusing on all the normal human stuff, he should perhaps take a look at their mission cloaks – not the outermost layer, but the structure. Marvin focused on the vibratory pattern of the quintet's physical forms and breathed a soft 'wow'.

"Check-out their particles, man, they bloody rock!"

Avory saw it too. There was barely anything out of whack. Transparent, harmonious, all particle dullness gone. Perfect hue and saturation. "Sleek," Marvin commented.

The cloaks were really state-of-the-art. A human in such a mission cloak would feel part of a greater plan – instead of like an isolated stranger in a strange land. They'd feel and correctly judge their own position and would better sense the position of others.

"Humankind," Victoria said softly, "will mature from 'I' to 'We,' and from 'have' to 'be' – a much more compassionate mental state."

This new perception would also mean a new interpretation of the moral code, which had been stored in every human being since the beginning, like a kind of compass. They would inherently feel what was right and true. Victoria concluded, "When thoughts, words and actions are in line, a human can harvest the combined power of all three. This new awareness will lead to absolute individual responsibility. And I mean absolute! You have to master your own life before you lecture others.... This also means, there's nowhere you can lay blame."

◆

The second day of the gathering did California proud. Reto felt right at home. He loved the view through the palms toward snow-capped Mt. San Jacinto, its peak an impressive 10,400' above the valley floor. After the intensity of the first evening, they decided to play golf before resuming their discussions. A bit of exercise would be a good thing, and Barb knew a fun Par 3 course where one had to walk rather than just sit and drive a cart.

The only one not completely happy with the outing was Reto. So sure of being the best player, he was forced to concede the crown to Shiv. He still couldn't get over how this giraffe could coordinate his long limbs into one perfect swing after another. The guy's iron play had the precision of a damn guided missile. What's more, Reto had to do his utmost not to be bettered by Barb, who played a fine game. But his having to give Haki a helping hand made losing a touch more bearable. He almost didn't mind at all, he proudly noted to himself.

At sundown they gathered by the pool, each with some combination of freshly pressed local citrus. Barb was the first to break the comfortable silence.

"This group silence thing would have driven me crazy before. I'd get more and more antsy, like a volcano waiting to erupt. Finally words just spewed out... Any words would do, just so they filled the void." She glanced at the four understanding faces. "But it's so different with you guys. Being silent with you is more like creating space – a lake into which we flow and merge. There is no need for words. On the contrary, words only disguise or distort how I perceive you." Barb shook her head impatiently. "See how inept words are." Again she looked at the others, who smiled and nodded. They seemed to know just what she meant.

Then Ali spoke up: "I know exactly how you felt, Barb. Stillness, immobility and quiet were my worst enemies for as long as I can remember. I used to feel I was dead if nothing moved around me or I didn't move myself." He flashed a smile that made her butterflies take flight again. "Until life pulled the rug from under me and sat me down for a while."

"Me, it flung down!" Reto chuckled as he looked at the others.

"Oh, and I got to experience how it is to move without a body at all." Haki hadn't really wanted to blurt that out. Her dark complexion couldn't hide the blush rising to her cheeks. Reto quickly took her hand and gave it a reassuring squeeze.

When he felt their eyes on him, Shiv felt compelled to add, "I'm not surprised to hear what you're saying. I too was impelled to change directions – inward and upward."

When no details were forthcoming, Ali spoke up again. "Look, we're not here in beautiful California just to work on our tans or our chipping and putting– as much as I like doing so," he added with a grin that made Barb's stomach flutter yet again.

"You're right. I did have a bit of a plan when I invited you here. You're under no obligation of course, but we could start by briefly sharing our stories. If my hunch is correct, I wouldn't be surprised if we have been led to similar conclusions, but via very different routes."

"Oh, I love the idea, Reto. I am curious...." When the others cracked up, Barb frowned at first then also started to chuckle. "I was born that way, right, I remember! OK, I'm still curious – a very important trait for the future – and I'm more serious than I used to be."

Remembering the tragic night of the party still made Barb sad. Bantering with her new friends and her dad in the gazebo – and having suddenly to let him go. But it was no longer a crippling sadness, more like a familiar melancholy, one you held close for a moment and then let go without regret. "Anyhow, I am all for this exchange. I'm sure there's more to come out of it than just talk. But this hotel just doesn't have the right vibes! Tell you what. I still have Dad's house down the road, and there's plenty of room for all of us without anyone having to share a bed." Now why had she said that? She didn't dare glance over at Ali. He'd probably think her a hopelessly seductive flirt and a bimbo.

Before Barb dug a deeper hole, Ali said quietly, "I second that idea. As comfortable as Reto made us here, for which I am most grateful," he glanced around at the perfectly styled luxury, "it's just a hotel with a hotel's atmosphere. I also feel we need to be somewhere more, I don't know, intimate maybe. And since Ethan had such a deep impact on our lives, I think it fitting to be in his house while we figure out what we are supposed to do.

It was a quick and unanimous decision. In the morning they'd move to the very place from where they had embarked on their journey.

◆

"Stop. Right. Now!" Victoria's voice left no room for objection.

The oranges stopped in mid-air, hovered for a moment above the sparkling pool, then vanished. Avory and Marvin, soaking wet and laughing wildly, shook themselves like large dogs, water arcing into showers of tiny rainbows. Shiv stared open-mouthed at the mesmerizing dance created by a million tiny bursts of color. He had just stepped out on the terrace while the others were choosing their rooms. As he took in the almost surreal contrast between the immaculately manicured fairway and the craggy, fractured mountainside rising just yards from the house, he was distracted by a commotion at the pool. He had not really seen anything save this amazing light show and before he could move or call out to the others, it was gone. Extinguished. Maybe he had imagined it?

"Phew! That was close. And it had to be the space cadet of course. Wonder what he saw? Hopefully not your naked butt hanging off the waterfall, dude! We'd have probably lost him there and then." Marvin whacked Avory's backside, as they quickly made their way across the lawn and through the hedge.

"Nah, I think we accelerated just enough to get above the range of human visibility. Gave him something to ponder though, the weird behavior of water!"

"One more of those stunts and it's back to the Plasma Cube! I'll be glad when we can wrap up this assignment," Victoria allowed herself a small sigh. "You are starting to identify a bit too much with your human form."

"Aw, come on, Miss Fusion, lighten up! You know perfectly well how restricting these mission cloaks are. May as well make the most of it while we're condemned to wear them."

Victoria smiled. They were right. Why not get the most enjoyment out of this mission? It would do Marvin good – increase his tolerance for what the human species had to contend with. "That's correct, Marvin. Fusion is what our five friends hopefully will achieve in the end. Fusion of different world views, of conflicting concepts, and – eventually – of time and space."

"C'mon ... it's not rocket science! All they have to do is read the ancient scriptures. It's been known and written about ever since they learned to use proper words. But we've chewed that cud already, haven't we?"

"Yes, but we need to focus on it again and again. It's the core part: humanity's destiny to integrate the eternal wisdom. Sure, the knowledge that has always been here on this planet, but..."

"...But they just didn't have enough RAM or a powerful enough processor to recognize it," Marvin just couldn't keep quiet. "It's like this morsel of truth had been hidden somewhere in their brain – like some sort of benevolent computer virus – waiting until the software was capable of reading and activating it."

◆

On the seventh day, when according to Genesis God ended his work and rested, the five friends set to work. They had enjoyed a grand week hiking amid tall ocotillo and barrel cacti, sagebrush and desert milkweed – coming upon miraculous groups of fan palms wherever the San Andreas Fault had arranged a water supply. After an outing to Joshua Tree, they had returned via the Salton Sea, another creation of plate tectonics and currently California's largest lake by virtue of a human misstep a century before.

They had played more golf of course, with Reto managing to come out ahead at least once. Tennis too – in the shadow of the stadium where the international circuit competed once a year. They had ventured out on bikes to sample the area's dining spots, trying local, Mexican, Chinese and Indian cuisine. Sometimes they had cooked at home, using Karl Marx as guide: from each according to his ability, to each according to his need.

And they had talked, opening up in ways they had not thought possible. However diverse their experiences, it was as if they spoke a common language – readily understanding what each had gone through and the conclusions they had drawn.

Now they were sitting as usual on the terrace amidst the profusion of orange and pink bougainvillea. "Could this really be the threshold of a new age?" Ali had asked, before quickly adding that the actual term was off-limits. It had been hijacked too many times already.

"It's not totally off the wall, is it?" said Reto.

"It's not only plausible, I think it's absolutely necessary!" Haki's quiet voice carried conviction. "We know humanity cannot continue on its current path, adhering to concepts developed when only half a billion humans roamed the planet."

Barb looked at Haki with shining eyes. "What I have learned – through life-shattering heartbreak and crippling emotional pain – is that at its core, all life is the same. The borders we draw between genders, nationalities, religions, cultures are only superficial."

"I have a little story about transcending borders, physical and mental ones." Shiv began slowly then went on to share his levitation experience with them. He was very sober about it, very scientific. He explained, in a way they all understood, how gravity could be overcome. Haki pointed out that Theresa of Avila had also levitated during deep meditation. And when Reto joked about the flying yogis in Switzerland, Haki set him straight by declaring that he in particular might appreciate this 16th century Spanish mystic, since she had not only been a very spiritual person, but also wielded considerable worldly power: reorganizing the Carmelite order, founding a number of monasteries and traveling extensively. This powerful and wise woman had been a constant inspiration to Haki, while she set up and ran her bush hospitals.

She turned to Shiv: "You see, your experience is proof of the potential we are now discovering." And these simple words removed any unease Shiv still felt when talking about his levitation.

"If I had to find the common denominator in all our highly dramatic stories, I'd say we've each, very obviously, matured. We are endowed with independence free of external influences. I would call it true or inner independence, because it cannot be taken away by anyone or anything." Shiv looked at each of them and found them nodding and smiling in agreement.

"You really get right to the point, don't you fusion man!" Ali grinned at the man he had come to admire so much, even though the palpable depth of Shiv's being and his awesome capacity for thought were more than a touch intimidating. But Ali had learned not to envy another's qualities, nor fear them. Part of inner independence lay precisely there – in liking someone for who they were, in appreciating aspects of their personality that might be lacking in your own. "I agree wholeheartedly. Through my burnout and inner search in the desert I have gained qualities that cannot be lost or taken away. They are always with me," he laughed out loud, "... just like the proverbial force!"

Barb started humming the theme music from Star Wars and wrapped Ali in one of her dazzling smiles.

"The qualities I've gained from my pain and fear have greatly increased my personal power," Reto said earnestly. "It's a different kind of power than before, not dependent on my legal victories or how fast I climb a mountain. Self-confidence from this new power does not rely on the external."

"I'm so glad you mention this, Reto," Haki said and lightly touched his arm. "You may remember me, barely out of my braids. I hardly dared open my mouth for fear of being ridiculed – always close to tears. I've learned there is no point trying to please others just so they might like you. What a fallacy! What matters is to think independently and act in accordance with your heart."

Barb gave Haki an affectionate squeeze. "You've turned into a real tigress, friend. I don't sense much pussycat in you anymore, even though you come across as gentle as always. I see you as the quintessential modern businesswoman." Barb continued, "And I know exactly what you all are talking about. You know what? We've gained these new qualities through experiences we believed at the time to be great misfortunes. It was complete devastation for me, when Dad died. And had I told you then that you, Reto, were about to fall off a mountain and break your back or that you, Ali, would loose all interest in your work and head for the desert in search of your soul ... you wouldn't have believed a word of it! But that's how we humans are, aren't we? Trying all the tricks to avoid sickness, pain, loss – the very experiences that might give us more maturity, strength and inner independence."

◆

"Has the penny finally dropped?"
Avory made a shushing gesture at Marvin and whispered:
"They got part of it, but are still one step away."

The twins were fooling around on the 12th hole – near where the fairway squeezed between the Bernstein mansion and the rocky hillside. Being consummate switch-hitters each wielded weird double-sided golf clubs. Needless to say, every shot went straight into the cup – despite the darkness. Victoria appeared beside them on the green. Together they moved over to a group of tall palms and lay down on the smooth grass. They shouldn't be surprised if humans were getting good at the games the twins created for themselves, Victoria forewarned them, since the upgrade bridged the two brain halves and stimulated the creative side. This would help people think calmly and confidently, knowing they have the capacity to solve problems that seem insurmountable at the moment – migration, world hunger, climate change, huge economic disparity, continuing conflicts. "Solving such challenges will lead humans into situations where they simply have to create new approaches, global approaches. And creativity, especially developing new solutions, has as we know a direct influence on brain structure."

The twins were familiar with this topic. They were aware that new thoughts induced the human brain to make new connections, kind of like rewiring itself. In fact, humans really shaped their brains with the input they received. Marvin figured the famous Apollo 8 earthrise image must have caused a synaptic tsunami. Floating against the inky blackness of space the sight of that exquisite blue jewel – then home to some 3.5 billion humans – must have caused a serious jump in mental development. For the brain network to change, humans didn't even have to act out their thoughts. Enough stimulation – such as learning a new skill, solving a problem, taking a journey, even looking at an issue from a fresh angle – caused new synapses to be formed, producing a permanent change in the brain. Kind of wonderful, wasn't it?

"Not kind of," Avory piped in. "It is wonderful! Wonderful knowing there's capacity for change – that you're not stuck with a hardwired blob of grey matter, but can directly influence the flexibility and mobility of the thing by purposeful thinking or learning."

♦

"I can't believe how completely I have misunderstood the term independence before." Reto looked at Ali whom he was sure would understand exactly what he meant.

The group had moved indoors. Barb had lit a fire in the open hearth. Reto felt right at home. All that was missing was the fragrant smoke of the cigars he had given up some time ago. Hampered his breathing, he realized, once he had discovered what breathing could really do for you. The five were lounging comfortably on low sofas and elegant fauteuils. A couple of large opaque spheres illuminated the spacious living room with a warm yellowish light. On one of the walls hung a large photo of a group of Peruvian kids grinning hugely into the camera. Looking at it, you involuntarily grinned back.

It was Haki who answered Reto. "Independence is a favorite word of warlords. What they actually mean is that they want the independence to exploit a country and its people for themselves."

Barb stayed quiet, apparently deep in thought. She was thinking of her own distorted sense of independence, which had led her on countless detours and down many a dead-end. Going against traditions, rules and regulations had felt freeing and radical at the time, until she realized she was hurting no one but herself. Even so, it had still felt right to set her own standards and follow her own laws – rather than marching in lock step with the dictates of convention.

"True independence is knowing you have direct access to your inner power source."

"Wow!" It was more like a sigh, from an Ali who seemed shaken to the core. He rose slowly and wandered over to the fire, before turning to look at Shiv. "There's no way you could have known, but I returned from the desert with the exact same phrase – direct access. Every human is rigged for it. There's no need for people to show you the way or tell you what to think or do. A human being contains a built-in module allowing him or her to access the highest truth. Somehow, seems to me anyway, this module is only now becoming active."

Barb got up, walked over to Ali, and stood next to him. "We have all experienced just that, haven't we? Hard lessons have taught us to let go of what we held closest and..." she gave one of her mischievous smiles "... tightest."

"But you stand no chance in this game of tug of war with life! What a tough lesson to learn for a guy who always wants to win." Reto was grinning too.

"I feel I have gone through a very personal version of the Theory of Everything – an idea which some of the most brilliant minds are trying to put into scientific terms." Shiv was looking at each of them, to make sure they understood what he wanted to convey. "In deep meditation I went where all knowledge fuses, where everything disassembles, dissolves and merges into nothingness. This neurochemical experience taught me that nothingness is the ultimate reality, just as the Theory of Everything proposes. Of course, you could call this nothingness 'fusion substance,' Brahman, God, Allah, Ishwara, Qi or whatever you want. I personally like the neutral expression 'it'. There are probably plenty of people intellectually, mentally and emotionally independent enough to come up with integrative philosophical concepts when looking at human life on this planet – but my experience taught me that at the end of all science, all philosophy, all religion lies this mysterious substance 'it'. We're talking fusion here, not fission."

Again Shiv paused to gather his thoughts. "I feel united in time and space with the mystics of all ages. And I am convinced that every individual has his or her independent path towards 'it'. All you have to do is take the first step. This fusion view marks a beginning, just like the five of us stand at a beginning; perhaps marking the end of this stubborn identification with only one country, one culture or one religion."

Barb was thrilled to hear Shiv's words, because she had played around with an idea for a couple of days now, ever since they had started closing in on this subject of true independence. Now Shiv had given her the right cue. Wasn't it still the most important piece of American literature: the Declaration of Independence as created by the Founding Fathers some 250 years ago? Of course, then it was a declaration of independence from an occupying power, but the words touched – to this day – people's hearts and minds. "And who said important thoughts, philosophies and such should all be male, pale and stale? We should write a new Declaration of Independence, the Declaration of Inner Independence."

The reaction was immediate. They all started talking at the same time. Ali pointed out that the original Declaration completely lacked any reference to what an individual should do with this 'independence'. This would have to be the key new part! Reto was talking about the recent finding in Jefferson's manuscript – where the term 'subjects' had been carefully erased and replaced with 'citizens', itself a major step up from the old ways. Instead of bowing to a king, citizens shared in the power and could rule themselves. Yes, Ali had interjected, but on what philosophical basis? A new democratic concept had indeed been crafted, but still based on religiously dominated, hierarchically structured philosophical concepts thousands of years old. Made for goat herders, living on a flat earth, with the sun revolving around them....

Reto said Jefferson seemed to realize this, since he and Benjamin Franklin then demanded the separation of church and state. Except the good citizens were left in the dark about this. "But now, more than ever in history, people around the globe begin to ask themselves: What does this mysterious, far away god want from me? Does he want me to kill for him or turn the other cheek? Who are his rightful representatives here on Earth? Does this far-away god care whether his self-appointed representatives are male, live in celibacy, are circumcised, or demand women be hidden underneath dark shrouds?"

When Reto paused, Haki added that if they were to take this direct access seriously, wouldn't the next logical step be to place the remote god inside every human? Wasn't that what this famous second coming was all about anyway?

"Yes, yes, yes." Reto had responded enthusiastically. "That's precisely what will happen, and then the 'citizen' will be recognized as a responsible and independent 'individual'! The right to vote for political representation is fine, but it hasn't much to do with real independence or self discipline."

Ali jumped into the fray again. "What today passes for democracy will seem like kindergarten in the future. Same goes for our traditional mosques, temples and churches. They have guided humanity to this threshold, but now we need to find our own answers to the questions 'why are we on this planet, where do we come from, what is our mission here, where are we headed?' Only then will true democracy and true caritas become possible. And true independence will be reached only when religious directives and political powers – legislative, executive and judicial – have become inner guidelines. After all, we are already equipped with a built-in, unerring moral compass."

Ali looked over to the now floodlit mountainside and said with a deep sigh, "True democracy would finally be achieved, further inspired perhaps by the first footsteps people have taken in my part of the world." Barb threw in her bit: "When you look at human DNA, we are all practically the same. Only about two percent make for all this diversity – and discord too. We all come into the world naked and we leave it naked. So what are we reasonably to do in between? Since we all belong to the same species, we should be able to come up with common answers, one would think."

And so they talked on – excited and thrilled by the possibilities they were uncovering together. Tossing around ideas, bouncing them off one another. They did agree that independence without direction would lead straight to chaos. Reto brought up the example of golf. Without flagsticks, where would you aim your swing? If all aimed in different directions, they'd probably soon use their clubs for other things! It was important to be clear about what one should concentrate on, what was sensible, reasonable, perhaps even wise.

"Any democratic society affording a certain amount of freedom to its citizens should agree on whether it wants to use that freedom wisely, as you say, or to acquire as many material goods as possible; or as much destructive power as its arsenals will hold." Barb's expression was very serious.

"Oh I agree so much, Barb." Haki picked up the thread. "But for society or humanity to decide on these vital matters, we must have an idea of what human life on this planet is all about – the true nature of man. Or, as someone we all knew said: Who and what am I?"

This was Shiv's cue. He too had thought about committing their insights to paper. It would be quite a challenge, he said, to find appropriate wording for a modern declaration. It would have to be understood by all, regardless of their cast, color, creed or education.... and moreover, without offending anyone. So that was the mother of all challenges right there! Plus there was another aspect, they were surely all aware of.

Shiv looked at four expectant faces. "You know how difficult it is to relate such deeply personal experiences. After all, Lao Tse once said 'those who talk do not know and those who know do not talk'. But, perhaps now is the time to talk, so why not give it a try, as long as we do not give out prescriptions."

Fully aware of the pitfalls but willing to give it a try, each agreed to put down a couple of key points, formulating as precisely and clearly as they could what true independence meant to them personally. It would help them focus.

◆

"Houston, hello, Houston, do you read me? We have lift-off." Marvin was playing ground control, fidgeting around with a handful of golf balls, making them rise and fall and whirr and spin in a crazy ballet.

"They are indeed doing great. This new software lives up to the promises of the designer." Victoria allowed herself a small smile. "Our job is nearly done. How do you 'feel' about that?"

Marvin leered at Avory and said: "Not having to look at your ugly mug all day long will be a serious relief, even if taking my shapely body out of the game is a great loss to humanity! Aside from that, I can't wait to give up form. I'm sure you know what I mean."

They wouldn't have to take form again to monitor the upgrade, Victoria said, placating him. The fusion-sense, which had become active in the five friends – since they had not only learned to focus their five senses inward, but also to align their individual wavelengths – let them recognize the secret knowledge of the ages: The one single player. And it was up to the best human scientists to strip away the complexity the human senses perceived, and uncover this stunning simplicity.

The increased particle speed in humans would allow individuals to understand that they were much more than the slower moving particles they called body and mind. Identifying with the fast-moving particles meant freedom from the dual forces – below and above, dark and light, good and bad, male and female.

"The 'I' will make a U-turn and realize all it ever needed – even its best friend and partner – is living within, and that the much-desired wedding chamber is a location in the brain, and not a bedroom!" Victoria smiled when the boys cracked up like teenagers. "The 'I' becomes aware of the unity of all creation and of the inherent divinity of man."

Marvin was down on his knees, hands towards Victoria like a sinner in the rapture of having found forgiveness. "Bless me, holy mother, bless your simple-minded child..."

"...Downright dimwitted, I'd say." Avory shoved Marvin, who pretended to fall, stiff as a board, onto his side.

"That's the only thing I'll be missing, bro." He grinned up at him. "Goofing around with you. This physical world definitely has its perks!"

"Isn't it just a tiny bit strange that we are here orchestrating this change to the third state of matter, but you, Marvin – who has had that knowledge for eons – you get attached to the first state, the slowest moving particles of the material world."

"But that's just it! I'm sure upgraded humans will finally appreciate the fantastic playground they've been given here. Tell you what: once that truth hits them, you'll see changes you won't believe. It's really going to be the Garden of Eden that their holy books have dangled in front of their noses from the word go."

Avory grinned and gave Marvin an affectionate squeeze, after helping him up. "What a wonderful sequel to that old tome. The key to entering paradise – the one they were kicked out of for hacking god's database – is knowing you don't need a key at all. It's always been open to everyone! All paradises are in the here and now, since it's a human's birthright to have direct access."

Victoria nodded. Time to write the next chapter in the great chronicle of evolution on planet Earth.

◆

The aroma of fresh croissants wafted under closed doors and warm duvets – so irresistible that soon the friends were seated around the breakfast table, sharing a companionable silence. Ali's special coffee, Shiv's delicious tea, an eclectic selection of baked goods Barb had hauled in on her bike, fresh juices blended by Haki, Reto's orange marmalade made to Nona's recipe – all elicited appreciative sounds and satisfied sighs.

With the table cleared, they followed Shiv out to their favorite spot on the terrace. "Haki, why don't you open this morning's session?" Shiv said and smiled at her. "I take it you've all done your homework?" The smiles coming back were equally warm and amiable.

"What surprised me most is that I didn't really have to think long and hard to come up with my answers. Once I focused on what Shiv asked us to do, it was almost immediately there. All I did was take time to properly phrase what I wanted to say. So, to me inner independence means

...Knowing death is nothing more than leaving the body behind and beginning an exciting new adventure.

...Knowing that everything, including our body, is a never ending dance of particles and that the inner eye can perceive the individual wavelength of these particles as the colors of the rainbow.

...Understanding that all of creation is steeped in compassion, and that compassion is the force that erases all differences and connects everything.

And perhaps on a very personal level, it means to me that you don't need to have your own child. All children can be your children."

Haki looked down at her hands folded in her lap, as if protecting her womb from this truth. She had, she knew, made peace with not having children; but her body still seemed to react to deep-seated patterns.

Shiv's eyes were filled with warmth that Haki felt, almost physically, on her skin. His nod said: thank you for opening up to us, for your courage to reveal yourself. Then he nodded at Reto.

"I assume we are not to comment each other's statements, even though I'd certainly like to hear more about perceiving solid matter as colored particle waves... So I'll just go on. I also had no difficulty coming up with the essence of what I've learned. Inner independence means to me

...Realizing that suffering is ultimately a path to power.

Suffering is a lesson in detachment, teaching you to turn inward. Inner independence therefore means knowing that real power lies within.

It might not surprise you that my insights focus on power. It's my main theme after all. So, again, inner independence means

...Knowing the real test of power comes when the external supports are removed – when the security we find in material possessions, in status, in a strong physique and in mental concepts is shattered."

"Suffering comes from clinging. This is the most excruciating lesson life has taught me." A subdued Barb glanced at her four friends. No, she wouldn't cry anymore. She had spilled enough saltwater to fill an ocean. Instead she smiled and added, "Inner independence is knowing that

...The Promised Land lies within, that it is a mental place. Those you love are never really lost to you.

You are never alone – you always walk with your master inside."

Ali was impressed. There was no sign of the finger painting he had made fun of at Ethan's funeral – a jest he was now ashamed of. What he saw was a woman in full bloom, glowing with an inner strength and serenity that had then seemed unattainable.

"OK, let me see what I can contribute to these really great thoughts. By the way, is someone writing this down or recording it at least?" When the others gave him a surprised look, he just shrugged and grinned. "Hey, I mean this is important stuff here, we might at some point want to share it with others!"

Barb jumped up, electrified. "Why hadn't I thought of this? That's my job, after all! I'm glad at least Ali's brain is working." Quickly she disappeared into the house and returned a couple of minutes later with her smart phone. "Let's just continue, OK? Then afterwards, we others should repeat what we said and record it too."

"I can make it pretty brief," Ali continued. "Inner independence to me is

...Keeping your self-confidence and composure wherever you are – in any culture, neighborhood or social circle – because you know and accept that everyone is made of the same stuff, and you have the flexibility to blend-in.

...After meditating and fasting I could finally read my in-built moral code, which I'm convinced, everyone has. I understand now what right action means. While running around in the busy world, you just can't decipher that code.

But most important to me is

...Knowing you always have direct access to your inner wisdom."

Shiv smiled at the expression. Great that the computer geek had come up with it too. Had a nice ring to it anyhow. He glanced beyond the flowering bushes, took in the golfers on the green, before turning to his small circle of friends.

"For me inner independence encompasses the following

...Knowing birth and death are just an illusion. Creation is simply particles changing from one state of matter to another. The total energy in the universe always stays the same – nothing is ever lost or added.

...Realizing that our bodies are made from stardust. We are a carbon-based species and carbon is formed within stars. Iron, the end product of fusion in the core of stars, gives our blood its color. We are stellar beings, not sinners.

...Knowing from personal experience that the essence of a human and the creating force of the universe are one and the same thing. So nothing is really 'man-made'.

...Realizing that this unity is the core of what has been called 'secret knowledge' – knowledge held back until now, especially in the West. And lastly I believe that

...Experiencing the unity of all things – fusion – is the sole purpose of human life."

The silence that spread after Shiv's declaration, spoken in his soft, lilting cadence, enveloped them in a translucent cloak of deep understanding.

"Let me tell you a story." Reto finally broke the spell. All eyes turned to him, alert and inviting.

"Years ago, before we met at that fateful party, a man paid a surprise visit to my Zürich office. My secretary announced him as Professor Benedetti, obviously Italian, but with no appointment save a bulging briefcase. He was elderly and frail, but impeccably turned out in an old-fashioned sort of way – you know, with that inimitable Italian elegance.

Roberto Benedetti held a post at the University of Padua – where Galileo had taught and Copernicus studied. Only later did I discover him to be one of the world's preeminent scholars of Latin, Coptic and old Greek. Modestly, he introduced himself as a simple translator of ancient scriptures. Then the story became really interesting. He was apparently one of the first scholars to set eyes on the Dead Sea Scrolls, which had been discovered in his youth. His special interest was the teachings of Jesus of Nazareth. Much of this he related when I met him a second time. This was when I resumed work after my accident." Reto smiled sheepishly "and my ensuing lessons in detachment."

More to himself he added, "He did give me an invaluable clue about how to view my personal suffering – advice from Jesus himself."

Then he shook his head as if to clear the memories and continued. "This encounter with Benedetti awakened my interest in what has become known as The Lost Gospels. I've closely followed their discovery and what has been learned from them – much of it thanks to Professor Benedetti's meticulous translations. Anyway, according to these texts, we have an extremely competent source validating what we – the five of us – individually have realized."

When the others looked at him expectantly he went on: "It is in Jesus' message to humanity: the kingdom of the father is within. In other words, the principle that animates the whole universe lies within every human and thus makes every human a divine being."

Reto shrugged. "Now after what we have shared these last few days, this might not come as news to you. But imagine, one of the greatest religious icons of humanity saying it so clearly and simply, with hardly anybody understanding the true meaning. Man has the divine spark within, and it is his mission – and his destiny – to bring that divinity forth in his lifetime. Jesus taught that the most sacred temple is the human body."

This time Ali broke in. "You mean this Benedetti had already discovered direct access decades ago, while we were still chasing after the next must-have gadget, ideal partner, or whatever was sure to provide lasting happiness? But look: our Islamic mystics – the Sufis – always maintained that god has imbued every human being with his divine spark. And there is a hadith, with words accorded to the prophet Muhammad. 'Each soul has its own religion and therefore access to god'. No surprise that the governing elite wasn't and still isn't interested in seeing this truth in print. It's not without serious consequences. Every human body a sacred temple – direct access to divinity." He shot a quick look at Shiv. "As I understand it, this is a core Buddhist concept as well, right?" When Shiv nodded, Ali continued: "It's not exactly in line with the orthodox doctrines of the times, let alone today. I'm sure the ruling Roman warrior class didn't like that kind of message, and neither do those who have built empires on the interpretation of god's will. He exhaled deeply and said: "This is a paradigm shift worth putting out on the world stage!"

"Yes, Ali," Reto smiled. "That's exactly how Benedetti felt. When these texts were written, the highest truth had to belong to Caesar and the high priests. But knowing that the highest truth resides in each individual is a deeply democratic principle. One fit for our times."

"Of course, I share your opinion that some initiates have known this truth for a long time. But they haven't kept it secret out of spite or from fear of losing power. They acted as guardians of this knowledge, until humanity was ready – on the right level – to really absorb it. No small matter, because the consequence is absolute personal responsibility. There won't be any guilty parties or circumstances anymore. The responsibility for your whole life – for whatever happens – lies with you, and you alone."

The others looked at Haki with new respect. So that was how a compassionate heart and mind functioned. By looking behind the obvious – untainted by sarcasm or cynicism or dogma – she was able to see further. But Haki didn't seem to notice her friends' reaction. Unperturbed, she continued. "What you just said, Reto, may also solve the riddle of the holy trinity, the father, son and this curious Holy Spirit! The son would represent the individual, each and every human being. The Holy Spirit represents that inner instance we all discover sooner or later – urging us to search for something greater, deeper, more meaningful. And the father, well, he would represent the ultimate divine principle that guides humans from within." With a satisfied nod, Haki concluded. "Yep, now a lot of things finally make sense."

Reto was quite overwhelmed by this soft-spoken but ever so clear-minded woman whose heart surely had room for a billion humans. He sprang up from his chair and began pacing beside the pool to focus his thoughts. "One last thing.... These texts speak time and again of 'the knowledge hidden in silence'. To me this means: as long as you follow your five senses into the noise of the material world, you can spend ten lifetimes and still not find this secret knowledge. Only the seeker looking inward, into the silence, will be rewarded."

Shiv glanced over at Reto who now stood by a tall saguaro cactus, a respectful distance from its impressive array of spines.

"This is where time and space fuse once again, my friend. A while ago my brain left me with a mantra – once the silence had finally descended on my inquisitive mind and I could penetrate the depth of my heart. For me, the words solved the ultimate human identity question:

I am the eternal, the immortal, the all-pervading. I am 'it'."

"It's the same message, isn't it?" Barb said softly. "We can therefore say, man is divine. That all the mysteries, secrets and riches of this world – and of the universe itself – are within. Within every single human being without exception."

"That's a very elegant way to put it, Barb." Shiv nodded at her. "Simplified, we could say: the individual 'I' is a spark of the underlying, unifying life force. We can even go one decisive step further. What the mantra is really saying is: the underlying life force, that what many people call god and I call 'it', and every individual being, every single particle in this universe are one and the same."

Now he also had Ali and Reto's full attention. "This would explain what brain research has revealed, that actions are triggered in our brain as much as a few seconds before the conscious I makes a decision. Seems 'it' pulls the strings we dangle on. Much like a cartoon character might believe it was an individual, self-determined character, when in actuality, it is a figment of the designer's imagination. And like you said, we can, we must take the ultimate step and conclude that we are the designer. I am 'it', you're 'it', we're 'it'."

Shiv laughed and added, "This new knowledge also answered one of my long-standing questions. How does an individual 'make' thoughts? Now I know I don't 'make' anything. An electric impulse is triggered in my mind, producing a chemical change in the body, inducing a reaction such as an emotion or muscle movement...."

Reto was deep in thought. There was this one sentence from the lost gospels that had always puzzled him. Under the title 'The secret sayings of the living Jesus' was written, 'He who finds, will be troubled. When he becomes troubled, he will be astonished, and he will rule over all.' He had not understood the meaning then. But now, in light of the way Shiv interpreted his mantra, it seemed natural that a human would be deeply troubled at the contradiction of being a mere remote-controlled puppet, yet at the same time 'ruling over all'.

When Reto related this story, an animated debate broke out, with one common aspect. This would be the ultimate question of identity and reality, wouldn't it? And before you could rule over anything, you had to twist your brain around this enigma! Wasn't it just like Plato's famous cave analogy? And so the ideas flew like ping-pong balls around the terrace – bouncing off one another, giving a different spin, following another trajectory.

Shiv finally summed up the debate and gave it clear form. "This means, on the ultimate level, the ruler and the ruled are one. In the finest of fine vibrations, in the subtlest of the subtle realms, all our energies are the same. In science we talk about Grand Unification – the merging of the electromagnetic, weak and strong forces. Everything is animated by the same energy, including you and me."

Now that put a silencer on the discussion. They all looked at each other, only half daring yet to think the unthinkable.

While Shiv had taken them into space, Barb brought them back to earth. "Now we've figured out the secret knowledge – wisdom passed along by initiates over thousands of years – what are we going to do with it? Tell people: hey, you are the only god? You're 'it'. All you see and hear and smell and taste and touch – and all else too – is a projection of a single energy? So get off your butts and start digging within for the truth?" She enfolded the group in one of her brilliant smiles. "Oh, and by the way, forget free will...."

Into the laughter she said, "Just thought of a really nice image! Maybe you don't recall, but on the fateful night of the party I was talking about jeans. How one piece of clothing conquered the world? Anyhow, jeans were the preferred clothing of gold-miners. Well, we could start a new gold rush!

Only this time people would be prospecting within – for a substance that never ages – surely a most noble quest." Again she smiled radiantly, before adding, visibly awed: "I just understood something else. It's the destiny of every human soul to turn into gold. That's what alchemists tried to tell us. We should all turn ourselves into gold."

"What a wonderful and plausible image, Barb." Haki gave Barb's hand a friendly squeeze. "And, yes the question remains, what do we do with this knowledge? I mean if we are serious about writing a 'Declaration of Inner Independence', we'll have to share what we've found. Is it time for people to realize they are divine – and thus immortal? To reveal the best kept secret of all time, expose the core knowledge of the mysteries, so to speak?"

"It's time, high time." There were laughs and shouts and high fives.

"It is time. Definitely." Shiv's voice had an immediate calming effect. "Look at where science stands today. With their Theory of Everything physicists stand on the threshold of great breakthroughs. They think that everything fuses into one substance at extremely high temperatures. There is new evidence that the whole Universe might be a projection, a hologram. Neuroscientists have found – we just touched on this – that conscious decisions are an illusion; another entity steers the individual. And then there is my own experience, where my I and the life force have fused."

Reto was nodding in complete agreement. "Remember we said independence needed direction? Our Declaration could perhaps contribute some of that, steering human endeavors in a direction where life makes sense. We could propose key points, summarizing our newly accessed knowledge – or gnosis, as the Greeks called it. And we now know from the lost gospels containing Gnostic texts of the second century that Jesus said: all knowledge is within, to be found only there."

"Funny you should say that, Reto. Buddhism has the same message: that every human has to walk the path to knowledge.

Budh actually means to awaken, to understand, to know. It is the Sanskrit root from which also Buddha is derived." Shiv gave a small sigh. "Knowledge, specifically about your own identity... it's not what I first thought, when I started university. It's not to be found in a book, it doesn't belong to east or west, past or future. Every human's destiny is to find higher knowledge within. Direct access is incorporated in every human being. Truth cannot be found through the five senses, only through bundling them into one introspective beam."

Into the quiet, Reto quoted: "It is hidden in the silence."

For a long spell the five friends sat quietly, looking at the flames dancing in the hearth. Barb broke the spell by suggesting that Shiv should be the one to formulate the 'Declaration of Inner Independence'. Agreement was quick and unanimous. With new enthusiasm they resumed the discussion and their individual input took the quintet deep into the night. Animated discussion filled the air until, at last, they were satisfied with their distillation of the infinite subject matter into a few key points – material for Shiv to work with tomorrow.

◆

"Hallelujah and such!" Marvin was doing a little jig behind the hedge. "I think they got it."

"They got 'it' all right." Avory grinned. "Now this much-trumpeted New Age can begin at last. The secret knowledge is finally revealed." Avory gave a deep sigh of relief.

"Yeah, bro, that's just fine and dandy. But even if they really trust their findings, they still haven't registered that it all happens according to the great game plan. Are you sure they will accept being nothing but characters in the endless book of life? Will they, dearest Miss Vicky, knower of the unknowable, ever get it? That all this" – Marvin's gesture swept the whole universe – "is just a mirage?"

Victoria graced both young men with one of her enigmatic smiles. "Yes, they will, dear boys, they will. After all, it is their destiny."

♦

Ali, Barb, Haki and Reto set out early the next morning. Barb had suggested a drive out into the desert, a hike among the fantastic palm groves where centuries ago the ancestors of the Agua Caliente Cahuilla Indians settled. They paid the fee and parked the car on the nearly empty lot, took their backpacks from the trunk and set off into the canyon. Soon they were captured by the spectacular scenery opening up around them. As they were climbing through stark, rocky gorges towards the arid, sun-baked ridge, the palm oasis at the bottom of the valley dropped away. They didn't speak until Haki called for a break when they had reached the cactus-strewn ridge. They drank water and enjoyed the magnificent view, the endless expanse of rusts and browns and grey and gold dappled with the intense green of small and large clumps of fan palms. All this breathtaking beauty spread out under a spotless cerulean sky. Still, no one was willing to break the silence beyond pointing out a bighorn sheep posing on a boulder like a model, or a particularly stumpy barrel cactus that looked like an enchanted dwarf. Gradually, the trail wound down towards the stately palms, scissoring the bright sun with their fan-shaped fronds, finally dipping into deep cool shade.

They walked mostly in companionable silence, on the sandy paths, listening to the palm fronds whispering stories from long ago. When Reto called out he wanted to explore a hidden side canyon, the others just nodded and watched him disappear between the heavily skirted trunks. Hesitant, they stood for a moment then went after him. They followed the trickle of dark brown water, enough to make brilliant green reeds thrive, turning gradually into a small stream. It felt like walking through a storybook. When the path turned sharply, they stopped and stared. Water tumbled over pale grey rocks, smoothed and shaped over centuries, then came to rest in a shallow pool. Wherever the sandy soil captured some of the humidity, it gave life to an array of vivid green baby palms, reeds and grasses. A myriad of rainbows danced in the spray.

The sun had already dipped behind the mountain when the four curious and excited hikers returned, eager to discover what their friend had forged from their collective ideas. But he was nowhere in sight. The large worktable in the living room had been cleared of papers, laptops, books and all other distractions. All that remained were four printouts – carefully placed in front of four chairs – and a note from Shiv. He had gone out for a late round of golf and would be back in time to hear their thoughts.

The Declaration of Inner Independence

1. **The goal of human life is to discover our true identity, and ultimately merge with it.**

   Body and mind are a complex molecular structure. Our thoughts, feelings and actions are determined by our unique DNA blueprint and input from the five senses. But true identity runs deeper than the senses and the intellect. Our true identity is 'it' – the one life force animating the universe and every single being.

2. **The laws of the universe can be identified within our own body.**

   The universe is always evolving, but the total amount of energy remains constant. None is ever added or subtracted – it just changes state. Therefore, the universe knows no birth or death. We will recognize our own immortality only when we identify with the underlying life force, and not with the constantly changing particles making up our physical body and mind.

3. Body and mind are just a costume for the soul – and only for one lifetime.

If we identify only with body and mind, we experience loss and death. Body and mind decay, whereas the soul moves on to play countless human roles. But even the soul – the subtle particle cluster carrying our DNA for countless lifetimes – will ultimately disintegrate. Whatever assembles will disassemble. Only the underlying pure substance – 'it' – is eternal.

4. Humans are the most advanced form of creation.

The human mind is uniquely equipped to understand the greatest secret of life. Only we have the ability to transcend our mortal humanness and identify with our eternal inner self. Only humans are capable of experiencing that all is one, and that each of us is part of this mysterious unity we call 'it'!

5. Male and female come from the same source and are equally valid.

Externally, our two different body types represent gender. Internally, they represent the left and right sides of the brain. Life's goal is to fuse all such duality into a grand inner vision of unity. This neurochemical experience of fusing the right and the left side of the brain has been called a 'mystical marriage'. Therefore, the human brain is the ultimate 'wedding chamber'!

6. Suffering is the direct path to inner strength and wisdom.

Suffering is the tool 'it' uses to pry our attention away from the external reality and focus it on the inside. Suffering is a concentration of the five senses on one particular mental or physical problem. Personal power and compassion grow through suffering.

7. We are all fellow travelers moving towards a common goal: to experience oneness.

Every moving particle in the universe is a manifestation of the same underlying energy. This subtlest of energies is our true identity. It moves us from within. Once we experience this, we understand: whatever we encounter is part of us. If we kill, we kill part of ourselves; if we hate, we hate part of ourselves; if we spread kindness, we grace ourselves with kindness as well.

8. Inner independence and a better understanding of human identity is the key to creating a truly advanced and democratic society.

Organized religions and cultural norms are like parents accompanying a child to the door of adulthood. From there we must begin our own quest for knowledge: learn that every action creates a reaction, and that we must face the consequences with courage and wisdom. The age of democracy will flourish only when we mentally mature from 'I' to 'we' and from 'have' to 'be'.

9. Live life cheerfully as if there were free will, while knowing there is no such thing.

There is only one life force animating the universe, so how can there be 'free will'? Free will is a concept tied to a world still unfamiliar with non-duality. Understanding free will starts from a point of duality where 'it' is outside the individual. The second stage lets the individual realize that 'it' is within. The ultimate insight is an inner experience of non-duality.

10. Know the reason for the existence of the universe.

The universal game is played by one single player: 'it'. 'it' plays the game by itself – for the joy of itself.

As if by silent agreement, each had picked up a printout and gone to find a private, comfortable place to read it. Barb was sitting by the pool, mesmerized by the cascading water, recalling the time she had sat right there for weeks and months, unable to do anything but watch the water fall. And now her difficult journey had led to this. The paper lay in her lap. She was filled with a deep sense of accomplishment and gratitude. Gratitude, that her pain had brought insight and peace. Suddenly she sat up, completely surprised, even a little shocked. What she had so long considered the most awful experiences in her life – the loss of son and father – now felt like just another scene in her very own movie.

Ali had retreated to the garden, where he sat on the close-cropped lawn under a floodlit orange tree. Shiv had done a splendid job writing the Declaration, condensing the wide range of ideas the four friends had thrown at him into ten succinct points! Awesome. Ali felt competent to judge Shiv's achievement, since his own competitive advantage in business resulted from the speed with which he grasped a complex issue, condensed it and extracted pertinent information.

Inside meanwhile, the figure snuggled up on the large sofa had her eyes closed, her face illuminated by a wondrous smile. She had carefully placed the piece of paper over her heart, not really conscious of what she was doing. How on Earth did she, little orphaned Hakika Hasina, end up here with these wonderful people, in this splendid house, contributing to something she could not fully fathom? Still, she knew this was exactly where she should be and what she had to be doing. There was really no alternative. Wasn't that what Shiv had formulated so clearly? She was here because 'it' meant for her to be here. So, why not relax and enjoy?

Reto couldn't look away. He was completely captivated by the peaceful figure with the radiantly happy face. Wow. If the Declaration could evoke this in people, they were really on the right track. He too was impressed with how Shiv had harnessed their high-flying ideas into ten concise statements.

Would others understand what they were trying to say though? Was it possible to understand this stuff if you hadn't experienced it? Well, as soon as Shiv was back, he'd pose the question.

After a while – unbidden – the four drifted towards the kitchen to prepare dinner. The result was a sumptuous couscous with all manner of veggies, topped with a spicy harissa sauce. Chocolate crème followed for dessert. After all, a celebration was definitely in order.

Shiv's timing was perfect. Just as Haki was setting the table, he strode through the door, greeted by smiling faces and a spontaneous hug from Haki that didn't even make him flinch. "Let's eat before we talk," Barb commanded from the kitchen, her chestnut mane curling around her face from the steam, eyes full of joie de vivre. Ali carried out platters of couscous, carrots, potatoes, beans and bell peppers, while Reto was busy re-creating his Nona's famous recipe for their well-earned desert.

Wiping the last traces of chocolate from his mouth, Shiv said with a sheepish grin, "Well?"

"Grand Unification, know what I'm sayin'?" Reto gave the Indian a wide smile and a high five, at which the whole group broke into hilarious laughter.

"You did a fantastic job, Shiv, simply fantastic." Haki beamed at him. "I wouldn't want to change a word of what you've written. And I'm sure the others agree. There's really only one question: will people who haven't experienced the things we have... will they take our word for it?"

After a long pause, Reto said "No, they will not take our word for it – at least I hope not." Into the puzzled looks, he threw the punch line: "Shiv has summed it up perfectly in the Declaration, that people should no longer follow gurus or recipes; they should make their own way to inner independence. Not take our word for it. But I'm sure some will take up the questions we pose, like Shiv's 'how do I make a thought?' That alone would start an inquisitive mind on an exciting journey – to discover what really powers a human."

"You're so right, Reto. Exactly!" Barb beamed at all of them. "And once you've stepped onto that path, you can't get off anymore. Still, until you really comprehend all points of the Declaration, you'll shed a lot of blood, sweat and tears. Believe me, here speaks an expert." She shrugged her shoulders and added, "Knowing the secret of all secrets will at least give suffering some meaning."

Shiv had been listening intently as they reacted to his draft. "What we are putting forward here is first and foremost an intellectual concept, right? And that's what people can start with. It's not a question of one faith or philosophy vs. another; it's simply a distillation of our experiences. If it makes sense to you intellectually, then you can begin perceiving it, living it."

"And that's precisely what I like about it." Ali got into the debate. "Doesn't matter where you start from, you'll experience these things in your own way. It was work, or rather overwork, that led me there. Work, work, work, all hours of the day, and having a ball...."

"Same here," Reto said with a deep sigh. "I too was having a great time pushing myself. Not so much professionally, where success came pretty easily. My kick was testing my physical limits – preferably against others," he concluded with a laugh.

"Sounds very familiar, only I did it intellectually." Shiv grinned at Reto.

"Yeah, and I'd try to max out my creative potential, constantly seeking new ways to express myself." Barb looked expectantly at Haki, who remained seated with a faraway look in her eyes.

"I went to the outer limits of pity, taking on other peoples suffering and trying to save whoever came my way," Haki said, "and now I know they didn't need saving." After a brief silence she continued, "And so we all walked our own paths with great dedication, didn't we?"

"...To the point where destiny decided to let us crash, right?" Barb piped in.

"To give us time to think, that's all. No ill will on destiny's part." Reto chuckled and signaled to Ali, who was obviously ready to put in his two bits.

"That was crucial, though, wasn't it? To have been ripped out of our daily routine and set down hard on our backsides. Like being sent to stand in the corner at school and consider if it was wise to put a frog in that girls desk."

"I wasn't exactly ripped like you guys," Shiv said with a slow smile. "I don't think I ever told you that dream I first alluded to in the gazebo. I not only encountered three of the four fundamental forces in the form of Hindu gods, but I also saw the goddess Cali – so clear and sharp I could have touched her. She invited me to her western abode, before disappearing with a lewd wink!"

"You mean California is Cali's western abode? Is that what you're saying?"

"Hey, what do I know? Sure drew me to California, where a dying man's question sent me on a journey to explore the science of the mind. And here I am, back again. As a scientist, I'll have to leave the Cali question open until I find proof." With a Cali-like wink, the usually frugal Shiv surprised them all by helping himself to the rest of the chocolate desert.

"Great story," Barb sighed. "We have all been on such different paths, haven't we? No common culture, education, religion or philosophy. And still, our paths have led to the same insights – giving added depth and new meaning to our lives. We have all learned how life's trials and tribulations lead to wisdom."

"The pot of gold at the end of the rainbow," Haki picked up the thread. "I don't think it's at all hard to reconcile our different paths." She consciously paused for a moment, to savor the amazement her statement had caused. "We are as varied as the rainbow's colors, yet ultimately we are made of the same light."

Her greatest triumph was to have shaken Shiv's preternatural calm. He actually jumped up... well at least as fast as his giraffe limbs would allow.

"You just did it, Haki. You extracted the essence of the Declaration, the Theory of Everything, the Grand Unification and everything else. Light strikes a falling raindrop and all of creation is to be found in the colors of the resulting rainbow. Ultimately, every particle ever created is a projection of the same light and finds its way back to the source."

Reto too was enthusiastic. "I've probably said it before, but isn't the rainbow a sign of the relationship between the creator and creation?"

"Said and heard and written and read a million times, but never understood." Ali was looking at Shiv, who stood and smiled at his four companions on the greatest adventure of their lives. "That's the thing!" Shiv said, "Only when we experience the universal animating principle within us will we know our true identity."

Epilogue

The Forces stood on the terrace of their empty house. All traces of anyone living there were gone; nary a molecule of furniture or technical equipment remained. Gradually the shapes who had been Victoria, Marvin and Avory began to waver and dissolve, their energies merging into a blinding light that almost instantly circled the knowledge belt on that tiny rock, third planet from the sun in a solar system far out on an arm of the spiral galaxy called Milky Way.

In Vegas, Johnny 'Chip' Dougan dropped a full house – aces over nines – and forgot his considerable pile of chips, as a flash of white light overwhelmed the casino's gaming rooms. It set off every last slot machine in a discordant cacophony, spewing credit tickets and coins to the unbridled delight of thousands of gamblers. In the Middle East, throngs who had taken to the streets to protest injustice and corruption took the strange phenomenon in the sky as a blessing and sign of support for their struggle for freedom. In the Himalayas, a small group of monks – huddled together on a snow-covered ledge, faded red robes drawn tight against the thin, cold air – stared, transfixed by the light streaking across the black sky. Calmly they turned toward their small monastery deep in the silent mountains, knowing the next stage had been initiated.

And on the Japanese island of Kyushu, the volcano that had been spewing ash and rock ahead of a major eruption heaved a deep sigh and simply died down. Marvin had heroically resisted temptation. And his aim, no longer constrained by human form, had been dead on.

The End

About the Authors

As a reporter and journalist, NORA BROWN has followed the trails of the Long March in China, interviewed survivors of a terrorist attack in Egypt and documented the misery of refugees in the Democratic Republic of Congo. She is the author of several books, has spent many years in Australia and the USA and now lives with her son in the countryside near Basel, Switzerland. Her passion for writing is only matched by her recently acquired taste for playing golf.

Nora

Stella

STELLA DUNN worked for many years as a journalist, editor and educational consultant. She has a degree in journalism, a postgraduate degree in career counseling and a profound knowledge of eastern and western philosophy. She lives with her husband John in the Swiss Alps and in Southern California. She enjoys golf, tennis, yoga and traveling the world. One of her favorite places is the Peruvian Andes, where she started a foundation providing educational funds for local farmer children. Nora and Stella have collaborated for over twenty-five years.

Multimedia Enhanced eBook Edition
Available on iTunes

Original Soundtrack
Available on iTunes

5470561R00154

Made in the USA
San Bernardino, CA
08 November 2013